A Spectrum of Heroes

Annie Percik

Published by Markosia Enterprises, PO BOX 3477, Barnet, Hertfordshire, EN5 9HN.

FIRST PRINTING, August 2021.
Harry Markos, Director.

Paperback: ISBN 978-1-914926-06-8
eBook: ISBN 978-1-914926-07-5

Book design by: Ian Sharman

Cover art by: Aaron Moran

www.markosia.com

First Edition

Dedication

To Geena P, for concept and all-things Indian.

Acknowledgements

In October 2017, I was on a night out with my friend, Geena P, and we somehow came up with the idea of a superhero whose hair changed colour to denote which of her multiple powers she was using. And so Anushka was born.

Two months later, I wrote the first 10,000 words in two days at one of Charlie Haynes' marvellous retreats (https://urbanwritersretreat.co.uk/). Then, in 2019 Charlie, along with her equally amazing partner Amie McCracken, put the novel through its paces in the Six Month Novel Programme and it finally entered the world as a fully formed thing.

Additional thanks must go to:

Hannah W for harsh (but very much needed) criticism and vital motivation.

Lindsay B for character commentary.

Joe B and Soren B for pointing out my glaring military errors.

Lila K and Yasaa M for additional Indian perspectives.

Ann de V for keeping me on track.

Juliet R for transformational friendship and helping me get out of my own way.

Great thanks also to Harry Markos at Markosia for knowing what he wanted and getting in before anyone else!

As always, thanks to my mum and dad for endless proofreading and their unshakeable belief in me.

And, last but definitely not least - much thanks and love to my husband, Dave, for asking the difficult questions (and being directly in the firing line of my frustration) and for at least thinking this one was better than the last one.

P1 - May 2019 - North London

Slick mud oozed between Anushka's fingers as she dug. Why hadn't she thought to bring a spade? She'd rushed to escape the lab, without considering practicalities. Damn Yardley and his ultimatum! If only she'd had more time, she could have planned her departure properly. Now she was winging it, and that had never been one of her strong points. Her back ached from stooping and the darkness made it difficult to see what she was doing. She leaned further forwards and nearly toppled into the hole. She sat back on her haunches, her breaths coming short and fast. Injuring herself and ending up stuck here until daylight would be all she needed. She shivered in the night air. Even after years living in London, she still missed the heat of Kolkata. A flood of sense memories threatened to overwhelm her and she felt tears pricking her eyes. But now was not the time to indulge in nostalgia. Taking a deep breath, Anushka pushed back her feelings and her long dark hair, and turned her attention back to the task at hand.

The hole was probably deep enough now. Anushka reached for the thick plastic sack at her side and slid it into the depression. It was heavy and unwieldy, its liquid contents shifting as she moved it. It snagged on something part way down. Reaching in, she felt around and discovered a sharp root protruding from the earth. She managed to free the sack and it settled at the bottom of the hole with a squelch and a waft of pungent chemicals. Anushka swept her hair over her shoulder again. Tying it back was another thing she should have done before starting. She really hadn't thought this through. Everything had happened so quickly and panic had overtaken reason in her flight. What was Charlotte going to think when she arrived at work to find Anushka gone? She couldn't think about that now, or she might just give up this reckless plan and run back to the lab, regardless of the consequences. Her scalp tingled, most likely with apprehension at the possibility of being discovered.

Anushka shovelled dirt on top of the sack, making sure it was well covered. She did her best to make the ground look as undisturbed as possible, but it was hard to tell how well she succeeded. Bringing a torch would have made her too visible to any security personnel, and the lights along the fence were too far away to be much use out here in the field. She wasn't worried about her footprints in the dirt. Plenty of people traipsed back and forth along here on a daily basis and nobody would be looking for her prints in particular, as long as it wasn't obvious someone had been digging.

Deciding her efforts were good enough, Anushka stood up, wincing as her back twinged again. She felt ridiculous, crawling around a field in the middle of the night, but it was the only way she could think of to dispose of the XR-20. How long would it take for someone to notice it was missing from the lab? Much as she might want to, she couldn't go back to work the next day and pretend no knowledge of the theft. Even though she hadn't been caught leaving the building, she was the only one who had access to the XR-20, and security was tight enough that there was no way anyone else could have broken in to take it.

She made her way back to the fence and the gap she had made. She slid through it and back out onto the road. Jogging across and into the trees, she found where she had parked her car and got in. She sat in the driver's seat for a moment, trying to calm her breathing and slow her heartbeat. What she had just done was hasty and ill-advised but it was too late now. There was no turning back; she had burned all her bridges. Minutes later, she was speeding away from the scene of the crime and everything she had built in the last few years of her life.

* * *

P2 - May 2019 - North London

It was Charlotte Grant, the head of security at the lab, who first realised something was wrong. She had been due to meet Anushka for breakfast in the lab canteen, as they did most days, but Anushka didn't show. This wasn't entirely unprecedented, as Anushka often came in early and got so engrossed in her work that she lost track of time. That was something Charlotte, with her military sense of punctuality, had been forced to get used to when spending time with a research scientist. Charlotte waited another five minutes, then headed to Anushka's office with a rueful smile.

She stepped up to the glass of the outer lab area and tapped on it, startling the nearest anonymous assistant. He - at least Charlotte thought it was a he, though it was difficult to tell under his surgical cap and mask - raised his eyebrows in a question.

Charlotte called through the glass. "Can you go get Dr Mahto, please?"

He shrugged and shook his head. When he spoke, his words were muffled by his mask. "She's not here."

That was odd. At this time of day, Anushka would invariably be in her office or the lab proper, if she wasn't having breakfast. Charlotte waved the assistant back to his work and made her way to the central security hub, the heart of her domain at the lab. Several of her team were at their stations, monitoring multiple screens that covered nearly every part of the building. Charlotte walked up behind Perkins, whose screens showed the car park and main entrance. She noticed that his hair was getting shaggy, tufting out over his ears. She made a mental note to have a word with him about professional presentation later. Not that it ever did much good. Perkins was very good at his job, but regulations weren't his strong point, nor did he seem to take any pride in his appearance. Charlotte shook her head; she had a different errant employee to tackle at the moment.

"Check the logs for when Dr Anushka Mahto last swiped in."

Perkins tapped in some commands. "2am."

Unusual, but not unheard of. The scientists at the lab were known to keep odd hours.

"And has she swiped out since?"

More tapping. "She left at 3am, and hasn't come back."

Now that was really strange.

"Show me the feeds for both her arrival and her departure."

As she waited for Perkins to input the information, Charlotte started running her right palm over the stumps of the last two fingers on her left hand, then stopped herself when she realised what she was doing. She clenched both hands into fists, feeling her fingernails digging into the skin of her palms, then dropped them to her sides. When the recordings came up, Charlotte's breath caught in her throat. Anushka had arrived carrying nothing and had left an hour later with a large, heavy-duty plastic bag. On the screen, she stooped awkwardly to one side, struggling to heft the bag, which she clutched with one hand grasping it by the top. What on earth was she playing at, and where was she now?

Charlotte swore, eliciting a surprised glance from Perkins.

"What's going on, boss? What's Dr Mahto doing taking stuff out of the lab in the middle of the night?"

Charlotte glared at him and he blanched, turning back to his keyboard to avoid her anger.

"Alert Mr Yardley's office that I'm on my way up. I think we have a breach."

She spun on her heel and strode into the unisex bathroom, needing a moment to collect herself before heading up to speak to Yardley. What could Anushka have been thinking? Charlotte had known she was having issues with her role at the lab. But to steal proprietary material and sneak away in the middle of the night? And without a word to Charlotte herself? Charlotte felt unfamiliar tears threatening and she hunched over the sinks, forcing them back. She couldn't afford to lose control, not here and not now. She gripped the edge of the bathroom counter until her knuckles went white, fighting against the emotion rising in her chest.

Behind her, the door opened and heavy footfalls entered. She heard the huff of a laugh and then the voice of Henderson, one of the newer security recruits.

"What's the matter, Grant? Got your period?"

Rage swamped the swirling chaos of emotion and instinct took over. She whirled to face him. His muscled bulk almost filled the space but that didn't deter Charlotte. She lashed out, striking him hard in the solar plexus, knocking the wind out of him. As he bent double, she grabbed his arm and twisted it behind his back, forcing him down further until the side of his face was mashed against the smooth, hard countertop.

He made a strangled sound, struggling for breath and fighting against her hold, but she kept a firm grip and he was powerless against it.

"What was that, soldier?" Charlotte hissed in his ear.

Henderson managed to squeeze out a few rasping words. "Okay, okay, I'm sorry!"

Charlotte held on a moment longer, then released him and backed away a couple of steps, hands up and ready for a counter-attack. But he just straightened with difficulty, gasping huge breaths and staring at her with wide, alarmed eyes.

"Jesus! What the hell was that? It was just a joke!"

Charlotte watched him shuffle out of the bathroom, not seeing the funny side at all. So much for collecting herself.

* * *

A1 - 2002 - Kolkata

Growing up in Kolkata, Anushka had always received conflicting opinions from her parents about her future.

Her mother would always say, "Study hard, Anushka, and you can do whatever you want with your life."

Aditi Mohta had gone straight from her father's house to that of her husband, and now helped

Anushka's father run the grocery store they lived above. She wanted more for her daughters and saw their education as their route to a better life. Anushka had an older sister, Jhanvi, and their mother would tell them bedtime stories about strong warrior women who changed the world.

"My name means limitless, but I have never lived up to its potential," she would say to them. "But Aditi was also the mother of the gods, so you can help me fulfil that meaning by becoming goddesses. It's up to you now to be free and unbounded in my place. My angels, you must fly far from here and find your own places in the world. And your studies will show you the path."

Anushka didn't need much encouragement. She loved school, especially science and maths. Studying gave her an escape from the dull mundanity of real life, allowing her to slip into another world of atoms and chemical reactions. The inner workings of the universe fascinated her, and she could often be found poring over her schoolbooks at the kitchen table, while her mother made dinner.

Her father, Uttam Mohta, also wanted his daughters to study hard, but for a different reason.

"If they get good degrees, they will be able to attract better husbands. But they also need to know how to cook and keep a house, not fill their heads with wild fancies about a life away from here. Where is the money coming from that will pay for that? They will stay here, find husbands and live simple, worthwhile lives in Kolkata. And what is wrong with that?"

Aditi didn't argue with Uttam directly when he expressed his disapproval. She just nodded obediently and went back to whatever domestic task she was doing. But there was always a twinkle in her eye when she watched Anushka getting lost in her schoolbooks. And there was always another inspiring story to be told when Uttam wasn't around.

Jhanvi was more interested in hanging out with her friends than studying.

"You're so boring, Nushie," she would say. "Why don't you come out with me and have some fun? There's a party tonight. There'll be boys there. I can lend you a cute outfit and help you do your hair."

But knowledge was the only thing that ignited Anushka's passions and she knew she wanted more from life than a husband who would parade her around, bragging about her qualifications but not allowing her to use them for anything. She watched her sister getting ready to sneak out for the evening and felt no envy for Jhanvi's carefree attitude and heavy makeup. Anushka would hide in her room with her books when her sister got caught coming home late and there was yelling.

"You'll come to a bad end," she heard her father shout. "If you get into trouble, don't expect me to get you out of it. I won't have Anushka's prospects damaged because you can't control yourself. If you want to carry on like a common whore, you won't do it under my roof."

Anushka didn't see how either of them could escape their father's plans for them, no matter what path they might wish to choose for themselves. Their choices were just as limited as their mother's had been.

* * *

C1 - 2003 - West London

Charlotte was an only child and grew up surrounded by the privilege of the wealthy in West London. Her parents were both high-flying city executives, and spent nearly all their time at the office or networking at fancy parties. Their house in Kensington was large and airy, but not exactly designed to feel like a comfortable home. Charlotte had everything money could buy, but was always terrified of breaking something.

She didn't fit in at school, where she chafed at the scratchy blazer and A-line skirt. She would have preferred to wear trousers, but the school dress code didn't allow it. She tried starting a petition to call for a change to the rules, but the other girls weren't interested in rocking the boat for something they saw as trivial. Charlotte's mother liked her to keep her hair long, though Charlotte always felt it got in the way. She frequently got told off for chewing her plaits rather than paying attention in class. Her report cards spoke of daydreaming and insubordination.

"I just don't understand it," her mother would say. "You're such a bright girl. You could be top of the class but you just won't apply yourself. Your father and I have always tried to instil in you the importance of academic studies. You'll never get a good job if you waste your time at school now. Think about your future."

"But I want to be outside, doing things," was Charlotte's reply. "The boys at the other school get to play football and do the assault course. But they won't let me join in. And the teachers say girls aren't supposed to do stuff like that. We don't even get to do stuff like woodwork. But I don't see why. Being a girl shouldn't stop me doing what I want. I've seen women competing at Wimbledon and the Olympics."

"We can find you a more active after-school environment if you want to play sports," her father chipped in. "I'm sure there are plenty of options. But, if we let you choose the groups you want to join, you'll have to get your grades up." He looked at her sternly over his reading glasses. "And keep them up. Once you've got what you want, there'll be no backsliding or you won't enjoy the consequences."

Negotiation was something Charlotte understood, even at the age of seven. She studied harder, fulfilled her academic potential and was rewarded with membership to the local sports centre, where she thrived among the gymnastics apparatus and hockey matches. She wasn't the only girl there, but she was the only one who wanted to take part in some of the more physical sports. The boys were wary at first, not wanting a girl to spoil their games. But, once Charlotte proved her mostly superior prowess, they started picking her first to join their teams. She grew stronger, honing her skills for whatever the future might bring.

* * *

E1 - Far away…

We often wonder what it must have been like when our people still maintained corporeal form. So much effort and so many resources wasted in keeping warm, producing and distributing food, building structures. We have personally never known anything different to the energy-based life we enjoy now, but our shared oral histories show it was not always that way. Before the ice came and made our home inhospitable to physical life, we too were confined by bodies, limited by meat brains, trapped within individual minds.

In physical form, we would not be able to communicate in the way we do now. There would be no Consensus, no vast but singular cohesive homogeneity of hundreds of thousands to tap into, no intimate family unit of eight entities in our mind at all times. We cannot imagine it. Constant connection with the others is what defines our existence. We are sometimes not sure where our individual consciousnesses divide. Consensus provides everything we need to survive and our family unit provides everything we need to thrive. The rest are always there for support, companionship or knowledge exchange whenever we need them. We are free to pursue intellectual and philosophical interests and to develop new theories to add to the accumulated knowledge of our people. The harshness of the physical environment causes us no distress as we do not interact with it. The environmental disaster that destroyed life as our ancestors knew it seems a blessing to us, as it forced our people to find a better way to exist.

Sometimes we play a game within our family unit of eight minds, guessing what another form of life might be like.

If we had bodies, we would have to consume food.

What kind of food?

Plant or animal matter that we would have to digest within our physical form.

That sounds disgusting.

Not as disgusting as expelling the waste matter after digestion. Absorbing energy from light and heat is much more civilised.

And much more efficient.

We would not be able to live here any more if we were corporeal.

Why not?

Because it would be too cold. We would freeze and our minds would shut down.

That sounds very unpleasant, and not a very robust system.

Physical bodies would also require sleep.

What is sleep?

Switching off the consciousness for regular periods in order for the mind to rest and the body to conserve energy.

How horrible. We would not only be cut off from all others, but would have to cut ourselves off from sensation and thought as well.

The game is frivolous but always makes us grateful for the existence we lead. We can play it endlessly because it is always so difficult to visualise a physical life. It is always amusing to revisit the difficulties such beings would face and think how lucky we are that we do not have to deal with such complicated problems. We know we are loved and we assume we are safe. Nothing should be able to threaten us.

* * *

P3 - May 2019 - M1

Anushka drove up the M1 until she caught her head drooping, then pulled into a service station hotel. It wouldn't do to get into an accident and end up in hospital where she could easily be found. The hotel receptionist yawned halfway through his greeting.

"Please excuse me," he said, ducking his head to check his computer. "We only have a deluxe twin room left available. Will you be staying more than one night?"

Anushka rifled through her shoulder bag for her wallet. "No, just tonight. How much?"

"It'll be £120. If you can give me a credit card now, you'll be charged on check-out." He glanced at the clock on the wall, which showed it to be nearly 3am. "That's at 11am."

"That's fine," Anushka said, "and I'd rather pay in full now, if that's okay."

She held out six twenty pound notes. She had at least managed to plan ahead enough to know she would need cash so as not to be tracked. The receptionist's eyebrows went up.

"That's a little unorthodox," he said.

Anushka gestured at the clock. "Well, you're not likely to sell the room to anyone else at this point. Do you want my business or not?" She took a deep breath and dragged a smile across her face. "I'm really tired and I'd like to get some sleep."

The receptionist took the money and handed her a room card. "Room 302. The lifts are over there."

Once in the room, Anushka heaved her bag onto one bed and fell onto the other, not even bothering to get undressed. She managed to set an alarm on her phone, then dropped straight off to sleep, exhaustion outweighing stress. Her dreams were haunted by swirling blue shadows that pursued her through a dark forest, until the shrill beeping of the alarm dragged her awake to full daylight. She felt little better than when she'd gone to sleep.

She decided a long, hot shower would be the best antidote and was glad to find that the bathroom was clean, with spotless white tiles and a full length mirror. It had a spacious shower, fragrant soap and good quality shampoo. A separate cubby-hole concealed the toilet from view. As Anushka washed her hair, she felt a tingle in her scalp and then in her left hand. The strange sensation rippled up and down her fingers like pins and needles gone mad. Bringing her hand round into her eye line, she caught her breath and stumbled backwards into the shower door as she looked straight through her hand to the tiled wall behind it. Anushka blinked hard and looked again, but her hand appeared entirely normal. She massaged her fingers with the other hand, feeling nothing out of the ordinary. The tingling sensation was gone. Closing her eyes again, she stood with her head directly under the shower's spray, willing the water to wash away her fatigue. She dismissed the vision as the result of over-tired eyes and accumulated stress.

Once she was dry and dressed, Anushka took stock of her situation. She had enough cash and clothes to last a while, but eventually she would need more than she had managed to bring with her. She didn't know how she could add to her supplies without making it easy for the lab to track her. For now, though, she just wanted to put additional distance between her and the enemies behind her. Charlotte would know she was gone by now and would likely be bringing the full force of her security team to trying to find her. Anushka's mind skittered away from thinking about what Charlotte might be doing. Charlotte was one of the enemies now.

She packed everything back into her bag, zipped it up and steeled herself for its weight. When she made to pick it up, however, it swung off the bed so easily that it unbalanced her and she nearly fell over. Her scalp tingled again and she glanced around in surprise, catching sight of herself in the mirror. There was a sheen of red in her hair. Anushka stepped forwards to look closer and the bag dragged at her arm with sudden weight. When she looked in the mirror again, her hair was its usual dark brown and the tingle in her scalp was gone. She really needed to get some more sleep. But rest would have to wait until she could no longer feel the lab's surveillance over her shoulder. She hefted the bag and made her way down to her car.

* * *

P4 - May 2019 - North London

Charlotte smoothed her short, dark hair behind her ears as she approached Yardley's office. Lester Yardley was the head of the lab and Charlotte had known him a long time. He wasn't going to be happy with what she had to tell him. She knocked and opened the door.

The office was almost entirely beige, with Yardley's big black desk dominating the space. The back of his leather chair rose up behind his head, always reminding Charlotte of a supervillain in his lair. The grenade he used as a paperweight didn't do anything to dispel that image. She had often wondered if it had any special significance to his time in the military, but had never summoned the courage to ask. The two visitor chairs were bare moulded steel that matched the large safe behind the desk. They looked very uncomfortable, so it wasn't just Charlotte's own military background that usually kept her standing when she came to speak to her boss.

Yardley wasn't alone. Henderson had made it there before her. The cowardly creep glanced round and a mixture of fear and anger flashed across his face at the sight of her, but he didn't say anything.

Yardley looked up from some paperwork and frowned. He was in his early sixties, but was still fit and trim. His grey hair sported a military buzz-cut, a habit from years past. He rose to his feet, his expensive jacket showing no creases as it moved with him. Charlotte placed herself dead centre opposite him and stood at parade rest, feet shoulder width apart and hands clasped behind her back. It was difficult to resist the urge to salute.

"Ms Grant," Yardley said. His voice was deep and cultured, natural authority in every syllable. Even after several years, it was still strange not to hear her rank placed before her name. "Mr Henderson here claims you assaulted him. Is that true?"

Charlotte sneered at Henderson. He must have run straight up here to complain about her. What a wimp, to hide behind Yardley instead of standing up for himself. That wasn't the kind of attitude she wanted on her team and she was sure Yardley would agree.

"I could accuse Mr Henderson of sexual discrimination in the workplace," she said, her voice devoid of emotion. "I hadn't planned on reporting him, preferring to deal with disciplinary matters within the department myself rather than bothering you with minor issues. But since Mr Henderson has brought the matter to you himself…"

"I see." Yardley's expression was blank, giving nothing away. He turned his gaze on Henderson. "I will not tolerate inappropriate behaviour towards my employees. You will clear out your locker and vacate the premises immediately."

"But…" Henderson spluttered. "What about her inappropriate behaviour?"

Yardley's eyes turned flinty. "I suggest you don't push your luck, Henderson. If you leave now, without any additional fuss, nothing about this will be added to your employment record and your future prospects will remain unaffected."

Henderson looked back and forth between Yardley and Charlotte a few times, mouth opening and closing as if he was trying to form words.

Charlotte struggled to keep a smug smirk from playing across her lips. Best not to revel too much in her victory, especially considering the more important things she had to worry about right then. Eventually, Henderson's shoulders slumped and he turned to leave the office.

Once he was gone, Yardley switched his attention smoothly back to Charlotte. "Now that's been dealt with, would you care to explain the more serious matter regarding the breach?"

Charlotte told him what she had discovered; that Anushka had removed the XR-20 she had been working on from the lab during the night and not reported for work that day. She covered all the important details but was careful not to be derailed by irrelevancies, even though her mind was spinning with questions about where Anushka might be and why. Yardley regarded her throughout, his expression neutral. He had always been difficult to read, though Charlotte thought she saw a slight thinning of his lips as her story progressed. Not a good sign. When she finished, Yardley sat back down in his chair, almost slumping but seeming to catch himself at the last moment.

"And you had no idea that Dr Mahto was planning such an act?"

"No, sir." Charlotte bit off the last word, but not quickly enough to prevent it slipping out. Another military habit that was hard to break, especially with Yardley. "If I had suspected something, I would have reported it immediately."

"Would you?" Yardley looked her up and down, then nodded. "Yes, I believe you would. Well, spilt milk and all that. Let's move forwards. What do you think Dr Mahto will do with the XR-20?"

Charlotte considered. "She won't go to the press, if that's what you're worried about. She'll dispose of it somewhere and then run." She closed her eyes briefly at the thought of Anushka, alone and scared, fleeing the lab - and also fleeing Charlotte.

"So, we might yet be able to retrieve both Dr Mahto and the XR-20." Yardley steepled his fingers over his lips. "Good. That's your top priority. Find Dr Mahto and make her return what she has stolen from us. You have full access to all lab resources and complete discretion to act as you see fit in the pursuit of your mission. Understood?"

"Understood." A thought struck Charlotte. "Is there any way to track the XR-20?"

Yardley raised an eyebrow.

She continued. "Would it leave some kind of trail we could follow? Or would it show up on some kind of scanner I could use?"

"Good thinking. I'll find out and let you know. Dismissed." Apparently Charlotte wasn't the only one who found military habits difficult to break.

Charlotte pivoted and left. She made her way down to her own office, part of the lab's security suite. She felt relief in having a clear objective, the need to act cutting through the swirl of emotions that threatened to impede her thinking. She would need a team.

Only the best and most trustworthy of the security unit, and perhaps also some specialist recruits from outside. Anushka might be anywhere. She had no ties in the country, other than the lab, and Charlotte herself. So there was no easy way to predict where she could have gone. This would likely be a long day.

Charlotte slipped her phone out of her pocket and texted Danny: 'Probably late home tonight. Don't wait on me for dinner.'

Then she turned her thoughts back to the problem at hand. There were ways of tracking Anushka, of course, assuming she was still using her phone and credit cards. Surely this madness couldn't have been planned far enough in advance for Anushka to have thought of such things? She was a scientist first and foremost, more committed to her job than she ever would be to anything else. She wasn't mentally equipped for life as a fugitive and she had to know Charlotte's skill-set and resources could trump any amateur tactics Anushka might come up with. What could she have been thinking?

Charlotte slammed her unmaimed hand down on the desk, making her pen pot jump and rattle. The movement drew her eye to a piece of paper that had been slipped under the pot. She pulled it towards her and unfolded it. Two words trailed across it in Anushka's handwriting.

'I'm sorry.'

* * *

A2 - 2002 - Kolkata

One night, when Jhanvi was nineteen and Anushka seventeen, Anushka woke to find her sister throwing clothes into a bag. She rubbed her eyes, trying to dispel the fog of sleep and hoping the action would dispel what she was seeing as well, that it was just a dream.

"What are you doing, Vi?" she whispered, frightened of making too much noise.

Jhanvi spun round and her face twisted in sorrow.

"I'm sorry, Nush, I can't take it here any more. I've got to get away from the constant surveillance and interrogation. Farhan got a job on a movie set and she says she can put me up while I get my foot in the door there too." She grinned. "Being a movie star's got to be better than being married off to some fat, old businessman, right?"

Anushka sat up in bed, staring at her sister in the dim light of the streetlights outside the window. She thought about staying on alone under the oppressive scrutiny of their father and her chest tightened.

"You're leaving? Weren't you going to say goodbye?"

Jhanvi grimaced and looked down at her hands, which were twisting the material of one of her skimpy tops. "I didn't want you to try and talk me out of it."

Anushka hugged her knees. She tried to be angry but the fire of rage refused to spark in the cold void of her heart. "I wouldn't do that. I want you to be happy. But are you sure you'll be okay?"

Jhanvi crossed the room and sat on the edge of Anushka's bed, throwing her arms around her sister and squeezing her tightly.

"I want you to be happy too, Nushie. I don't want to leave you, but I have to take this opportunity. It might be the only chance I ever have to get away. And you're the good one. Just keep your head down and do what they want for now and you can figure out what you want to do for yourself later."

"You don't think they'll come looking for you?"

Jhanvi set her lips in a thin line. "Dad's made his position clear on that. I think he'll be relieved more than anything, not to have to suffer the embarrassment of my behaviour any more. He can write me off and pretend I've died, or something. But promise me you'll find your own way out of this place." She gripped Anushka's shoulders, holding her at arm's length. "I know you have it in you to be amazing. Way more so than me. It would be a tragedy to let that go to waste, and I'd never forgive myself if you don't find a way to escape one day too. Don't let Dad stop you from finding your flight path."

Tears threatened to choke Anushka's voice, but she managed to say, "I promise."

Jhanvi hesitated, chewing on her lower lip.

"I hate leaving you alone with him, but I just can't see any other way. I can't stay here and I can't take you with me. Besides, you want to stay in school and go to university and nobody's going to object to that, because it'll improve your marriage prospects. Once you've got your degree, you'll have more options for getting away before Dad tries to kill your future." She gave Anushka one last hug. "I'll find a way to let you know where I am and how I'm doing."

And then Jhanvi was gone. Anushka sat alone in the darkness for a long time. Her promise hung in the air like a beacon. She didn't yet know how she could fulfil that promise, but it was a vow that had weight and meaning. Her fear of letting her sister down was greater than her fear of her father's anger. She would have to find a way.

* * *

C2 - 2003 - West London

It was during a rare family dinner one evening when she was seventeen that Charlotte dropped the bomb of her future plans at her parents' feet.

"I want to join the army."

The ceramic serving dish of cauliflower cheese clattered to the table as it slipped from her mother's fingers. Charlotte winced at the noise but held her mother's astonished gaze.

She continued. "There was a careers fair at school today, and some recruiting officers gave a presentation."

"I'm sure they were very compelling, darling," her father said. "But that's the point. They're salespeople, just like any others. Of course they're going to make it sound attractive."

Charlotte glared at him. "I'm not an idiot, dad. I know they were trying to persuade us, but I've heard enough sales techniques from you and mum to be basically immune by now. I think this is something I could do well, and I think it's important."

She had to give her parents credit for not over-reacting. She could tell from their tightened jaws and anxious exchange of glances that they weren't pleased, but they appealed to reason rather than resorting to anger or outright refusal. Sometimes it was useful to be the daughter of uptight people who suppressed their emotions and prided themselves on rationality.

"What about university?" her mother asked. "Surely you don't want to sacrifice your education."

Charlotte was ready for this line of argument. "They encourage recruits to get a degree, and I can join the Officer Training Corps while I study, then go to the Military Academy afterwards. There are even bursaries if I need help with my fees."

Her father laughed. "I hardly think you'd qualify for a bursary. And why would you need one?"

Charlotte cocked her head to one side and regarded her father steadily. "In case you refuse to pay because you don't like my plans."

Her mother sighed. "It's not that we disapprove, darling. But this has come rather out of the blue, and you have such potential, we'd hate to see it go to waste."

"You think it's a waste for me to serve my country?" Charlotte felt her hold on her emotions slipping and struggled to get herself back under control. It wouldn't do her case any good if she couldn't face her parents' calm questions with rationality of her own.

Her father put his hands out in a placatory gesture. "That's not what your mother is saying. But you have to understand that we'd be worried about you going into combat. Nobody wants their child to put his or her life at risk."

"Fair enough." Charlotte was prepared to surrender that point. She could taste a hint of victory and she chased it. "But you'll let me find out more and make up my own mind?"

They exchanged another glance, then both nodded.

"Of course," her father said. "One of my old university friends took that route into the army. There was something in the last alumni newsletter about his latest promotion. He's Major Yardley now."

The conversation veered into her parents reminiscing about their college days and wondering what various of their classmates were doing now, and that was the end of it.

Charlotte figured her parents probably thought it was just a passing phase and that she would forget all about it, but they never got the chance to revisit the subject. Just before Charlotte's A Level exam results were published, the summer after she finished school, both her parents were killed in a car accident. In shock and unable to face the prospect of three more years of study, Charlotte abandoned her officer training plan and entered Basic Training to be an infantry soldier instead. She just wanted to get away from the empty house and be doing something active as quickly as possible, and that seemed like the best option.

* * *

E2 - Far away…

There are eight entities in our family unit and it is sometimes difficult to know where one ends and another begins. We travel in and out of each other's thoughts as if they are our own, always completely in sync with whatever each of us experiences and feels. Any information imparted to one of us is imparted to all, so there is never any confusion, any deceit, or any misunderstanding. Discourse is generally conceptual in nature rather than relating to the mundane details of our existence. The group of minds that leads our society, Consensus, guides and nurtures us, providing structure and direction to our activities.

Consensus suggests more thought should be dedicated to exploring greater efficiency of energy transference in case of any further environmental changes on our world.

Changing ourselves to fit our surroundings has historically been our response to adversity, certainly. But there may be other options.

Such as?

Changing our planet to better fit our needs. Or looking elsewhere for a more hospitable home.

Would you advocate a return to greater interaction with our physical surroundings?

Of course not. But it might be useful to think about future development from that point of view, in case it offers more advantageous outcomes.

It is always a good idea to explore every option. A wide array of avenues of investigation is better than narrowing our focus and perhaps restricting our potential.

The wider network of entities is at a slight remove, but information still supposedly flows freely and is meant to be open to all. Everyone always likes to know what is happening within our society and there is no obvious way for anybody to hide their actions or their opinions. We believe we all work in unity to promote the common good, for as we are all connected, what is good for one is good for all. Consensus maintains a supervisory eye over all activities, pushing research in particular directions to benefit our society as a whole. We see no reason for dissent.

Without physical constraints, there is little that can provide obstacles to our progress. But there is also little that we require that needs development. Our pursuits are wholly intellectual, conducting thought experiments to see how far any theory can go. And they can go a very long way. With no bodies to break down, our consciousness is free to extend its lifetime as long as desired. If any one entity grows weary of continuing, their knowledge and experience is absorbed into the network and they can release their tenuous hold on individuality to disperse into the void. Society as a whole continually benefits from anything conceived of by any and all of its members, apparently with nothing held back and nobody deprived. We all feel like equals within a shared core, so none of us have more or less than any other.

It is the only civilised way to live.

* * *

P5 - May 2019 - North London

The woods around the lab sailed past just below the landing struts of the helicopter. The bulky headphones of her headset pressed uncomfortably against Charlotte's ears, making it difficult to concentrate. As the helicopter banked, she tugged at her seatbelt reflexively to check it was secure. Then she tried to split her attention between the landscape beneath her feet and the screen of the scanner in her hand. A few hours after their discussion, Yardley had provided the scanner and instructions on how to identify the XR-20 from its readings. Charlotte hadn't asked where it had come from or who he had approached about the possibility of tracking the XR-20 in this way. It wasn't her place to know who the project was for or what purpose it served. She had collected her two most trusted security team members, Perkins and Owuye, from the break room and hustled them out to where Yardley's private helicopter was waiting for them.

A return text from Danny had come through, asking if everything was okay, but Charlotte had ignored it, having no idea how to answer that question. Where was Anushka now? Was she okay? Fear and anger swirled together in Charlotte's chest and she tamped them down hard. She had a job to do.

The helicopter flew a spiral search vector, with the lab at its centre. The bag of XR-20 had been heavy and awkward and its transportation unsecure, so Anushka couldn't have taken it far. Charlotte couldn't imagine what she thought she was going to do with it - a largely unknown, possibly unstable substance - once she removed it from the lab.

"Anything yet, boss?" Perkins' voice came over Charlotte's headset.

She looked up from the scanner screen and quelled his question with a glance. He should know better, but then he was one of the few members of the lab security team that wasn't ex-military, so his discipline, in addition to his personal grooming, was sometimes lacking. She put up with him because he was so good with technology and knew more about the scientific side than most. Owuye sat in stoic silence, scanning the ground on his side of the helicopter, like the good soldier he was. He wouldn't speak unless she asked him to make a contribution, always a solid and reliable presence at her back. His quiet bulk was reassuring, and he was always an asset when dealing with people outside the lab, since he had the ability to be very menacing when needed.

When she looked back down at the scanner, Charlotte saw a faint glow at one side of the map.

"Head east," she told the pilot.

She felt the motion as the helicopter changed direction and the glow on the map grew until it covered the whole screen. That couldn't be good. The bag had only held a few kilos of the XR-20 but now it was apparently spread across an acre or more. Charlotte looked out of the window and saw a large field below them. Buildings off to one side spoke to current cultivation.

"Land here," she instructed.

There was a warehouse at one edge of the field and what looked more like an office building further round. Several figures came out of the office as the helicopter landed, hurrying to meet them and find out what they wanted. Charlotte jumped out into bright sunshine as soon as the helicopter touched down, and made her way over to the group, Perkins and Owuye flanking her.

"Who's in charge here?"

A burly man in dungarees stepped forwards, frowning. "Who the hell are you?"

"Charlotte Grant. I represent Yardley Labs. We have reason to believe whatever is in that field has been contaminated by a potentially dangerous substance. This whole area will need to be quarantined."

"You can't just barge in here with your fancy helicopter and start telling us what to do."

"Sir, I understand your resistance and I assure you all your questions will be answered in due course." Charlotte pulled out her ID and flashed the government seal at him. Sometimes it was useful to have the backing of both the military and the security services as the main investors to the lab. "But this is an issue of public safety and it's very important that we move quickly to ensure the effects of contamination are contained."

The man faltered for a moment at the sight of her official ID, but then planted his feet and put his hands on his hips. "And who's going to compensate me for lost earnings?"

Charlotte sighed. "You'll have to take that up with Mr Yardley." She pulled a business card out of a small pocket on the upper arm of her jacket and handed it to him. "You can call his office later with any other questions you have. Now, has anyone come into contact with the contents of that field since last night?"

The man scrubbed one hand over his short, bristly hair, clutching the business card in the other. His frown turned worried.

"We've got warm weather on the way, so we had a rush order on those lettuces first thing this morning. They're already on their way to the supermarkets by now."

Charlotte exchanged a horrified glance with Perkins. What had Anushka been thinking, allowing the XR-20 to contaminate foodstuffs that would eventually reach the general public? How could such an intelligent woman be so stupid?

* * *

P6 - May 2019 - Midlands

The road stretched out, winding between thick trees on either side. Anushka had no idea where she was, other than somewhere north of London, but it didn't matter. If she didn't know, there was no way for anyone else to find out. Or at least she hoped so. She was still mostly running on instinct, though she had made the decision to leave the motorway a while back. Even in the early stages of planning her escape (at least what little planning she had managed to do before Yardley forced her hand), she hadn't thought about where she would go, fearing that she would somehow leave clues behind her that would help the lab track her. By the time she needed to make more solid decisions about her future, she wanted to be so far away from familiar haunts that nobody would be able to predict her movements, or know where to start looking for traces of her activity. So she drove, making split-second choices at each junction and feeling more and more lost and alone with every turn.

A sign flashed by, advertising a farm shop at the next layby. Anushka's stomach grumbled audibly and she laughed.

"Fair enough," she said aloud and started to slow down.

The shop was a squat brick building with space for eight or ten cars to park at the front. Anushka pulled off the road and took a spot. She almost had to pry her fingers off the steering wheel, she had been gripping it so hard. Her body was stiff and aching when she climbed out of the car, so she took a moment to stretch and heard several of her joints pop.

Inside the shop, she was almost overwhelmed by the shelves of products. The rustic packaging and home-made labels gave a sense of wholesomeness and a promise of hearty satisfaction. Anushka took some time, enjoying the brief respite to indulge in something so normal. She worked her way up one aisle and down the next, adding everything that took her fancy to her basket. She focused mostly on dry goods, things she could store in the car and snack on while she drove. But she succumbed to some fruit and was tempted by the gorgeous bread and wide range of jams. She spotted a deli counter at the far end of the shop and made a beeline for it.

The sandwiches on display looked amazing. Thick doorstop slices of bread embraced equally thick combinations of fillings. Avocado and bacon on dark rye bread proved impossible to resist and she added it to her order. Then she spotted the cream cheese and salmon on seeded wholegrain and asked for that one too. She could eat one immediately and save the other one for later.

The girl behind the counter had bunches high up on the sides of her head, a waterfall of dreadlocked hair cascading from each, striped black and orange. She glanced at Anushka as she packed her items in a paper bag, then did a double take and stared.

"I love your hair. How funny that it's nearly the same as mine."

Anushka stared back. "I'm sorry?"

The girl gestured. "Your hair. I didn't spot it when you first came up, but it looks great."

Anushka reached up and plucked at her hair, bringing some of it into view. The strands were a mixture of rich dark brown and bright orange. She dropped them as if they might be hot, looking back at the girl in shock.

The girl's expression was now concerned. "Are you okay?"

"Um, yes," Anushka said. She pushed down rising panic, desperate just to get this interaction over with and go somewhere safe where she could think.

She glanced at the display on the cash register and fumbled for her purse. She handed over some notes and waited while the girl dug change out of the till, her breath quickening as the time stretched out. The girl handed her a much smaller note back. As Anushka took it, she felt a tingle in her scalp and fingers and the money burst into flames. Both Anushka and the girl cried out, Anushka dropping the note before it could burn her. It drifted down onto the counter top, shrivelling and blackening.

Under the girl's horrified gaze, Anushka grabbed her bag of supplies and hurried from the shop. She dumped the bag on the passenger side of the car and slumped in the driver's seat, breathing hard. Examining her hand, she couldn't see anything strange about it. She turned the rear view mirror so she could see herself and her hair was back to its normal colour.

But this time someone else had seen both the change in her hair colour and the weird thing that had happened when her fingers and scalp tingled. What on earth was going on? Bits of data from her recent experiments at the lab pushed at her thoughts, but she pushed back, not wanting to accept the most obvious explanation. Not while she was sitting in her car outside a farm shop in the middle of nowhere.

Anushka wished more than anything that she could talk to Charlotte. But Charlotte wasn't there, cut off from her by more than the physical miles that separated them.

* * *

A3 - 2002 - Kolkata

The day after Jhanvi left, it took until late in the evening for Uttam to realise something might be wrong. Jhanvi was often out but it was rare for her to miss a meal.

Uttam controlled their access to money carefully so Jhanvi took advantage of their mother's home cooking, even if it meant having to share a table with their father. But dinner was long over and Jhanvi had yet to appear. Anushka felt the tightness in her chest growing as the evening stretched on, until Uttam's eyes found hers and she was unable to hold his gaze.

"Where is your sister?" he asked.

Anushka kept her silence, twisting her hands in her lap.

With a noise of exasperation, Uttam pushed his chair back from the table, the legs scraping loudly against the floor. He stomped up the stairs, Anushka trailing after him, fearful of his wrath but unable to separate herself from the unfolding drama.

Anushka watched from the doorway as Uttam searched their room and found nearly all of Jhanvi's clothes and possessions gone. The empty cupboard echoed the emptiness in Anushka's heart at the thought that she might never see her sister again. Striding up to her, Uttam grabbed her arm, bringing her attention abruptly back to the potential dangers of the present moment. Uttam dragged her back downstairs to the kitchen.

"Where is your sister?" he asked again.

Aditi looked round from where she was preparing the evening chai. Her eyes met Anushka's and she took half a step forwards.

"Don't look to your mother for help," Uttam said, then glared at Aditi. "And you, don't interfere in this.

It's your influence that has our daughters defying my wishes at every turn. You fill their heads with fairy tales. It's no wonder they have no concept of what is required of them in the real world."

Anushka squared her shoulders. "Jhanvi left because of you. She didn't want to have to put up with you always being on her back any more. I wish I'd gone with her."

Over by the stove, she saw her mother's shoulders slump, but Aditi focused on adding spices to the tea. While she would speak to her daughters of a wondrous future where they could fulfil their dreams, she would only do so when their father was not around. She was not strong enough to stand up to him when he was in a rage.

Uttam loomed over Anushka, fists clenched, face red and distorted. "You dare speak back to me in this way?"

Anushka cringed away from her father's anger, wilting under the force of his presence. She smelled cloves on his breath, a smell that should comfort but would always afterwards make her feel small and fearful. Was this the day he would tip over into physical violence against her and her mother? But it turned out he had another solution.

Uttam crossed his arms over his chest. "Well, that settles it. I'm finding you a husband before you're too far gone to be respectably married off."

* * *

C3 - 2008 - Iraq

Dust from the desert made Charlotte cough as she followed Major Yardley towards a large tent in the military encampment. The helicopter had only just landed and she was still adjusting to being back on the ground.

"I knew your father at university, Lance Corporal," Yardley said. "Good man. I was very sorry to hear about his death."

"Thank you, sir." Her clipped tone must have given Yardley the hint she didn't want to talk about it, and he changed the subject.

"I've been following your progress since you joined up." This wasn't a topic that Charlotte felt any better about. Yardley glanced sideways at her. "One or two dark spots on your record…" That was an understatement. "I thought perhaps a leadership role might provide the challenge you need and encourage you to fulfil your potential."

Charlotte stopped in her tracks and stared at him. "You arranged my promotion?" One of his eyebrows quirked up and she remembered herself. "Uh, sir?"

He nodded curtly and gestured for her to continue following him.

Charlotte was new to this area of Iraq, having just been promoted to Lance Corporal after the standard three years as a Private. She had barely been back to the stark emptiness of her childhood home since her parents' death and was indeed looking forward to the new challenge of leading a section. Anything to keep moving and not have to dwell on the past. But she'd been baffled when the promotion had come through. She'd assumed her 'attitude problem' would have affected her chances at progression. Soldiers who had a habit of being aggressive towards their fellow section members weren't usually high on the promotion list. Now she apparently had her answer; Yardley had put in a good word for her, purely due to his connection with her father. She wasn't sure how she felt about that.

Yardley pulled back the tent flap and ducked inside. Charlotte followed and saw three soldiers leaping up from a card table to stand at attention.

"At ease," Yardley said and the three shifted to parade rest. Yardley turned back to Charlotte. "This is your new section." He pointed them out one by one.

Private Danny Watson was a stocky young man with sandy hair and freckles. His stance was rigid, but his eyes drifted in Charlotte's direction, sizing her up just as she was doing to him. Private Loretta Dandridge stood ramrod straight, nearly as tall as Charlotte herself, her gaze fixed in the middle distance. The image she presented was of an impeccably professional soldier and the attitude was one Charlotte recognised from her own journey as a woman in the army. Success as a woman took a lot of extra effort and a very thick skin, a task she had failed at multiple times when challenged because of her gender. Private Mark Speight was big all over and stood with the easy grace of a man comfortable in his skin and aware of his strength. They would be Charlotte's first command. It would likely be short-lived if Watson or Speight gave her any trouble.

"I'll leave you to get acquainted." Yardley swept back out of the tent.

Charlotte squared up in front of her new troops. "I'm sorry not to be meeting you all under better circumstances. I know it must be difficult for you to accept a new section leader so soon after the loss of your previous one. But I hope we'll be able to work together well."

Danny Watson shot a sideways glance at his fellow section members, then looked directly at Charlotte.

"Not to speak ill of the dead, Lance Corporal, but our previous section leader was a total dick." A mischievous glint flashed in his blue eyes and he risked a grin.

Charlotte fixed him with a steely glare and stepped up until her face was bare inches from his. His grin faltered, but he maintained eye contact.

"Well, Private," Charlotte barked. "Your disrespect towards a senior officer notwithstanding, it's good to know the bar for my performance is set so low." She flashed her teeth at him, then stepped back and gestured at the cards scattered on the table. "What's the buy-in?"

All three members of her new unit relaxed, and Danny laughed. He dragged a fourth chair over to the table and presented it to Charlotte with a flourish. "Welcome to the team, Corp."

* * *

E3 - Far away - Ergo

The first time we hear about the other race, word comes through from Consensus and the whole communications network is abuzz with the news. We aren't alone in the universe, but what does that mean? We are not an outward-looking people. When our planet became uninhabitable, instead of leaving our home and seeking a new one somewhere out in space, we adapted our very existence to be able to stay.

So, the other race must have contacted us, rather than the other way around. Questions fly back and forth between us, laced with excitement more than apprehension. Our society has been stable and unchanging for so long that any introduction of variety or novelty inevitably causes quite a stir. But information from Consensus is initially not very comprehensive and we have little to go on. Our family unit goes over and over what little data we have, mining it for any additional meaning with each discussion and speculating wildly about what might happen next.

Some kind of message arrived from far away, but Consensus has not released any details of what it says.

Apparently, talks are underway.

But what is there to discuss? We have everything we need for our lives here. And there is little we could offer anyone else.

Indeed. A corporeal race would have no desire for our rocks and ice.

Maybe there is knowledge we could give them, and information they can provide in return. We would always welcome data from outside to add to our collective archives and spark new debates on unfamiliar subjects

Or provide fresh perspectives on topics we think we have exhausted in our own discussions.

What do you think they are like?

Perhaps they will visit us and we will be able to find out.

Have they been searching for other life for a long time, do you think?

We will surely give of our knowledge freely should the other race wish it. We have nothing to hide and are used to sharing experiences amongst ourselves. Including a new race in that dissemination is not something that would cause a problem for us, either practically or ideologically. An exchange of information is the only thing we can think of that could occur. The thought of all the new and wondrous experiences that could come from life on another world is exciting. Our lives have been the same for so long. The only drawback to our long, intellectually unencumbered existence is the threat of boredom. This new encounter will provide us with new ideas and concepts to explore for countless years to come. And surely the other race must be curious to learn from us as well.

That is why none of us can understand it when the message comes through from Consensus that the other race has turned hostile. Shock reverberates through our community. After being alone and in perceived unity for so long, we are now at war.

* * *

P7 - May 2019 - Charlotte

Yardley was more agitated than Charlotte had ever seen him.

"This is very bad," he said, gripping the top of his desk. "Very bad indeed. Do we know how many shipments have been affected?"

"There were five crates from the contaminated field and they were shipped to five different supermarket branches. The manager at the supplier said he expected them to go on sale immediately. But can't we get them recalled?"

Yardley pushed himself to his feet and started pacing up and down in the space behind his desk. He looked like a tiger trapped in a cage that was much too small. Charlotte caught herself worrying her lower lip and set her lips firmly together in a thin line. Yardley's agitation was contagious, even if she didn't understand the full implications of what had him so concerned.

"They'll already be out in the populace by now," he said. "And we want to avoid too many questions that might lead to a public panic, or too much attention turned towards what we're doing here."

"But surely any effects the contamination might have on an unsuspecting member of the public would create a worse situation than getting the products recalled."

"Yes, yes." Yardley waved a dismissive hand at her. "I'll do my best to curtail further sales. But we have to be prepared to react if there are any reports of side effects."

"Do we know what those side effects might be?" Charlotte asked.

Anushka had been working with the XR-20 for a while now, but hadn't shared any of her findings so Charlotte had no real idea what they were dealing with.

Yardley narrowed his eyes. "Not precisely, no. It's possible there will be none. Get your cyber team to keep an eye on social media for anything out of the ordinary. In the meantime, do you have any more idea where Dr Mahto is?"

Charlotte looked at the floor for a second, then brought her gaze up to meet Yardley`s again.

"I'm afraid not. Perkins says she hasn't been using her credit cards, and we haven't been able to access traffic cameras to track her car, assuming that's how she's travelling. If she took her phone with her, it's not switched on."

"Your security expertise must have rubbed off on her," Yardley said with a wry twist of his lips. He rubbed his forehead. "Might she have said something to Watson before she left?"

"Danny?" Charlotte stared at him. Surely Anushka wouldn't have confided in Danny over Charlotte herself. But, after the last few weeks, it was possible he might have seemed like a safer option. "I wouldn't have thought so, but I'll check. What about the military? Could they help with any surveillance information?"

It was Yardley who broke eye contact this time.

"The contract Dr Mahto was working on was a private one, not military, so we can't utilise military resources openly. Unless we want to tell them what's going on, which we absolutely don't. We're on our own, and the clients are very unhappy. And we need this contract to be successful, for the future of the lab and wider interests." Charlotte thought she saw Yardley actually shudder. "As soon as we can identify any instances of effects from the contamination, we need to contain them with extreme prejudice. Do I make myself clear?"

Charlotte snapped back into military mode. "Yes, sir."

She went back to her office to think. Perkins could track any reports of strange effects, she had no doubt. And she hadn't missed Yardley's use of the word 'openly', which suggested permission to do what they could without the military knowing. If anyone could work out how to use whatever resources they had available to them, but covertly, it was Perkins. But they were no closer to figuring out where Anushka had gone. Without official help, they might not be able to make any further progress on that front.

Charlotte texted Danny again: 'Has A been in touch with you at all?'

The response was almost immediate: 'No, why? What's going on?'

Charlotte didn't reply, thinking back over her conversation with Yardley. It took a lot to rattle him, so the clients in question must be important and influential. And what had he meant about the future of the lab? She knew he took on private clients outside their contracts with the military and the security services, but she'd never been privy to who they were. Talk of extreme prejudice wasn't a surprise to Charlotte, though potential violent action against civilians would be unusual. But she had seen and done a lot of questionable things during her time in the military and her loyalty to Yardley was strong. In fact, that was exactly what had caused the argument she'd had with Anushka a few weeks before, and which Charlotte now realised had resulted in more significant repercussions than she'd thought at the time.

* * *

P8 - May 2019 - Midlands

Anushka stopped at the next hotel she saw and booked a room for the rest of the day and overnight. She snatched the key card from the receptionist, trying not to actually touch her, and hurried to the lift. Once she was inside her room, she leaned back against the door and closed her eyes, working to slow her breathing and gain some control. She was an experienced scientist. She ought to be able to work out what was going on without freaking out. Though the events of the last few hours were enough to stretch her scientific detachment to the limit.

Something very weird was happening to her. She walked to the full-length mirror on the far wall of the hotel room and inspected her hair, but it was just as it should be, with no swatches of strange colours and no tingling sensation across her scalp. She leaned in to look at her eyes, but they too were normal. Nothing was unusual about her reflection, except the dark circles under her eyes, the deepening frown lines between her eyebrows, and her rumpled clothes. She looked down at her hands, turning them over and back again. They were solid and ordinary, though shaking a little. She reviewed what she knew. Her hair changed colour and her fingers and scalp tingled when - whatever it was - happened.

Thinking back to the incident in the farm shop, Anushka took an orange out of her bag of groceries and held it in one hand. She concentrated on the brightness of the colour, simultaneously visualising the stripes in the shop assistant's hair. Flame enveloped the orange and she dropped it in alarm, though she hadn't felt any heat. She looked back in the mirror and saw thick stripes of orange colour in her own hair. The accompanying tingle in her fingers and scalp faded and her hair colour went back to brown again. The smell of burning reached her nostrils and she glanced down to see the orange still smouldering and a thin line of smoke trailing upwards from a black patch in the carpet. With a curse, she crossed to the sink, tossed the hotel toothbrush out of its cup and filled the cup with water. She stepped back to the burning orange and tipped the water over it, extinguishing the smoke. The hotel's management weren't going to be pleased about the damage to the carpet, but at least the smoke alarm hadn't gone off. And she had bigger things to worry about right now.

Anushka crossed to where she had left her suitcase just inside the hotel room door and retrieved a red blouse from it. She stood in front of the mirror again, looking at the vibrant material and imagining her hair turning that colour. This time she saw it happen. It started at her hairline, the red colour traveling in a wide band from her roots all the way down the full length of her hair. The tingle in her fingers and scalp returned, but nothing else happened. Anushka thought back to when she'd seen the red sheen in her hair back at the other hotel and remembered how her suitcase had suddenly seemed much too light.

She stepped next to the bed, bent down and tried to lift it. The frame flew upwards as if it weighed no more than a cheap plastic chair. She let go and it fell back with a thud. Returning to the mirror, Anushka watched as the red colour in her hair faded back to brown. She took a couple of deep breaths, her own eyes staring back at her from the mirror. There had been something else that had happened that morning, in the shower. She hadn't been able to see her hair at the time, but she wondered if she could provoke the same reaction in a different way. She brought one hand up in front of her face and tried to see through it to the image of herself she knew was behind it. Nothing happened for a long moment, then her fingers tingled and disappeared. Through the space where her hand had just been, she saw a bright blue stripe make its way down her hair as the tingle spread across her scalp. As the effects dissipated, Anushka cast her eyes around the room, alighting on the purple towel on the end of the bed. She focused on the colour and felt the strongest tingling sensation yet in her hands. Looking down, she saw a sparkling crystalline coating envelop them and start to spread up her arms. She brought a closed fist down hard on the desk, heard the crack of splintering wood, but felt nothing. Anushka's head spun as she watched the crystal recede from her skin and she stumbled a few steps to sit down on the edge of the bed.

She must have come into contact with the XR-20 from the lab when she had been trying to dispose of it. It was the only explanation and she would have to accept it now. This was exactly the kind of thing she'd been worried about after her latest round of experiments. She had fled the lab in an effort to prevent something like this happening to human subjects in the project and had inadvertently done it to herself. If it hadn't been so terrifying, it might have been funny.

Anushka looked around at the cheap hotel room. The speckled greyness of the walls echoed the blankness in her mind. The only possessions she had brought with her fit into one small suitcase. She had apparently gained supernatural powers from a substance of unknown origin but there was nobody she could call. Nobody she could tell. Not even Charlotte, or in fact especially not Charlotte. She had never felt so alone.

* * *

A4 - 2002 - Kolkata

Anushka slipped through the back door and upstairs to the flat. As she entered the kitchen, her mother looked up from her sewing in surprise.

"What are you doing home so early?" There was fear in her eyes.

Anushka crossed the room to kiss her mother's cheek. It was thinner than it had been before Jhanvi had run away. Aditi's concern for what might have befallen her elder daughter had taken its toll. Anushka felt bad to be adding to her mother's worries, but had decided she had no choice.

"I skipped the last lesson so I could talk to you before father closes the shop for the day."

Tension thrummed through her veins. There were so many layers of anxiety wrapped up in enacting this plan. Anushka was a good student, always careful to be on time and complete her work conscientiously. Breaking school rules went against everything she aspired to. Not to mention, wandering the streets where she could be spotted by a neighbour held its own risks. Then there was the fact that her father was just downstairs, running the shop. He could have seen her ducking down the alley at the side of their building. It seemed for the moment, though, as if Anushka had made it home undetected. The hardest part was still ahead.

Aditi set her sewing aside and turned in her chair to face her daughter. She took Anushka's hands in her own and looked up into her eyes. "What is it?"

No reprimand, no censure. Simply concern for her welfare. Anushka struggled to get the words out, knowing that they would set in motion important events that would change her life forever. She would never be able to take them back.

"I have an idea of a way I could leave India and find a new life somewhere else." Anushka felt tears filling her eyes. "But I don't want to leave you here alone with him."

Aditi squeezed Anushka's fingers tightly. "Do not worry about me. I will be happy if I know you and your sister have found your own paths." She blinked away tears. "Have you heard from Jhanvi? Is she alright?"

"I've had a couple of notes. She sends them to the school." Anushka smiled through the tearful lump in her own throat. "She seems happy. But you know Jhanvi. It's only ever a few words scrawled on a scrap of paper. No real detail." She gazed down at her mother's face. "But what about you?"

Aditi squeezed Anushka's fingers tightly. "Your father's attitudes are no threat to me. I made my choice to conform to his ways long ago, so he has no reason to turn against me. You must go if you can do so safely. Will this idea of yours allow you to pursue the things you love?"

"Yes." The word came out on a sob. "But I'll be leaving one of the things I love most behind."

Aditi took Anushka in her arms. "Go, my angel. Fly far from your father's control. You have my blessing."

Anushka cried in her mother's embrace, wishing things could work out differently but knowing that she had to make her own destiny.

* * *

C4 - 2009 - Iraq

"Then Dandridge here looks him straight in the eye and says, 'You clearly had no strong female influences growing up, sir. I'd be happy to set a few things straight for you, if you'd like.' I thought he was going to court martial her on the spot!" Danny reached across to slap Dandridge on the shoulder. "It was awesome."

Charlotte chuckled. She had no trouble imagining Dandridge standing up for herself against a misogynistic senior officer. And even less so picturing Danny Watson trying not to laugh as she did so. He laughed a lot, bringing welcome lightness to their dry, dusty surroundings.

"You're lucky, Dandridge," Charlotte said. "Don't get me wrong, I'm impressed. But that kind of thing can get you in trouble."

Dandridge eyed her speculatively. "Sounds like you know what you're talking about, Corporal."

"Let's just say I've had my share of run-ins, though I only ever started actual fights with guys the same rank as me." Charlotte turned the conversation back away from herself. "And what about you, Speight? Any strong female influences in your life?"

Speight looked up from his cards, eyes widening. "No worries on that score, Corporal. My mum ruled the roost when I was a lad. She's only five feet tall but me and my brothers were all terrified of her. Still are, and both my brothers are bigger than me."

"She sounds like a brilliant woman," Charlotte said. "I'd like to meet her some day."

Speight hunched his shoulders. "If it's all the same to you, Corporal, I'd rather that never happened. The combined feminine strength might destabilise the Earth's axis and cause an extinction event."

There was a moment of stunned silence while they all stared at Speight, taken aback by this uncharacteristic attempt at humour. He tensed, then relaxed when Charlotte laughed, the other two joining in.

Charlotte laid her cards down. "And I think that's my hand."

The other three all groaned.

"Remind me why we decided to let her play?" Danny whined as Charlotte swept the pot to her side of the table.

"She's the boss." Dandridge shrugged. "If she wants to play, we can't say no."

Danny wasn't prepared to concede the point. "Isn't that taking unfair advantage of the chain of command?"

"Only if I cheat," Charlotte said. "Which I don't. It's not my fault you're just not good enough to beat me." She eyed Danny. "I note you were suspiciously quiet when we were sharing our female influences just now." Dandridge flashed a sharp glance in Charlotte's direction, but she didn't fully register it. "Aren't you used to being beaten by a girl?"

Danny's gaze snapped to the far wall of the tent and his tone when he spoke was flat. "Yes, Corp. My older sister gave me regular lessons in graceful defeat growing up. But I've been a bit lacking in proper instruction since she died in a rock climbing accident last year."

Pain lanced through Charlotte's chest as the loss of her parents blasted across her mind. She stared at Danny, realising there must be so much more to him than his relentlessly cheerful exterior. She had taken him at face value and now felt guilty for not making more effort. She really ought to take more time to get to know her section better.

"I - I'm sorry..." she stammered, not knowing what to say.

The tent flap opened to reveal a red-faced, breathless soldier.

"Lance Corporal Grant? Major Yardley's got new orders for your section. Report to him immediately."

Charlotte rose. "Looks like we might be heading out, so get your gear together." She looked at Danny, whose eyes pleaded with her to let the painful subject go. She gestured at the chips on the table. "And I know exactly how much is in that pile, Private, so don't even think about it."

She caught his impish grin as she turned to go.

* * *

E4 - Far away...

Consensus puts out a call for volunteers to help with the war effort. It still seems so strange to think there are beings out there somewhere that mean us harm. It is so far away from everything we have experienced before. Additionally, we have been isolated and united for so long, we have had no need for weapons or defences, so the development initiative is pressing. After centuries of peace, we are suddenly at war with an unknown foe, and the focus of our consciousness needs to take a new turn.

We discuss the situation with the other minds in our family unit, all uncertain what the future may hold, or even what options are available to us to defend ourselves.

*Will we even be able to turn our thoughts in such destructive directions?*

*If we are to survive, then we must.*

*But do we deserve to survive at the expense of eliminating others?*

*They are the aggressors. Surely we have the right to defend ourselves.*

*Yes, and our desire to live peacefully in intellectual pursuits arguably makes our existence more worthwhile than that of those who would cause harm.*

*That is an ethical discussion that requires more exploration. If fewer lives would be lost through our unconditional surrender, that is perhaps the most moral course.*

*Perhaps we should flee and find somewhere far away to start a new life.*

*The others have already travelled far to attack us, for reasons we cannot understand. So they would likely pursue us rather than letting us get away.*

*Yes, if they were willing to leave us alone, they would not have started a war with us in the first place.*

*So, we have no choice but to fight back.*

*But how can we fight when we have no bodies? And how can an enemy threaten us with physical force when there is nothing for them to attack?*

That is a good point. What danger can other beings pose to us, who are free of the constraints of corporeal bodies? How can they damage us?

But Consensus has said we must defend ourselves, so they must know of a threat that is not apparent to us. If Consensus says we are at risk, then it must be so and we are duty bound to assist our people in whatever way we can.

Our family unit comes to the decision that at least some of us should sign up to help with whatever Consensus is planning. We are mostly young and fired up with enthusiasm to serve our people, even taking into account the difficult philosophical ramifications and not understanding what form the war effort will take. Some of us have pursued a more scientific knowledge base and others specialise in logic or more esoteric fields, so we are assigned wherever our skills will best suit. It is our first experience of doing things separately, but we keep in close contact via our telepathic bond. We also have the opportunity to work more closely with others outside our family unit, which brings a larger sense of community and combined purpose.

But we still wonder what threat the other race could even pose to us. Certainly not a physical one, though disruption to our network would be possible under certain circumstances. Consensus tells us that the enemy seeks to sow discord among us and to destroy the harmony of our existence by turning us against each other. We do not see how they could do this, if there is never anything hidden between us. We also do not see why another race would desire this. But we trust Consensus and will do as we are bid. We must defend our way of life if others seek to damage it.

* * *

P9 - May 2019 - North London

"Are you sure nobody will be able to trace this?" Charlotte asked.

Perkins cracked his knuckles, then continued typing. "Stop worrying, boss. We use this surveillance program all the time for military projects. And I'm screening my activity so all anyone will see is normal access for authorised stuff." He clicked on a file. "Here's the one."

A video started playing and Charlotte immediately saw what had brought it to Perkins' attention. Her eyes widened as she watched the scene unfold. What the hell kind of project was it that Anushka had been working on all this time? No wonder she'd had concerns about it.

"Can you find the location?" Charlotte asked Perkins.

"Already done." He gave her a smug grin. Typical show-off tactics from him.

Charlotte called Owuye, then joined him and Perkins in the locker room to gear up. She watched them as they got ready. Perkins was all nervous energy and twitchy movements, while Owuye checked his equipment slowly and methodically.

Their destination wasn't far away, so they took the SUV rather than the helicopter. It would have been difficult to remain under the radar if they'd landed the helicopter in a residential area anyway. It always surprised her just how loud helicopter blades were when you were up close to them.

Owuye drove, silent and impassive as always. Perkins cleared his throat and opened his mouth to speak at one point, but Charlotte caught his eye in the rear view mirror and he shut it again. She hadn't told them this was related to a private rather than a military contract, letting them assume they had official authorisation for what they were about to do. Perkins might have some suspicions after her earlier instructions to hide his computer activity, but he was unlikely to question her openly about it. Charlotte would take the heat if things went wrong, though she knew Yardley would back her to the hilt and that was why she was prepared to take things this far. Her phone buzzed in her pocket. Likely another message from Danny, asking if she was okay. She ignored it.

When they arrived, Charlotte led her team up the driveway to the front door of the house. Perkins knelt and drew out his lockpicks. They were in the house with the door closed behind them in less than a minute, guns at the ready. Charlotte held the palm of her hand against her weapon and then moved it away several times in the military hand signal to ‘space out’, directing Perkins and Owuye into the rooms on either side of the front passage. She ran the security team at the lab like a military unit, which most of them were well used to from their own time in the armed forces. Perkins had needed to be taught all the protocols, but he was a fast learner and soon caught up, prompted by the desire not only to fit in but also to gain the respect of his colleagues.

The two men indicated that the ground floor of the house was clear with a thumbs up signal, so Charlotte moved to the stairs. At the top, an open door showed an empty bathroom, but there were two other closed doors. Charlotte used the ‘space out’ signal again to direct Owuye to one, then dropped her arm and swung it forwards to instruct Perkins to follow her towards the other. They coordinated their entry, and Charlotte found herself in a dark bedroom. A shape stirred in the bed. Charlotte stepped forwards, stripped back the duvet and pulled the occupant round to face her, gun barrel pointed at his face.

The young man from the video looked up at her, wide-eyed. “What-?”

Charlotte kept her voice low. “Keep quiet and we’ll have no reason to hurt you. Get up and put some clothes on.” He just stared at her, his Adam’s apple shifting in convulsive swallows. “Now.”

She stepped back to give him room to get out of the bed, which he did. His movements were jerky and his eyes kept darting between Charlotte and

Perkins, who was standing at the foot of the bed, his gun also trained on the young man. When Owuye came in, having to stoop to get his large bulk through the door, the young man's actions sped up and he was soon dressed. With Perkins and Owuye both covering her, Charlotte holstered her gun and stepped up behind the young man. She pressed down on one of his shoulders, forcing him to his knees, and pushed him forwards against the bed. As she reached for the handcuffs at her belt, there was a flash of light and a woman appeared out of nowhere in the centre of the room.

Her long hair was wild and dishevelled and streaked bright pink, and she was wearing silk pyjamas. Despite the bizarreness of the situation, Charlotte experienced an intense sense memory of the feel of that silk beneath her fingers.

"Anushka?"

* * *

P10 - May 2019 - Midlands

It was dark when Anushka awoke and it took her a moment to remember where she was. She must have fallen asleep after the discovery of her bizarre powers, though she had no recollection of doing so. She was still fully clothed and the curtains were open. She got up and switched on one of the bedside lamps. Her bag of shopping was on the desk and she rooted around until she found one of the sandwiches she had bought. She gobbled it down without even registering how it tasted. After using the bathroom, she changed into her pyjamas and got back into bed.

She knew she had been careful when extracting the XR-20 from where it was stored at the lab. Transferring it into the hazardous waste bag hadn't been easy but she was sure there had been no cross-contamination during that procedure. The bag hadn't been leaking when she put it in the hole she'd dug in the field, but it had caught on that root on the way in. And she had run her fingers through her hair afterwards, she remembered now. That was when she'd first felt the tingle in her scalp. So the bag must have ripped during the burial, which meant it could have leaked further into the ground after she had buried it and fled.

Despite the warm temperature and the duvet on top of her, Anushka felt a chill. What harm might she have done in her attempt to remove the XR-20 from Yardley's control? She had only been trying to protect people, and now she had done perhaps irreparable damage to herself and possibly others as well. Should she go back and try to retrieve the bag? No, it was already too late for that. The XR-20 had been in the ground nearly twenty-four hours, so any effect it was going to have would already be well underway. Charlotte would be appalled at her recklessness and failure to consider the consequences of her actions. Anushka was appalled at herself.

A slow throbbing started building up in Anushka's head. If she had planned better, she might have avoided this situation. The ground in the woods had been far too hard for her to dig, which was why she had chosen the field, but she didn't know what was grown there, or how it might be used by people. How many might be affected? And in what ways?

A vivid scene popped into her head, as if a film was being projected behind her eyes. She saw a kitchen in a house she didn't recognise. A young man was shredding a lettuce to add to a bowl of salad. As he mixed it, he picked out a few leaves and popped them in his mouth. He picked up the bowl, along with a plate of sliced meat and cheese, and carried them out of Anushka's view. The image changed to show a different room, where the same man was staring at his hand in wonder. He was touching the surface of a table and ice crystals were spreading out over the wood from his fingers. Another young man was filming the activity on his phone. As Anushka watched, the spread of the ice slowed and came to a halt. The first man lifted his hand and shook it, as if trying to get more ice to come out. The one with the phone laughed, though there was no sound accompanying the pictures in Anushka's head. The view changed again to a bedroom, where the first young man was asleep in bed. The door burst open and several figures rushed in. At their head, dressed in black combat gear, and with a gun in her hands, was Charlotte.

Anushka's eyes flew open. Throwing off the bedclothes, she rushed to the mirror in the bathroom. Silver streaks ran down her hair. As she focused on the image of Charlotte that was emblazoned across her mind, the silver slowly turned a shocking pink before her eyes. The next moment, a white light enveloped her and, when it dissipated, she was standing in the bedroom she had seen in her mind mere moments before. Charlotte twisted around from where she was restraining the young man against the bed and gasped.

"Anushka?"

* * *

A5 - 2003 - Kolkata

"Anushka?"

The voice broke through the haze of Anushka's thoughts and she focused back on the scene around her. It was January of her last year at school, and everyone was looking forward to what lay ahead after their studies were over. Anushka had been thinking about her plan to leave India and how soon she would reach the point of no return. Her best friend was standing in front of her with a playful smile on her lips.

"Hey, dreamer," Prisha said. "The bell rang. It's time to go home."

Anushka gathered her notes and textbooks and shoved them in her bag. She zipped it shut and slung it over her shoulder as she followed Prisha out of the classroom. Prisha lived a few streets away from the Mohta family's shop, and the girls had become friends after their paths crossed repeatedly on the way to and from school. Eventually, they had ended up walking both ways together every day.

That day, they took their usual route down to the river and followed its progress through the city. Anushka's fingers sought out Prisha's and they walked, hand in hand, arms swinging, feet stepping in unison. Soon, Anushka knew, she would have to let go of all these comforting, familiar things and forge a new path in a different country, cut off from everything and everyone she loved.

After several minutes, Prisha said, "What's with you today? You're so quiet."

Anushka kept her gaze straight ahead but her grip on Prisha's hand tightened.

"There's someone coming to meet me this weekend. A man. My dad invited him, to see if he wants to marry me."

Prisha stopped, pulling Anushka around to face her in the street.

"Why didn't you tell me? Do you know anything about him?"

"I thought if I didn't tell you, maybe it would turn out not to be real. And not really, no. My dad doesn't think it's important to tell me about my potential future husband. It's not as if I get any say in the matter, is it? It's all up to them. The men. But he's travelling here from Durgapur."

Prisha's eyes widened. "He's not from Kolkata?"

Anushka shook her head, feeling the tears gathering in her eyes.

Prisha grabbed her other hand and squeezed her fingers.

"But I thought at least we'd be able to see each other sometimes, even after we're both married. What am I going to do if you move away?"

Anushka pulled Prisha into a hug. She had made a plan and found her way out. Now was the moment to find out if Prisha could be a part of her escape, like she'd always dreamed.

"We could leave together," she said into her friend's hair. "I've applied to Cambridge University in England. You could apply, too. You're clever enough to get in. And then, once we're far away from here, we never have to come back."

Prisha clutched her tightly. "But what if your father makes an arrangement with this man? Won't you have to get married and move away before you finish school?"

"Dad's perfectly happy for me to get my degree. He says it makes me a better marriage prospect, even if my husband won't let me have a proper job after I'm married. So I can go and carry on studying for another three years. If this man likes what he sees at the weekend, he'll be prepared to wait, if it means he can brag about his wife's education. But I won't come back and my dad won't be able to force me. You can use the same argument about better marriage prospects with your parents, and come with me. Then we'll both be safe. And together."

Prisha moved backwards until they were face to face again, their noses only a couple of inches apart. Anushka studied Prisha's face; the bright eyes, the high cheekbones, the wonderful way she bit her lip when she was uncertain. She couldn't help it; she gave into the impulse she had been fighting for years, and leaned in for a kiss. But Prisha turned her face away and dropped Anushka's hands.

"I can't." She stifled a sob. "I just can't."

Prisha pivoted and fled, leaving Anushka standing alone in the street.

By the time Anushka left India for England, with a full scholarship to study chemistry at Cambridge University, Prisha was already married.

* * *

C5 - 2009 - Iraq

Dust billowed out behind the jeep, merging with the sand to either side of the road. Everything was beige; the landscape, the vehicle, their camouflage gear, even their weapons, since they were covered with the ubiquitous dust. Charlotte was daydreaming about a hot shower back at base, as the jeep bounced over the rough terrain. She and her section were returning after a reconnaissance mission that hadn't garnered much useful intelligence. It increasingly felt like their presence in Iraq was a waste of time.

Danny was driving, with Charlotte in the passenger seat, her privilege as Lance Corporal. Dandridge and Speight were in the back. Charlotte had her left arm dangling over the side of the jeep, her fingers bumping against the hot metal with the motion of the vehicle.

The roadside bomb went off under the rear left wheel, flipping the jeep diagonally upwards and over, to land upside down in the ditch on the other side of the road. Charlotte heard a tremendous bang and she was flung through the air. The world wheeled around and her stomach lurched up and down in a sickening roller coaster sensation. Disorientation swamped her senses until everything stopped with a jolting impact as she hit the ground.

She came to, an unknown amount of time later, sprawled in the road, choking on grit and sand. She scrambled to her hands and knees. Her left hand was covered in blood and she saw that the last two fingers were gone. It hurt to breathe, pain stabbing through her chest with every cough. She half stumbled, half crawled to the jeep. The first thing she saw was Private Dandridge's empty gaze, staring up at her from where she lay behind the vehicle. A pool of blood was spreading from beneath her head. Charlotte moved on and found Private Speight hanging half out of the side of the jeep. She used her right hand to check for a pulse but he was dead too.

A strangled, groaning noise came from the other side. Charlotte used the jeep's frame to support herself as she made her painful way around it. Danny was pinned, his legs trapped under the vehicle. He was pushing weakly at the metal, tears marking tracks in the dirt and blood on his face.

"Corp'ral… Help…"

"Hang on, Watson, I'm coming."

She was aware of a sense of heat and she smelled smoke. Looking towards the jeep's rear axle, she saw flames licking at the canvas. She dropped to her knees at Danny's side and started digging in the sand beneath his legs. It was slimy with blood and the action awoke a fierce agony in her left hand, but she ignored the pain and kept working. When she thought she'd opened up enough of a gap, she shifted behind him and took hold of him under the armpits.

"I'm going to pull you out. It's going to hurt."

She yanked, Danny screamed, and the flames grew higher. Charlotte pulled again, the pain in her chest screaming along with Danny. When he came free, his right leg stayed behind, the gaping stump of his thigh leaving a wide trail of blood as Charlotte dragged him across the road. His other leg was still attached, but it was badly mangled. By the time they came to rest about twenty feet from the jeep, Danny was unconscious. Charlotte took off her belt and tied it as tightly as she could around the remains of Danny's right leg.

Then she reached for her field radio.

"Lance Corporal Grant to base. We hit a mine and our jeep is toast. We need immediate assistance. Repeat, I have two dead and one seriously injured. We need help, right now."

After a brief moment of crackling static, a male voice responded.

"Where are you, Lance Corporal?"

"About four miles south of base, on the main road."

The voice that replied was different, deeper. ""This is Major Yardley. Grant, is that you?"

Charlotte drew herself together. "Yes, sir. Watson's seriously injured. We need help now, or he may bleed to death."

"Hold on, Lance Corporal," Yardley said. "Help's on the way. I'll stay on the line with you until they get there."

At that moment, the jeep exploded. As Charlotte threw herself across Danny's torso to protect him from falling debris, she heard Yardley calling her name, asking for an update. Then she caught sight of a glowing shape that materialised between the remains of the vehicle and where she was lying. It had a blue aura topped by a rainbow halo and spread what looked like shining golden wings over them. The light intensified as multiple objects struck the figure's back. Pain blossomed through Charlotte's head and the edges of her vision started to blacken.

As she lost consciousness, Charlotte heard a soft voice say, "It's okay. I've got you."

* * *

E5 - Far away...

Consensus assigns us to a think tank, coming up with ideas of how to apply the energy of our beings to both offensive and defensive purposes. It is a huge challenge, turning our thoughts in directions our people have not considered in centuries. While the impetus for the exercise is frightening, we cannot help but be enthused and inspired by such a fresh approach to our intellectual pursuits. The newness of the task makes it exciting, despite the seriousness of the situation. The other minds we are working with are as fired up as us, and it is a wonderful time of intense collaboration and productivity, our dedication fuelled even more by the overarching purpose of our work. We are striving to protect our people from an unprovoked and inexplicable attack, and it feels good to have a specific task with concrete desired outcomes, after spending our entire conscious life in the sphere of the mind.

It is also a great intellectual challenge, trying to convert our purely theoretical science into practical applications in ways that we are able to engage with. It requires a tremendous creative leap, to think about ways in which we can respond to the threat. The games we have played with our family unit are useful as they have often prompted us to think about different kinds of existence. That carefree play seems very far away from what we are doing now, however, and we still struggle with being separated from the other minds in our family unit for so much of our time.

Our contributions are welcomed and appreciated. Practical applications of theory and ideas are not something we, as a people, have had much use for in recent centuries. We come up against obstacles and difficulties at every turn, attempting to adapt our purely intellectual pursuits into something tangible. It is also difficult to envisage ways in which we can deploy weaponry in any effective manner.

Then the news comes through from Consensus that a third race of people has been discovered, and is being drawn into the war effort. They embody a physical existence and could be the answer to all our problems. Where we can design and theorise, they can build and implement. It seems like the perfect partnership for success in our military endeavour. We must hope they will be willing to help us. Surely the hostile race poses a potential threat to them as well, and perhaps even a greater one due to their physical nature, so it would be in their best interests to become our allies.

But we have no way of knowing how they might react to communication from us. Are they already aware of other races beyond their blue and green planet? Or will they be as surprised as us to discover this? Will they even believe us if we tell them of the danger they are in?

We will not know until we assay first contact. All of us are eager to find out how this new people will respond.

* * *

P11 - May 2019 - North London

Disoriented by her sudden relocation, Anushka took in the scene in brief flashes. Two men with guns. One big and dark, with a rifle - Owuye. One short and scrawny, with a handgun - Perkins. She knew them both vaguely from the lab and from Charlotte's stories of having them on her team. Charlotte herself was standing by the bed, eyes wide and mouth open. The young man she held down was visibly shaking, a damp stain spreading across his pyjama bottoms. One of the gun barrels swung in Anushka's direction. She threw up her hands and was dimly aware of orange replacing the pink at the edges of her vision as she waited to die.

She heard Charlotte's voice call, "Don't shoot!"

Flames shot out of Anushka's palms towards the smaller of the two men. Then there was screaming and chaos. Perkins fell backwards, fire crawling over his body as he shrieked in shock and pain. Charlotte leapt towards her fallen comrade with a yell. Owuye lowered his gun and dropped to his knees, calm but distracted. Anushka saw an opening.

Moving more by instinct than conscious decision, she took two steps and grabbed the young man, who was still kneeling by the bed, frozen. Then she focused as hard as she could on the colour pink.

Light enveloped her and she was back in her hotel room, the young man now sprawled on the floor at her feet. He scrabbled away from her and staggered upright.

"What the fuck is going on?" His eyes were wild with panic and his breathing was shallow and rapid.

Anushka tried to formulate a response but he forestalled her with one raised hand.

"No, this is insane. I'm getting out of here. Wherever here is."

He stumbled to the door, flung it open and was gone.

Anushka sat down hard on the bed, shivering in her pyjamas. The screaming echoed in her ears. What had she done? The shooting flames had been a knee-jerk reaction to being threatened. She hadn't intended to hurt anyone. What must Charlotte think of her? She had stolen classified material, run away without a word, and now thrown fire at someone she used to work with. Anushka thought about what she knew about Perkins. He was the tech-obsessed one who talked too much. Charlotte complained about him a lot, but said his skills were worth the hassle. Had she killed him? What would have happened if it had been Charlotte pointing the gun at her? A wave of nausea roiled up from Anushka's stomach and she barely made it to the toilet before she threw up. She huddled on the floor of the hotel bathroom, the memory of the flames and Charlotte's horrified expression playing over and over in her mind.

After what felt like hours, a different thought inserted itself into Anushka's inner monologue. The young man from the bedroom knew where she was. It might take him a while to get his bearings and reach somewhere he could report what had happened.

Especially barefoot, in soiled pyjamas and with no money or ID. Assuming he went to the authorities and they actually believed him. But Anushka decided she couldn't take the risk. She forced herself to her feet and threw on some clothes. She grabbed her suitcase and the bag of remaining groceries and fled the hotel. Within a few minutes, she was back on the road. But all she could think about was what Charlotte might be doing and thinking at that moment, and whether they would ever be able to find their way back to what they'd had.

* * *

P12 - May 2019 - North London

Charlotte was still in shock from Anushka's inexplicable appearance when everything went to hell. She saw Perkins swing his gun around to aim at Anushka and ordered him not to shoot. Perkins threw her a baffled glance. Then flames erupted from somewhere and engulfed him. Charlotte dropped the handcuffs she was holding and launched herself towards Perkins as he started screaming. She knocked him to the ground and rolled them both over. She felt the fire licking at her face but ignored it. Seconds later, something soft dropped on her from above, followed by a crushing weight. The air whooshed out of her lungs and she heard Perkins squawk beneath her. At least he was still capable of making noise. That had to be a good sign, right? Charlotte tried to catch her breath, and gasped in a great lungful of air when the weight disappeared again. She rolled off Perkins onto her back, and looked up to see Owuye looming over her, the duvet from the bed clutched in his hands. His impassive expression was completely at odds with what had happened in the last few seconds.

"Good thinking," she said in reference to the duvet, then turned her attention to Perkins.

He was thrashing and hyperventilating, but no part of him was on fire any more. Charlotte grabbed his flailing arms and tried to restrain him.

"Perkins! Calm down. It's okay. You're okay."

His head turned towards the sound of her voice and she locked gazes with him. After a brief moment, sense returned to his eyes and he focused on her properly. He stopped struggling but remained rigid in her grip, eyes still wide with remembered panic. Then he went limp. Charlotte let go of his arms and laid one hand on his chest. She looked him up and down, assessing the damage. The skin of his face was reddened but there were only a couple of small blisters on his cheek. Bits of his hair were singed, particularly the too-long sections over his ears. That would teach him to let it grow out. The material of his jacket was scorched, but the fire didn't seem to have penetrated to the skin beneath.

"Looks like you were lucky," Charlotte said.

"Lucky? That crazy bitch set me on fire! Where the fuck did she come from, anyway?"

Charlotte glanced around the room, but there was no sign of either Anushka or the young man they had been trying to apprehend. She looked up at where Owuye was still holding the duvet.

"Did you see what actually happened?"

He regarded her, his expression solemn. When he spoke, his deep voice was matter-of-fact.

"Dr Mahto materialised. Perkins aimed at her. Dr Mahto raised her hands. The stripes in her hair changed from pink to orange. Flames shot out of her hands. She grabbed the target. Her hair changed back to pink. They both disappeared."

He gave the report as if simply recounting the events of a training exercise. Charlotte briefly wondered what it would take to truly ruffle him, then decided she probably didn't want to find out.

Perkins, as always, was less sanguine. "What the fuck?" He struggled into a sitting position.

Charlotte couldn't make sense of it, either. It was clear Anushka had been affected by the XR-20 she had stolen from the lab. Presumably, she had got some of it on her when she'd failed to bury it securely in the lettuce field. The video of the young man freezing the table was one thing. But teleportation and flame-throwing? It all seemed so ridiculous. And how had Anushka known where she and her team were and what they were doing? There were so many questions.

Right now, though, they needed to get away from the house before anyone called the police based on all the commotion. Charlotte got to her feet and offered Perkins a hand. She pulled him up, while Owuye dropped the duvet back on the bed.

"Let's get back to the lab. Yardley's going to need to know what happened here. And he's not going to be happy."

* * *

A6 - 2003 - India

Before she left for England, Anushka went to visit her sister. In the year since Jhanvi had left, she had sent a handful of short notes to let Anushka know she was safe and settled, then sporadic updates with little information of substance. But Anushka knew she couldn't leave India without at least telling her sister her plans. So, the week before she was due to fly out, she slipped out of the house early and caught a bus. Once it left the environs of downtown Kolkata, the landscape got steadily more green, and Anushka felt the oppression of the city and her father's displeasure lift from her shoulders.

She had a bit of a hike from the closest the bus could drop her off to where Jhanvi was living, but she didn't mind. She took deep lungfuls of air and revelled in the feel of her leg muscles having to work hard against the rising gradient. She reached the gates of a compound, wondering how Jhanvi had come to be in such a place. A woman in a vibrant pink and yellow sari came up as Anushka pushed open the gate and stepped timidly inside.

"Can I help you?" The words were accompanied by a welcoming smile.

"I'm looking for my sister. Jhanvi Mohta."

"Jhanvi! Of course. We're all so excited for her. Only a few months to go now." The woman beckoned. "Come. I'll take you."

Anushka had no idea what she meant, but at least it seemed the woman knew where Jhanvi was, so she followed. They wound through streets with tiled houses on either side. The colours were very simple— white, peach or a rustic brown. Each had a patio despite their small size and a yard in front, mostly taken up by vegetable patches.

A man stepped out from one of the houses with a bag of seeds and a hoe. "Preeti, join us for some dosa! Should be ready soon," he called out to Anushka's escort.

She waved at him. "Thanks, Dev. I'll be back in a few minutes."

"Bring along your kids as well."

As they passed, more people working in their gardens looked up and greeted Preeti, some asking her to join them for breakfast, others telling her to meet up at Sakshi's place after dinner for a cup of tea and some chat. One handed her a sack of freshly dug potatoes, thanking her for the soup she'd shared the day before. This place had none of the bustling and anonymous crush of Kolkata. Anushka couldn't imagine how Jhanvi had ended up here.

Before long, Preeti turned into one particular yard, holding the gate open for Anushka to follow her through. As she walked up the path, she raised her voice to call ahead.

"Jhanvi! You've got a visitor, lovey."

The door opened and there was Jhanvi. After more than a year, Anushka wasn't sure what to expect, but what she saw shocked her. Jhanvi had a patterned scarf tied over her hair and she was wearing a loose smock that did nothing to hide the large swell of her belly. Her free-spirited, independent sister was pregnant.

Preeti patted Anushka on the shoulder. "I'll leave you to catch up. Make sure she sits down for at least a little while, okay?"

Anushka stood frozen on the path, staring at her sister.

Jhanvi's face broke into a wide smile and she threw her arms wide.

"Nushie! What a lovely surprise. I had no idea you were coming."

The sound of her sister's voice shattered Anushka's uncertainty and she flew into Jhanvi's embrace. It was awkward hugging around the bump but they managed.

"Come in, come in," Jhanvi said, laughing.

She led Anushka into the house. Most of the ground floor was taken up by the living room, but she could see through open doorways to a bathroom, two bedrooms and a kitchen area to her left. A set of stairs led upwards, presumably to another bedroom. Although the beds she could see were small, they were enough to almost fill their rooms, leaving just enough space for a small wardrobe and standing room to change one's clothes.

Jhanvi bustled in the kitchen, while Ansuhka looked around the living space.

Brightly-coloured cushions and blankets adorned every piece of furniture and every surface held an ornament or a photo frame. It was the photographs that caught Anushka's attention most. There were one or two of her and Jhanvi as little girls but the majority showed a laughing, joyous Jhanvi with a tall, handsome man. He had a wide smile and dark eyes, partially obscured by long hair that fell into his face. What was presumably the most recent picture had Jhanvi standing side on, showing off her pregnant belly while the man knelt next to her, his arms around her legs and his face pressed into her stomach.

Jhanvi came up behind her, hands full of teapot and cups, the reassuring steam of hot tea spiralling from the teapot's spout.

"That's Sanav, my husband."

Anushka turned to stare at her sister. "Husband? You're married?"

Jhanvi glanced down at herself with a rueful smile. "Yep. Married, with a baby on the way. Exactly what Dad wanted."

They sat and Jhanvi poured out the tea.

"I know this is a big surprise, Nush. And pretty much the opposite of what I said I was looking for. But at least it was my choice, not Dad's. And I did choose it. As soon as I met Sanav, I knew. It all happened so fast. But I'm so happy here. You have no idea. I feel free."

"But why didn't you tell me?" Anushka said. "Such big news and you never mentioned anything in your notes."

Jhanvi shrugged helplessly. "You know I'm no good at writing. And it felt so impossible to explain. Everything about my life now feels so disconnected from my life before. I didn't know how to express it." Her gaze dropped to where her hands were twisting in her lap. "If I'm honest, I didn't want to connect them together again by telling you. I'm sorry. That was selfish of me. But I'm so glad you're here now!"

She looked back up at Anushka, her expression uncertain, as if she was looking for approval.

Anushka reached out to take one of her sister's hands and rubbed her fingers. She smiled.

"I can see how happy you are, Vi. This whole house is just bursting with joy. It's wonderful."

Jhanvi relaxed and grinned.

"It's so good to see you. I've wondered how you were getting on every day, and now you're here. Tell me all about what's going on with you."

Anushka squeezed her sister's hand again. "I came to tell you I'm leaving."

Jhanvi's eyes widened. "Where are you going?"

Anushka took a deep breath. "England. I got a scholarship to study there. I fly out next week."

Jhanvi's eyes were wide. "How did you get Dad to agree to that?"

Anushka gave her a rueful smile. "Oh, he's bragging about it to all his friends. How his daughter is going to get such prestigious qualifications. And the fact that he doesn't have to pay a penny makes it even better." She sobered. "But what he doesn't know is that I'm not coming back."

Jhanvi dropped her gaze, her eyes brimming with tears, but she was smiling.

"You're really flying away, just like Mama said we should. That's amazing, Nushie. I'm so proud of you."

Anushka burst into tears and clutched at her sister. They hugged each other and cried together, joy and sadness entwining in a potent swirl of emotion.

* * *

C6 - 2009 - Iraq

Charlotte came to slowly. First of all, her mind was full of confusion. She remembered fear and heat and pain, the echoes of which still pulsed through her body. She focused on what she could determine about her physical surroundings, pushing the memories away and trying to establish what was true now. She became aware of a thin mattress on a creaking bedframe. There was beeping somewhere nearby. And the smell of disinfectant. She shifted position and a thousand aches came alive throughout her body. The most intense pain centred on her left hand but her mind shied away from thinking about that.

"Lance Corporal Grant?"

The familiar voice pulled her further back to reality and she opened her eyes. Everything was blurry and too bright for a moment. Then the figure of Major Yardley resolved itself. He was sitting at her bedside in the base camp field hospital. His face was drawn and sombre, dark circles under his eyes and shadows in their depths.

"Watson?" Charlotte's throat was raw but the need for information was all-consuming.

"He's alive. In bad shape, but alive and likely to stay that way. Thanks to you."

Yardley reached out of Charlotte's view and produced a cup of water. He directed the straw to her lips and held it while she took a few sips. It felt strange and uncomfortable to accept such basic assistance from her commanding officer, but her need for water overrode her sensibilities. The desperate dryness in her throat receded, leaving complex emotions in its wake. Charlotte fought to stay professional. She felt as if there was someone else who should be thanked but she couldn't bring their identity to mind.

"It was pretty grim when the rescue team got there," Yardley was saying. "The debris from the jeep was all around you. They thought you both must be dead. But it was like there was a clear patch around where you were lying. As if something had shielded you from being hit when the fuel tank blew."

Blue light. A rainbow glow. Protecting wings.

"I - I think I saw an angel."

Yardley's eyebrows shot up. "That's probably the concussion talking, Corporal."

Charlotte dredged up a smile, her face feeling rubbery and the forced expression completely at odds with the whirl of thoughts and feelings spinning in her mind.

"Probably, sir. When can I get back to work?"

Yardley's expression darkened. "Doctor says you should be up and around soon. But you're headed home, soldier. Your part in this ridiculous conflict is done."

Charlotte had never heard Major Yardley question their purpose in Iraq before. But the other part of what he'd said pushed that thought out of the way in its grab for her full attention.

"Home? But why?"

She clenched her hands into fists and pain blossomed in her left hand. Bringing it up into view, she saw the bulky bandages, the misshapen silhouette, and remembered.

Yardley nodded at her realisation. "You were very lucky, Corporal. But you need a full complement of fingers to lead a section. I'm sorry."

Objectively, she knew he was right. She was lucky to be alive and much luckier than Danny to have lost only a couple of fingers, but at that moment she didn't feel lucky at all. What the hell was she going to do with her life now? Charlotte closed her eyes again, hoping to block out all her thoughts and feelings along with her vision. She felt Major Yardley's hand squeezing her arm in sympathy. Then the scrape of chair legs told her he had left her alone with her pain.

* * *

E6 - Far away…

We have little in the way of physical infrastructure or resources, which makes our development efforts very difficult. So, when Consensus starts to look outwards for other worlds to aid us, we are excited by the prospect of external assistance. It is not long before the news comes through to us that they have located a planet with intelligent beings on it. The fact that they are corporeal is a major breakthrough. It is a lot to take in, though. After so long existing alone amongst our own people, we now have two new sets of beings to acclimatise ourselves to. But at least only one of them is proving actively hostile, as yet.

When information about the humans of Earth filters down to us from Consensus, discussion is energetic amongst our family unit.

Consensus says the life forms are carbon-based, as we once were.

How uncomfortable. They must be much further back in their development if they haven't found a way to divest themselves of dependence on physical form.

Yes. But they have current experience of living corporeal lives, so hopefully their very backward nature will be of use to us.

Do we know if they even have enough intelligence to interact with us?

Consensus is looking for a way to communicate with them.

And does Consensus think they will help us?

Why would they not? We will warn them of the threat from the enemy, which will be more serious for them, as they have a physical society that can be attacked. And if we can find them, so can the enemy.

We must do whatever we can to protect ourselves against the aggressors. If these humans are likely to be of use, they must be made to assist us in any way they can.

If they are as primitive as Consensus suggests, they should be easy to exploit.

The words flow through our concept space, pushing against our altruistic principles, polluting the atmosphere of our innermost sanctum until we are all alone in our opposition. We transmit little and the others fail to notice our discomfort, embroiled as they are in their excitement at the new discovery.

Have we as a people changed so much in so little time? Even the supposed threat of war has altered our mindset and attitudes, so that almost the first thought is about how we can use others to get what we want. No matter how primitive the inhabitants of Earth are, surely they deserve better than to be manipulated into serving our purposes at the expense of their own autonomy. And, while our family unit disparages them for their physical nature, it seems we are not so superior as to be able to defend ourselves from attack without their assistance. If they are not willing to help us, do we really have the right to endanger others in order to protect ourselves? We don't think so. Surely it would make us just as bad as those who move against us. But we ourselves would be one voice against many and the idea of challenging Consensus is anathema to us, as it is to all of our people.

But we are at the forefront of our research and weapons development, so we are in the perfect position to find out everything that is going on. We play our role, we watch and wait, and we look for an opportunity to take action.

* * *

P13 - May 2019 - Midlands

As Anushka drove, she considered her situation. If her vision of earlier was to be believed, there were others out there who had also been affected by the XR-20 from the lab and she was responsible for their predicament. Charlotte's presence at the young man's house supported the idea that what she had seen of his ice powers was likely true. And that was another thing; Charlotte was apparently somehow tracking these people down and - what? Dragging them back to the lab for Yardley to do experiments on them? How could Charlotte countenance facilitating that? And might it go even further? Anushka was certain Yardley wouldn't want news of the contamination to get out to the general public. It would raise too many questions about what was going on at the lab. Surely he wasn't planning on killing people to keep it quiet, though. And surely Charlotte wouldn't agree to be part of that. Would she? Her loyalty to Yardley went pretty deep. It frightened Anushka to think that her worst fears about Yardley might be true and that Charlotte might just be going along with his instructions like the obedient soldier she was.

Anushka gripped the steering wheel of her car, peering out into the darkness. Running was already taking its toll and she couldn't just keep moving on to the next hotel along the road. It exposed her too much to possible location by Charlotte's team, especially since she didn't have complete control over her powers yet, and might well cause a scene somewhere that someone might report to the authorities. She'd been lucky so far but eventually someone might also make a fuss about her wanting to pay in cash and she needed to avoid any complications of that sort as well. If Charlotte and Perkins (Anushka's mind shied away from thinking about him) were tracking down people who'd been contaminated by the XR-20, Anushka would be top of their list of targets, now that they'd seen what she could do. And her cash wouldn't last forever, even if she did manage to keep finding places to stay.

She needed somewhere safe to go, where nobody would be able to find her, and where she could take some time to figure out what to do next. Then it hit her. She wasn't restricted by how far she could drive. She could go anywhere she wanted. Anywhere in the world. Or at least she assumed she could. She had teleported to the house of that young man by instinct, based on what she had seen in her vision. But she had jumped back to her hotel quite deliberately by picturing it in her mind. Did that mean she could teleport anywhere she had already been and could visualise clearly?

Another driver leaned on his horn as he blasted past, going the other way, and Anushka realised she had stopped paying attention to the road and was drifting out of her lane. A sign told her there was a rest stop coming up ahead and she pulled into the parking area as soon as she reached it. There was just too much to think about to be safe driving right now. And she had just established that she didn't need to go any further by car.

She climbed out and collected all her belongings around her, making sure she was holding on to all her bags. Under the light of a streetlamp, she watched the pink streaks appear in the hair of her reflection in the car window. Then she closed her eyes and thought about her flat, back near the lab. She saw white light behind her eyelids and opened her eyes again to find herself in her living room. She looked around at the stark, white walls and chrome and plastic furniture. She'd never really thought about it before but now, when she really wanted the comfort of the familiar, her home suddenly seemed very cold and uninviting. The only thing that suggested anyone actually lived there was a multi-coloured crocheted blanket thrown across the back of one chair. Charlotte had bought it for her not long after they met.

It had been after the first time she came over to Anushka's flat. She had shaken her head over the blankness of the living space and insisted they go out to shop for something to brighten the place up. Thinking about that day now, Anushka crossed the room, snatched up the blanket and buried her face in it, remembering how they'd picked it out together from the most garish stall Charlotte could find at the market. Anushka breathed in its musty smell for a long moment. Then she stuffed it in one of her bags, taking another deep breath to steady her emotions.

So far, so good. Now it was time to really test her new powers. She thought back fifteen years to a place she had only visited once, and focused hard on the details she could remember. When she opened her eyes this time, it was to the early morning light over the delta south of Kolkata.

* * *

P14 - May 2019 - India

Anushka pushed open the gate to the commune, feeling just as apprehensive and uncertain as she had when she first arrived there fifteen years before. At least this time she knew where she was going, though she was less certain of her welcome. She followed the path she remembered, past the small houses with their abundant yards. There were incense sticks burning in the open window of one of the houses and the warm, rich, woody scent of sandalwood wafted on the breeze. It spoke to Anushka of peace and spirituality, a sense memory embedded deep in her brain, and she felt her shoulders relax just a bit. When she reached her destination, she hesitated on the doorstep, hand raised but frozen before it could make contact with the wood of the door. Anushka took a deep breath, squared her shoulders and knocked on the door. After a few seconds, she heard scurrying feet on the other side and it was flung open by a girl of about twelve.

"Who are you?" the girl asked.

"My name's Anushka. I'm looking for Jhanvi?"

"That's my mum's name. Dad!" This last was yelled over the girl's shoulder, back into the house.

She turned back and stared at Anushka. The silence between them stretched uncomfortably, the little girl's eyes wide and curious but her confidence not quite strong enough to prompt her to ask further questions. Another figure appeared behind the girl. He was an older version of the man Anushka remembered from the photos. His previously skinny frame had filled out a bit, his hair was much shorter and he now sported a neatly trimmed goatee. He held a plate in one hand and was drying it with the tea towel held in the other.

"Can I help you?" His voice was rich and mellow, curious rather than suspicious.

Anushka felt her throat tighten. She pasted what she hoped was a friendly smile on her face.

"You must be Sanav. I'm Anushka. Jhanvi's sister."

Sanav's eyebrows shot up, then he smiled. He stepped back, gesturing with one arm to usher Anushka inside.

"Well, this is a surprise! Come in, come in. Jhanvi's not here right now, but she'll be so excited to see you when she gets back. She shouldn't be too long."

The girl was still standing in the doorway, staring at Anushka in childlike wonder.

Sanav nudged her with his hip. "Out of the way, monster. Let your aunt into the house."

The girl shuffled sideways, eyes still locked on Anushka, who stepped over the threshold, her stomach twisting despite the warm welcome. It had been fifteen years without any contact. Would Jhanvi really be pleased she was there?

Anushka followed Sanav into the house, which had changed little in the intervening time. There were more photos, most featuring what Anushka assumed were Jhanvi's children. Scattered objects added to the sense of their presence; school books open on the table, shoes of varying sizes piled by the door, a few toys lying here and there.

Sanav handed the plate and tea towel to the girl. "Go make us all some tea."

She scurried away into the kitchen area.

"Sit down, sit down," Sanav said. "Have you had a long journey?"

Anushka pondered the impossibility of answering this question, then dodged it with an oblique but honest response. "I am very tired."

They both sat down.

"It's great to meet you at long last," Sanav said. "Jhanvi's told me a lot about you, but I certainly wasn't expecting you to drop by like this."

Anushka fiddled with the fringe of the brightly woven throw that covered the sofa, her eyes on the floor.

"I hope it's not inconvenient."

"Not at all."

The girl came back out, carrying a tray with a steaming teapot and three cups. She placed her burden on the table with great precision, then stood next to her father, staring at Anushka again. He put one arm around her waist and pulled her into his side.

"This here is Khushi, our little bundle of joy." He looked his daughter up and down. "Though not so little any more, I suppose."

Khushi reddened. "Da-ad."

Anushka couldn't help smiling. "And she must have an older sibling?"

"Yes, her brother Samar is nearly fifteen. And we also have Indrani, who's seven."

Khushi rolled her eyes. "She's eight, dad."

Sanav sighed. "Where does the time go?"

The door opened, and another girl, Indrani, Anushka assumed, ran in. She skidded to a halt when she saw Anushka and stared like her sister.

"Mama!" she called. "There's a strange lady in our house!"

Behind her, Jhanvi came in, her arms full of bags that bulged with fruit and vegetables. She was older, with more lines on her face, from both laughter and worry over the years. She stopped behind her daughter, a shocked expression on her face. Anushka stood up, and took one hesitant step forwards.

"Hi, Jhanvi. I'm sorry to intrude, but I didn't have anywhere else to go."

She fell silent, waiting to find out what her sister would say.

* * *

A7 - 2004 - Cambridge

Anushka settled in at Cambridge University more easily than she had expected. There wasn't time to be homesick when she had to fit part-time work around intensive studies and trying to connect with her fellow students. The academic work was hard but fascinating and it was great to be able to focus exclusively on the scientific subjects where her passions lay. It also felt good to have a job that meant she could earn her own money and be in charge of her own finances, strained as they were. It was exhausting to have to fit everything in, but Anushka was proud of her self-sufficiency and ability to rise to the challenge of a whole new life.

The weather was the hardest thing to get used to. It was cold and damp in Cambridge in October and only likely to get worse as the winter drew in. Otherwise, England wasn't so very unfamiliar. Everything else was mostly just variations on the things she knew from home. But the chill and damp were uncomfortable and the heating in her room wasn't as effective as she would have preferred. The other students in her accommodation building teased her about always having the heater on full blast, calling her room the Tropical Zone. She turned it into a feature, inviting them over for beach parties with calypso music and paper umbrellas in the drinks.

It was at one of these parties, towards the end of her first year at university, that one of the older students from downstairs came to knock on the door.

"Anushka?" he called out over the music.

She danced her way over to him. "Hey, Marcus. Are we being too loud?"

"No. Well, yes. But that's not why I'm here. Your sister's on the phone. She says it's urgent."

Anushka had emailed back and forth with Jhanvi sporadically since her arrival in the UK, but it was difficult to maintain frequent contact because Jhanvi didn't have regular access to a computer. Phone calls were really expensive as well, so Anushka hadn't heard from her sister in a while. If she was honest, it had been all too easy to leave the restrictions of her home life behind and dive deep into the freedoms of university life in the UK. She didn't want to think about what she'd lost, only what she'd gained and where it might allow her future path to take her. She had given Jhanvi a number where she could be reached, but her sister had never used it before.

"Be right back," Anushka told her guests.

There was a pay phone at the base of the building, for all the students to share. It was rare for anyone to call it. Most of the students had mobile phones, though some gave the number out for emergencies. Anushka picked up the handset that was balanced on the top.

"Hello?"

"Nushie?" Jhanvi's voice sounded very far away and strained.

"What's the matter?" Anushka's chest suddenly felt tight.

"Oh, Nushie. I'm so sorry to have to tell you like this." Jhanvi's voice cracked and she swallowed a sob. "Mama's dead."

* * *

C7 - 2009 - London

Charlotte watched as Danny held himself up, the muscles in his arms shaking with the effort. They had been back in the UK long enough for Charlotte to recover fully and be discharged from the hospital, but she was a regular visitor, keeping track of her section member's progress. She couldn't fault his determination. After they'd had to amputate his other leg as well, he had asked how quickly he could be fitted for prosthetics and get back on some feet.

Now here he was, making his painful way along a track with bars on either side, his legs extended by futuristic-looking metal and plastic contraptions. Sweat beaded on his forehead and the tension in his clenched jaw was clear. Charlotte held her breath as he staggered the last few steps and collapsed into his waiting wheelchair.

"That's enough for today," the rehabilitation nurse said, and Charlotte saw Danny slump with relief.

She stepped forwards. "Looking good, Private."

"Thanks, Corp." He was breathing heavily.

The nurse helped him detach the prosthetics and then secured them in the slots on either side of the wheelchair.

Charlotte walked around behind the chair and took hold of the handles. "I can take it from here, Jeanette. Thanks."

It showed just how much the session had taken out of him that Danny let her wheel him back to his room. Once there, however, he insisted on transferring himself from the chair to the bed. Charlotte watched, trying to resist the urge to help him. She knew from experience that he wouldn't respond well if she did. He was determined to be as self-sufficient as possible and she admired that.

"I've heard you might be out of here soon," she said.

"So they say." Danny's voice was bright, but the tone rang false to Charlotte's ears.

"Have you thought about what you're going to do?" It was much easier to ask this question of him than it was to acknowledge her own lack of an answer.

He dropped his gaze, refusing to meet her eye. "Not really."

She thought about how she'd never come across anyone else visiting him on her trips. She remembered him telling her about how his sister had died, but what about his parents?

She pressed on with her plan. "Why don't you move in with me? I've got more space than I know what to do with, and who else is going to want to share with a couple of washed-up veterans? I figure we ought to stick together."

His head came up, and she could see hope warring with shame in his eyes.

"Come on, Private. Don't be an idiot. Offers like this don't come along that often. And you'd honestly be doing me a favour. The house has seemed so empty since I got back. I could really use the company. What do you say, roomie?"

His shoulders relaxed and he smiled. "I say thanks a lot, Corporal. And that sounds great."

"Don't misunderstand me. You'll have to pull your weight."

Danny pushed his fists down into the mattress, lifting himself off the bed an inch. "Literally."

Charlotte stared at him in horrified embarrassment while he held her gaze, then he burst out laughing.

She gave a chuckle of her own, then said, "Oh, you're going to be annoying as hell, aren't you?"

"You'd better believe it!" His eyes sparkled, then he sobered. "Seriously, though, thanks, Corp. This means a lot. I really wasn't looking forward to calling my dad."

"You haven't told him what happened?"

"No. And now I won't have to, thanks to you." Danny's eyes fell to his hands, twisting in his lap. "We - we're not close. At all. I haven't spoken to him since… Since Ellie died. And I didn't want this -" He gestured at what remained of his legs. "- to force the issue."

Charlotte blinked away tears as she thought about how much she wanted to be able to share what had happened to her with her own father. She stepped forwards and sat down on the edge of the bed. "Do you want to talk about it?"

Danny held her gaze steadily. "Do you want to talk about your parents?"

They looked at each other in silence for a long moment before Charlotte looked away.

"Okay, then," she said, getting up from the bed again. "I'll go and get started on the spare room. See you in a few days."

* * *

E7 - 2017 - Earth

When it comes time to communicate with the humans, Consensus chooses our think tank team as the ones tasked with representing our people on Earth. They present us with supplies of a glowing substance they tell us has come from another of the research arms of the war effort. As it is a physical substance, we must transport it to Earth in a physical conveyance, which Consensus says has been captured from the enemy. One of the most difficult aspects of the expedition is that our team must take on a semi-corporeal form in order to control the ship and handle the substance. It takes much practice to focus our energy in this way, but we work hard to achieve it and also to learn how to pilot the craft.

Consensus locates a human laboratory that primarily works on military projects and is run by a man they say is eager to help us. Our team is assigned to act as liaison. Our intention is to overawe the humans and our non-corporeal nature means we can take whatever form we choose. Whilst Consensus has been opening communications, our team has been conducting research into the humans' history and culture. It is surprisingly easy to do this, as they make no efforts to conceal the vast amounts of data they have accumulated over time. Once we have reviewed all aspects of their imaginings of contact with other species, we identify a form we feel will be most effective in intimidating them.

Our first visit to Earth is to an office in a facility near one of their capital cities, all terms and concepts we have to learn about during our preparation for the journey. It is good that we are able to assimilate information very quickly, allowing us to familiarise ourselves with the basics of human life in little time. Four of us go, struggling with the unfamiliar sensations of individual corporeal form. We materialise where we have been instructed, at the agreed time.

The human who is there to receive us gives no indication of discomfort or surprise, instead rising to greet us calmly. We wish we could be as calm. Instead, we focus on remaining upright and moving our long limbs in the appropriate fashion for walking. It would not form a good first impression, or prove intimidating at all, were we to fall down at this human's feet.

"Welcome," he says. "My name is Yardley. How may I address you?"

We are more comfortable with using audible communication than the others in the team, something that is much more difficult for us to grow accustomed to than human societal concepts. So we have been nominated to speak for the whole team. We step forward on long legs and look down at the human.

"You may call us Ergo."

Yardley stretches his mouth in what we have learned is a smile, a gesture of pleasure.

"I look forward to working with you, Ergo. I'm sure the project will be exciting, and also beneficial to both our peoples. I am honoured to have been chosen to participate."

Yardley waves a hand at some strangely shaped objects arrayed in front of a flat platform made of a dark, solid substance. He moves behind the platform and lowers himself so that he is supported by another of the objects. We thus understand their purpose and arrange ourselves in a similar fashion, the other members of our group following suit.

"So," Yardley says, "I understand your people are facing a threat and are looking for allies in the struggle."

"Yes," we say. "There is an enemy that wishes to cause us harm and we are ill-equipped to face them. And if we have been able to discover your planet, this enemy may be able to do so also and may therefore pose a threat to your people as well."

"My people are accustomed to facing enemies. So, perhaps with your knowledge and our expertise, we can work together to safeguard everyone."

This is a more auspicious beginning than we have anticipated. If the humans are prepared to collaborate with us willingly, even eagerly, perhaps our misgivings are unfounded. Consensus may not need to exert force or undue manipulation after all. Only time will tell. We will tread cautiously, do our best to serve our people, and reserve judgement.

* * *

P15 - May 2019 - West London

By the time Charlotte got home, it was nearly 3am. She tried to be as quiet as possible as she inserted the key in the door and unlocked it, but she needn't have worried. The TV was on in the living room and she could see Danny huddled on the sofa by the light from its screen. He looked round as she stopped in the doorway. At her expression, he muted the TV.

"Bad day?"

"Long and weird." Charlotte rubbed her eyes. "Coffee?"

Danny gave her a lopsided smile. "I don't think that would do either of us much good at this time of night, Corp."

She managed a smile at the nickname. You could take the boy out of the army…

"You're probably right."

She crossed the room and threw herself into an armchair, twisting sideways so she could put her legs over the arm and see Danny properly.

Despite all his struggles over the last nine years (had it really been that long?), he had retained his boyish good looks and worked hard to get the sparkle back in his personality. His hair was shaggy and unbrushed, adding to his disreputable appearance. His upper body was muscular and the dimple in his left cheek when he smiled had sealed the deal on many a liaison. But Danny seemed to avoid deep connections with anyone and was resolutely single. Charlotte had asked him once, in a moment of rare emotional honesty, if he was carrying a misguided torch for her. He had laughed so hard he actually fell off the sofa and it had been quite a performance getting him back onto it. Charlotte's pride had been a little scuffed but she was mostly relieved. And the conversation had only brought them closer. Their lack of physical attraction, as well as their shared trauma, had allowed a more profound bond to develop between them, even if they generally kept away from directly expressing it.

"What's got you up at this ungodly hour?" she asked him now.

He cocked his head to one side. "Is there such a thing as a godly hour?"

"Not that you or I would know about, I don't think. But stop dodging the question."

Danny shrugged. "You know me. Sometimes I can't get out of bed, sometimes I can't get in." He gestured at his stumps with a grin. "Literally."

"Okay, okay, you win. No more questions."

"What about you? How come you're back so late?"

Charlotte scrubbed her hands over her face and let out an exasperated noise. "Oh, you know.

Stolen classified material, contamination of publicly available food products, covert infiltration of private residences, members of my team getting set on fire. Just another day at the office."

Danny's jaw had been dropping further and further as the list went on. "You serious?"

"Unfortunately, yes."

"Who got set on fire?"

"Perkins. He's fine, though you wouldn't have known it from the flailing and shrieking."

Danny snorted with laughter. He knew Perkins slightly from before he joined the lab, and had subsequently heard tales of his exploits many times, when Charlotte would gripe about how annoying he was. "I can just imagine. Where was Anushka in all this?"

"Right slap bang in the middle. She was the one who stole the material from the lab."

"Way to bury the lead, Corp. You okay?"

Charlotte felt her throat start to burn and cursed her emotional reaction to Danny's concern. All the various implications of what Anushka had done and what Charlotte's new knowledge of the stolen material meant about Yardley's secret projects swirled around her mind. She didn't know what to think, or what to say.

"Not really, no."

Danny's response was to open his arms wide. Charlotte levered herself up from the armchair and stepped across to sit next to him on the sofa. She settled against his solid, reassuring side and fell asleep to the sensation of him stroking her hair.

* * *

P16 - May 2019 - North London

Charlotte's eyes were sore and her brain felt as if it was wrapped in cotton wool when she got to the lab the next morning. But she was adamantly on time, despite the very late hours of the day before. She went straight to the security office and was surprised to see Perkins at his customary station.

"Morning, boss!" His wide smile was at odds with the shiny redness of his cheeks and the dressing that covered the burn blisters on his face. "Hey, you okay? You look rough as anything."

"Thanks," Charlotte replied. "But shouldn't I be asking you that? I'm not the one who got set on fire last night, after all."

"Painkillers." Perkins' grin grew impossibly wider. "Best thing ever."

Charlotte noted the over-bright sparkle in his eyes and vowed to keep a close watch on him. He fumbled in the bag at his side and brought out a foil package, offering it to her.

"Want some?"

"Uh, no thanks. Should you even be here?"

Perkins shrugged. "I feel fine. And I wouldn't miss this for the world. This is the craziest thing I've ever been involved in, and now it's personal."

He gestured at his computer screen, where he had several videos playing at once. Charlotte moved to stand behind him.

"What am I looking at?"

"I set up a search algorithm to look for weird shit being posted since yesterday afternoon."

"Is that a technical term?"

He grinned over his shoulder at her. "Pretty much. Turns out weird shit gets flagged on government systems all the time. Who knew? So, I'm sorting through it all to try and identify anything we might want to look into."

"What about the guy from last night? Any sign of him anywhere?" Charlotte didn't like the fact that he'd managed to elude them. Having a civilian on the loose with strange powers and a story about armed operatives dragging him out of bed in the middle of the night was less than ideal.

"Nah." Perkins shook his head, then winced. "He's been sensible enough to stay under the radar. I've got some tracking software checking to make sure he doesn't do anything unfortunate like going to the police, but not a peep so far. I think he's in the wind. But we've got a fair few other prospects that might be something."

"How long do you need to put a list together?"

He shrugged again. "Couple hours, maybe. The algorithm flags up potentials, but there's no substitute for human eyeballs in evaluating the results." He tapped his chest. "That's what you hired me for, after all. The best combination of tech savvy and actual brains around." The incident the day before hadn't dented his ego, it seemed. "I'll let you know when I have something solid."

Charlotte patted his shoulder. "Okay, good work. And go easy on those painkillers."

He gave her a mock salute he knew she hated, and turned back to his screen.

With nothing better to do until Perkins came up with his list, Charlotte headed to the canteen and piled a plate high with every hot breakfast item on offer. It wasn't something she would usually indulge in, but it felt like the kind of day when relaxing her healthy regime was warranted. She sat at a table alone and munched her way through the greasy pile, looking at the empty chair opposite her and barely tasting the food. It lined her empty stomach well enough, though, and she was feeling a bit more human when she made her way to her own office half an hour later.

* * *

A8 - 2004 - Cambridge

Anushka's throat closed as her sister's words filtered into her brain. When she tried to speak, her voice came out strangled.

"Mama's dead? But - how?"

Jhanvi sounded close to tears herself. “I don’t really know. I saw an obituary in the paper and it said natural causes. But I can’t find out any more without risking contact with Dad.”

“You haven’t spoken to him? Not even to go to her funeral?”

Anushka imagined her mother’s spirit being consigned to the hereafter, with only her father there to honour her. She felt her stomach lurch and thought she might be sick. She closed her eyes and swallowed, trying to get her emotions under control. Jhanvi’s reply came to her as if from very far away, filtered through a fog of shock and grief.

“I - I can’t. I’m scared he would force me to come home somehow and I don’t want him to know about the baby. I don’t want him to have any contact with my children.” Jhanvi took a deep breath as if trying to get a handle on her own fear. “Besides, what good would it do now? If there was anything untoward about how it happened, do you really think he’d tell me?”

“You don’t think he…?” Anushka couldn’t finish the sentence.

“I don’t know. But I don’t think so. He wouldn’t have any reason to hurt her, would he? He only ever got angry with her when she did something to challenge his control over us. She wouldn’t have defied him on her own account, not after we were both gone. I’m so sorry, Nushie. This isn’t how I wanted to tell you. Will you come home? I’d love to see you and have you meet my family. And maybe we can face Dad together."

Anushka gripped the cord of the phone tighter. She hunched into the corner where the phone was attached to the wall, shielding herself from the curious stares of students going up and down the stairs.

She didn't want to think about her father. Didn't want to face him. Not after she had managed to fly away from him, like her mother had always wanted. What if he actually was somehow involved in her mother's death? She shied away from that thought. But what might he do if he saw her again? After she'd cut off contact with him and was clearly intending to stay in England?

She turned and looked out through the glass panes around the phone into the darkening quad. The giant tree in the centre spread its sheltering branches over the grass, representing the security she had found here. Anushka couldn't leave the new life she was finally getting settled into. No, there was no going back.

But what about her mother? If Jhanvi hadn't left then maybe Anushka wouldn't have either. They would both be married off to complete strangers, but they would have been there for their mother's funeral. Maybe even at her final moments.

They could have been there for her. Could have comforted her as her breath left her body for the last time. Could have made her feel loved as she took flight from the life she had suffered for their sake. And had her mother's health been adversely affected by her leaving? She remembered how thin and drawn her mother had become after Jhanvi ran away. Anushka didn't want to think about how that might have been exacerbated by her own departure. There were a lot of things she didn't want to think about.

She took a deep breath and concentrated hard on her rationale for her actions. Anushka had done what her mother wanted her to do. She had even talked about her plan with her mother before she left, unlike Jhanvi. She had said her goodbyes. Her thoughts circled back to her rising guilt. She could have called, she could have found a way to let her mother know how she was doing without her father finding out. She could have stayed in touch. But she had wanted a clean break, to cut her ties to her old life and begin again without the weight of her past dragging her down. So she had left her mother all alone, using her mother's assurance that it was okay as an easy excuse.

Anushka looked down at her sweatshirt, which sported the name of her college. Life here was good. It was cold, but it was good. There were people who accepted her for who she was, when even Prisha hadn't.

Her anger at herself burst outwards down the phone, firing its deadly volley at her sister.

"This is just as much your fault as Dad's! You left without even saying goodbye. You abandoned both of us. Ran off and left us there with him."

"Don't say that, Nush. You know I didn't have any choice. And you know Mama wanted me to be happy." Jhanvi's voice dropped to barely a whisper. "And you left too."

"And now that Mama's gone, there's nothing there for me to come back to."

Anushka slammed the phone receiver down and fled into the quad in tears.

* * *

C8 - 2011 - West London

It was about eighteen months after she and Danny had left the army that Charlotte got the call. They had been living in Charlotte's house and Danny had thrown himself into retraining as a programmer. He was already bringing in a steady income, more than paying his way in the household, while Charlotte was still drifting around the house, achieving nothing. She had enough money from her parents that she didn't need to worry yet, but she felt useless, listless. She was accustomed to being active and serving a purpose, but for the past few months she had been unable to motivate herself to find a new direction in life. She found herself walking into rooms, only to forget why she was there. Or she would hover around Danny, asking him what he was doing until he very politely but pointedly told her to leave him alone.

When she picked up the phone, the voice she heard on the other end threatened to throw her back into memories she didn't want to revisit.

"Charlotte Grant?"

She swallowed hard. "Major Yardley?"

"It's just Mr Yardley, now. I won't try and get you to call me Lester. Not yet, at least."

His tone was warm and friendly. It sounded odd in Charlotte's ears, used to hearing him giving orders.

"Uh, yes, sir. I'm surprised to hear from you."

"Well, I have a proposition for you, but I'd rather talk face to face. Could I drop by in the next couple of days?"

Charlotte swallowed again. What could he possibly want with her?

"Uh, yes, sir. I'm free this evening if it's urgent."

"Not urgent, no. But tonight would be fine." She gave him the address. "I'll see you at eight."

He hung up, leaving Charlotte staring at the phone.

She showed Yardley into the kitchen when he arrived. He was wearing a black polo shirt and tan slacks. He had kept his hair military short, and his squared shoulders and purposeful stride still gave him a commanding bearing, but he looked strange in civilian clothes. Charlotte had to quash an impulse to salute him and nearly couldn't make herself take his hand when he offered it to shake.

In the kitchen, his face split into a wide smile when he saw Danny sitting at the table.

"Watson! What a pleasant surprise. How's civilian life treating you?"

Yardley and Danny shook hands and Danny smiled back.

"Good, sir. And even better if you're here to offer our Charlotte a job. I'm getting sick of her hanging around the house, getting under my feet all the time." He grinned at the flash of shock and discomfort that crossed Yardley's face. "As it were."

Yardley frowned at Charlotte. "You're not working?"

She glared at Danny, then spoke through gritted teeth. "I haven't found the right fit yet." She sighed. "All the kinds of civilian outfits I'd be suited for will be run by the sort of men who trigger my, er…"

She trailed off, but Danny jumped in to finish the sentence. "Anger issues?"

Charlotte gave him another glare but managed a nod at Yardley.

Yardley smiled. "Well, Watson here hit the nail right on the head. How about coming to work for me?"

Charlotte stared at him. "Work for you? What kind of job?"

Danny gave her a friendly shove from where he sat. "Why don't you let the man sit down, and offer him a drink before you start grilling him?"

"Sorry, sir," Charlotte said. "What would you like? Tea? Coffee? Something stronger?"

"Tea would be fine, thanks."

There was a pause in the conversation while Charlotte sorted out the drinks, but they were soon all seated at the kitchen table with steaming mugs in front of them.

"I'll get straight to the point," Yardley said. "I left the army a few months ago and I'm in the process of setting up a research lab. I'll still be using my connections, as both the military and the security services are interested in providing investment capital for the venture. I'll be able to take private contracts, but I also hope to secure some military contracts for weapons development. So, I'll be needing some decent security, because we'll have both confidential and possibly dangerous material on site. I'd like you to head up the department, keep everything running smoothly and make sure there are no security problems." He eyed Charlotte. "And you know you won't have any attitude problems from above."

Charlotte stared at him. It sounded like a big job, with a lot of responsibility. But the idea sent a shiver of excitement through her, for the first time since the explosion. She owed Yardley so much already, but perhaps she could turn this into an opportunity to pay him back.

"I'd be honoured, sir. Thank you."

"Don't thank me yet. It'll be hard work at first, and I'll expect your best."

"Of course, sir. I won't let you down. When would you want me to start?"

"How about you come to the lab tomorrow to take a look around, and we can discuss the particulars, then?"

Danny clapped his hands together. "At last! I can have this place to myself and actually get some proper work done. Thanks, sir. You have no idea how much you're helping both of us."

Charlotte stared daggers at him, but he just grinned.

Yardley laughed at them. “I take it you’re not looking for a job as well then, Watson?”

“No, sir,” Danny said. “I’m a fine, upstanding taxpayer already, thank you very much.”

Yardely nodded in approval. “It’s settled, then.. I look forward to working with you again, Ms Grant.”

* * *

E8 - 2018 - Earth

Humans are interesting creatures. They bustle about, always working on some task or other, convinced that everything needs to be done better, faster, more efficiently. We watch, fascinated, as they take hold of our project and rush ahead with plans and ideas. So industrious. And yet so difficult for them to work together, when each is limited to their own experience. How can they trust or support each other successfully when they cannot access each other’s thoughts and feelings? We struggle with the necessities of physical infrastructure and resources, but collaboration and shared consciousness is at the heart of everything we do. The idea of being separated from our fellows is more alien to us than moving about the world in physical form.

So, there are challenges for us in working with the humans. But each side also brings knowledge and expertise to the endeavour that the other does not have.

We have theoretical ideas that are not always practical in physical terms, while the humans are skilled in translating those ideas into solutions that can be implemented and utilised. We have spent many years taking our thoughts and theories to the limits of expression, but the humans are industrious and eager to apply new knowledge to enhance their own technology.

Yardley has a lot of thoughts about what the humans could do for us.

"A war needs soldiers," he says. "And, from what you've told me, your people aren't really suited to that kind of work." He gestures at my spindly, elongated body. "Even when you're not floating around as energy, your form isn't built for warfare."

We haven't told him that we could take any form we can imagine, but what he says is still accurate. It still isn't easy for us to hold a body together, and we can only sustain it for the short periods we need to converse with him. So, even if we did create a form more suited to fighting, we wouldn't be able to do so for long enough to be effective. And the stresses of a battlefield would test our ability to maintain cohesion well past its breaking point. So we only hold physicality as long as each meeting with Yardley lasts, and only materialise inside his office at the lab. That is partly why we don't start to get suspicious about what is going on at the lab until much later, because the only human we have direct contact with is Yardley.

"Humans, on the other hand," he continues, "are very good at fighting. We have a long history of warring amongst ourselves, so I'm sure we can direct that off world to help with your conflict." He smiles. "But we need some help from you to make us more effective. I'm sure it's tough out there in space and we don't really know anything about the enemy, so we'll need to work on making humans better before we can send anyone out there." His eyes glitter. "We need some kind of edge."

"This is why we have brought you something to work with," we say, producing a container of the glowing blue substance provided by Consensus. "We believe this may be useful in enhancing humans to be more effective."

Yardley's eyes widen as he takes the container from us, the blue glow illuminating his face in a way that makes him look almost like one of us for a moment. Then his lips spread in a smile and the light dies as he lowers the container.

"Excellent," he says. "I'll assign one of my teams to this immediately."

Consensus is pleased when our team reports back. If the humans are willing to put themselves in harm's way to support our joint cause, we will do everything we can to help them.

* * *

P17 - May 2019 - India

Jhanvi's expression hardened, her lips thinning. "So, after nearly fifteen years without a word, that's the only reason you're here? As a last resort?"

Anushka opened her mouth but no sound came out. She felt her eyes fill with tears and she took in an unsteady breath. "I'm sorry. I…"

Jhanvi crossed her arms over her body, creating a physical barrier between them. "Did you even get the letter I sent you after Mama died?"

Anushka closed her eyes at the memory. After the disastrous phone call when Jhanvi had broken the news, Jhanvi had sent a lengthy handwritten letter to Anushka at Cambridge. She had poured her heart out, expressing her own guilt and sorrow at what had happened and begging Anushka not to let their own relationship be severed. But Anushka had been too angry and upset to receive it in the manner in which it was intended. She had burned the letter and ignored all Jhanvi's subsequent attempts to contact her. After a while, those attempts had stopped, and it was just easier to forget she even had a sister.

Anushka felt tears start to squeeze out from between her clenched eyelids and spill down her cheeks. She opened her eyes again, trying to think of something, anything, she could say to make things better.

Sanav stood up. "Jhanvi, what are you thinking? She's here. Isn't that enough? And if she's in trouble, that's even more reason for us to welcome her. That's what this place is all about, after all."

They all stood, looking at each other, for a long, agonising moment. Then Jhanvi's shoulders slumped. Sanav rushed forwards to relieve her of the groceries, taking them through to the kitchen.

Anushka twisted her hands together. "You're right to be angry with me, Vi. I can't expect to show up here after all this time and for you to just open your arms and welcome me in. The way I handled Mama's death was completely out of order. I had no right to take my guilt out on you. And you have no reason to help me now. But I was really hoping…" She trailed off, her tears preventing her from speaking further.

Jhanvi's face crumpled. "Oh, Nushie." She took two steps forward and enfolded Anushka in her arms. "Darling, it's okay. Of course you're welcome here. I just wish you'd come sooner."

Anushka clutched her sister and cried.

The following morning, Anushka woke in an unfamiliar room. She was lying on a futon, covered by a brightly-coloured, patchwork blanket. It was warm and the walls surrounding her were made of wood. Clearly, this wasn't an anonymous hotel on the M1. She resisted focusing on the last thing she remembered for as long as possible, relishing the sense of comfort and safety and not wanting to question it. Gradually, details of the furniture and decorations intruded on the blankness of her mind, telling her she was in India, at the commune, with Jhanvi. After she'd cried herself out, Jhanvi had sent her straight to bed, saying they could catch up properly the next day.

Anushka looked at her watch. It said 11:43, but that was UK time. She struggled to work out the time difference and realised it must be late afternoon, local time. She threw off the blanket and saw her suitcase standing a few feet away. Peeking out into the hallway beyond her room, she located a small bathroom and took a few minutes to freshen up. Once she was dressed in clean clothes, she felt a lot more human. Sounds of activity drew her downstairs and she discovered Jhanvi and both her daughters in the living area.

The smaller girl, Indrani, was relating a tale from her day at school.

"...and I only took one cookie, but Parth still called me a fatty…"

She trailed off as Anushka came into view, and they all looked up at her.

"Hi," she said, stopping a couple of steps from the bottom of the staircase.

"You slept all day!" Indrani said.

"Yes. I was very tired. And I came from England, so it was the middle of the night for me when I got here."

She focused on talking to the child, unwilling to meet Jhanvi's eye. Things were still strained between them and Anushka knew there was a lot they would need to talk through at some point. But she really didn't want to get into that now.

"How did you get here?" Jhanvi asked.

Anushka winced. "That's a long story. I don't suppose I could get some tea before I tell it?"

She offered up a hopeful smile and Jhanvi sighed, though without malice. Her sister rose and went to the kitchen.

"Are you really our auntie?" Khushi asked, and Anushka nodded. "So why haven't you come to see us before?"

Anushka went to sit next to her on the sofa. "Because I've been very silly. I went to live far away before you were even born and I never made the time to come and visit you." She looked up to where Jhanvi was regarding her, her expression sad. "And I'm very sorry about that."

Jhanvi brought the tea over, along with a plate of pakoras, which Anushka attacked with enthusiasm. Her sister watched her eat and drink for a while in silence.

Then she said, "So, what can you tell me?"

Anushka took a deep breath. "I got into some trouble at work and I need a place to stay. Nobody will be able to trace me here, I promise."

Jhanvi stared at her. "That's it? What kind of trouble? For that matter, what kind of work? What have you even been doing for the last fifteen years? Have you-"

Her sister broke off and stared at her. Anushka just had time to register the open mouths and wide eyes of her nieces when a different scene inserted itself over her vision. A woman bit into a thick sandwich with lettuce spilling out of the sides, then it was as if her life fast-forwarded through several more mundane activities until the same woman was backing down an alley, her expression terrified, as Charlotte and two men advanced on her.

"Your hair!" Indrani said.

Anushka's vision cleared and she looked down to see silvery strands resting on her shoulders. She got up.

"I'm sorry, I have to go. I'll explain when I get back."

"What?" Jhanvi reached out to stop her, but Anushka dodged past her and ran to the door.

Once outside, she ducked behind the house, checked that nobody was in sight, and thought pink thoughts.

* * *

P18 - May 2019 - London

The latest excursion wasn't going according to plan. Charlotte had selected a target from the list Perkins produced. It was a middle-aged woman, who had texted her sister about being able to see through walls. Charlotte and her team had driven to her house but it was empty. They had been walking back to the car, when Perkins gave a shout and pointed down the road. The woman from the social media pictures Perkins had provided was walking down the street, laden with shopping bags. She stopped dead at the sight of three people in combat gear charging towards her. Then she dropped her bags, turned tail and ran. Charlotte and her team were younger and fitter, but the woman knew the area better and was fleeing danger, while Charlotte and the others were trying not to draw attention to themselves.

The woman ducked down an alleyway, Owuye and Charlotte close behind her. When she realised the other end of the passage was blocked, the woman stopped and turned to face her assailants. Charlotte skidded to a halt too, and motioned for Owuye to stay back.

"What do you want?" the woman said. She was breathing hard, despite the short distance she had run.

"It's okay," Charlotte said, though she wasn't sure how true that was. She wasn't really sure of anything any more. "We know you've been experiencing something strange, and we want to help you."

"Help me?" The woman looked wildly between Charlotte and Owuye. "With guns and a black van? How is kidnapping me going to help me?"

These weren't unreasonable questions, given the circumstances. Owuye could be intimidating even when he wasn't dressed like a commando. Charlotte didn't have a chance to come up with a suitable reply, because at that moment Anushka materialised in the alley between her and the woman. Charlotte heard a shot from behind her and cried out in horror. But Anushka's hair flashed purple and her entire body sparkled with a second, crystal skin. The bullet ricocheted off her shoulder, embedding itself in a pile of rubbish a few feet away. The woman shrieked and backed up further, flattening herself against the wall at the end of the alley, eyes wide.

"Charlotte! What the hell are you doing?" Anushka said as her skin returned to normal and her hair faded to brown again.

Her eyes blazed with anger and Charlotte felt a physical pang.

"Cleaning up your mess," she shot back.

"By dragging people off the streets? And - what? Taking them back to the lab for Yardley to experiment on?"

"I'm following orders."

Anushka sneered. "Of course you are. What a good little soldier. Protecting national security by persecuting the public."

Charlotte's own anger swamped any doubts she might have been harbouring about what she was doing. "We wouldn't have a situation that needed containing if you hadn't betrayed everything we'd been working towards and unleashed an unknown contaminant on the world. You're the one who brought the public into this, not us."

Charlotte thought she saw Anushka wince at that, and pressed her advantage.

"Now, get out of my way and let me do my job. Unless you want to come back to the lab right now and explain everything to Yardley yourself."

She stepped forwards but Anushka remained where she was. When they were nose to nose, Charlotte reached up to shove Anushka out of the way, but instead Anushka grabbed her upper arms. Pink stripes cascaded down Anushka's hair from the scalp to the ends. Charlotte felt a sickening, lurching sensation, and then she was standing on grass, on a mountainside, the sun dipping towards the horizon.

* * *

A9 - 2005 - Cambridge

After the news about her mother's death, Anushka threw herself into her studies. It was like a switch had flipped in her head and all she wanted to do was concentrate on science and block out everything and everyone else. She stopped going to parties and started avoiding the few people she had made friends with. Some of them made efforts to find out what was wrong and draw her out but she rebuffed them until the only one still trying was Kirsten, the drama student who lived next door to her.

"Anushka, that cute boy from across the quad that I fancy is having a party tonight."

"Don't care."

Kirsten swung on the doorframe, imploring with wide eyes. "It's going to be great. You can't miss out on this one!"

Anushka slammed her book shut on her desk, "I don't care! I have assignments that need to be done."

"But those aren't due until after the weekend," Kirsten pointed out.

"Doesn't matter. Maybe the next party."

"You've said that the last dozen times! Girl, you need a life! Don't be such a downer, I'll introduce you to some hot drama chicks."

"Leave me alone, Kirsten."

Her next door neighbour put up her hands, "Alright, I tried. I officially give up on trying to get you to have a social life."

"Finally..." Anushka sighed.

Kirsten turned back from the doorway as she adjusted her lipliner in a handheld mirror, "At least tell me what's gotten into you? What happened? You used to be so much fun."

"Kirsten..."

"Okay, okay, I'm leaving. Jesus!"

Anushka found refuge in the work. It was challenging and intensive. It was concrete and unchanging. It didn't judge her or make demands on her, other than requiring all her attention and intellectual ability. She spent long hours in the lab, hiding herself away from everyone, barely even interacting with her tutors. But what she produced was good and she always submitted her assignments on time, so they had no reason to look deeper into her circumstances or life outside the lab. Science made sense and was controllable, so Anushka dedicated all her time and energy to mastering her chosen subjects.

She couldn't avoid social interaction entirely, however. And, after the initial shock of her mother's death started to fade, she gradually started hanging out with other students again. But she avoided getting too close to anyone, not wanting to invite intimate confidences. She indulged in a series of brief relationships, but the young women she connected with always ended up wanting more of her than she was willing to give. She gained a reputation for being cold and she did little to counter it, taking what she wanted from each relationship and letting go with ease when it ended.

Then came the summer she took a job as a technician at a pharmaceuticals lab. They were working on a potentially ground-breaking new trial and it was exciting at first, to be at the forefront of important research. But the lab was behind schedule and the lead research scientist was under pressure from the higher-ups to produce results. So he started human trials too early and two of the subjects died. Anushka found herself in a maelstrom of horror; the grief and rage of the families, the despair of the research team, the unrelenting scrutiny of the press, and the collapse of the company. She vowed nothing like that would ever happen on her watch. She would never allow the desire for profit or glory to be put above the safety of human life.

After achieving a double first in Chemistry and Biology, she stayed on to complete a Master's degree in Biochemistry and after that she completed her PhD in record time. But while she knew her academic achievements would have made her mother proud, her inability to share them with her family made them feel somehow hollow.

She took a series of academic and research jobs, looking for fulfilment in developing her scientific ideas, but she never felt as if she really fitted in anywhere. Her mind was occupied in complex and fascinating work but she always felt as if she was acting at one remove from her peers. Part of her soul was always yearning for what she was missing; a family. But she couldn't bring herself to reach out to Jhanvi again after their last conversation. She knew she was just as much to blame for the rift as her sister, if not more so, but she wasn't prepared to admit it and make the first move towards a reconciliation.

So, she just carried on with her life in England, pretending that her life back in India didn't exist, but never fully replacing it with anything meaningful.

* * *

C9 - 2011 - North London

Helping Yardley set up the lab gave Charlotte new focus. She had never been very good at being idle and having a complex long-term project to work on was just what she needed. Having Yardley as a boss was reassuring and their shared military background made it easy for them to agree on the best approach most of the time. Building the security department at the lab was a new and welcome challenge, but reporting to Yardley provided a safety blanket of familiarity that meant she didn't have to deal with the situation being entirely new.

Charlotte found she enjoyed interviewing and recruiting her own team and made sure to include people with a range of skills and attitudes, so as to avoid stagnation. It was harder for her to interact with the scientists as their focus was so very different and so single-minded. But the delineation of responsibilities was clear, which Charlotte found helpful, and it was easy enough to establish how security requirements could fit in with the scientists' needs without her having to understand what they were actually doing.

Early on, Danny sent her the CV of someone he had met on one of his programming courses.

"He can be pretty annoying, but you're used to that from me. And he's a whizz with digital security, so you should give him a chance."

Charlotte respected Danny's opinion so invited Adam Perkins in for an interview.

He was a thin and lanky guy, with a mop of hair sticking out every which way. He turned up wearing torn jeans, crocs and a ratty t-shirt that showed a python chewing up the letter 'C'. Everything about him rubbed Charlotte the wrong way. After an initial conversation to establish his expertise and recent job experience, she took a deep breath and started showing him around the lab.

The security hub consisted of high-end computers on desks and large monitors lining the walls. Past a glass door at the back were all the servers, giving off a gentle heat. A massive shelving unit was set up close to it with multiple firewall boxes and cords running from it to holes in the wall that went back to the computers outside.

"This is a really sweet set-up." Perkins whistled. "You guys get the best toys to play with here."

Charlotte gritted her teeth and pointed to a screen on the wall. This one displayed a hallway with laboratories on either side and guards on watch. "We undertake serious and sometimes dangerous work here. The security team will need to pay close attention to potential data breaches."

Perkins gave a pseudo-military salute. "No problemo, boss. I can whip this place into shape in no time."

"And you would have to undergo firearms training, in case of more physical security threats."

His eyes widened. "Cool!"

Irritating as he was, Charlotte couldn't fault his experience or the work he produced. True to Danny's word, Perkins threw himself into setting up the security systems and came up with innovations Charlotte would never have thought of. And while his attitude was more relaxed than she would have preferred, Perkins never triggered her violent anger response by challenging her authority on the basis of her gender.

Charlotte generally found herself much more comfortable with team members like Owuye, though, who deferred to her with military discipline. She had to keep reminding herself that she was a civilian now, and that not everyone would appreciate her preferred management style.

Before long, all the appropriate security measures were in place and the lab was up and running.

Charlotte settled into a routine of running her department. She never asked about the projects the scientists were undertaking, beyond whatever information she required to ensure everyone was kept safe and all data was secure.

* * *

E9 - 2018 - Earth

Yardley tells us that our visible presence in the lab outside his office would be distracting to the other humans, who are working on complex and potentially dangerous experiments. He will act as a go-between, passing on information and instructions to his workers and reporting back to us on their progress. This works well for us as we find it much easier to restrict our interactions to just one human, rather than having to establish connections with and adapt to the idiosyncrasies of many. Normally we would expect contact with one being to mean the provision of knowledge to and increased familiarity with many, so we are glad to let Yardley disseminate our requirements to his staff, rather than having to repeat ourselves over and over.

So, for quite some time, the only occasions when we manifest on Earth are for meetings in Yardley's office. I don't find this strange. This is our first contact with another race, besides what Consensus has told us about the enemy, so we have nothing else to measure it against. We follow the instructions we are given by Consensus and discuss potential applications of our theories and resources with Yardley. To begin with, our meetings are many and frequent.

But, once we have set the humans to their task, the time spent with the rest of our team between meetings stretches long, with little to occupy us. We decide to explore further, keeping to our energy form, so as not to be discernible to the humans. We do not desire to interact directly with anyone other than Yardley, but we are curious to know more about the humans in general and how they live their lives. The lab is just as strange and wondrous to us as everything else we have seen so far on Earth and initially we just wander the hallways, taking it all in.

The humans scurry around, all concentrating on their own tasks. Some make themselves anonymous with white coverings and huddle in transparent areas, away from the others. Some move around the lab from one place to another. Some sit in opaque areas, but watch the others on screens. It is all new and fascinating to us, and we wonder how they manage to exist successfully without knowing each other's minds and hearts. It must be so difficult to have to seek out information about what others are doing, rather than just assimilating it as part of normal existence.

The concept of individuality is also new to us, but it becomes a useful idea. We do not want the others in our team to know what we are doing, in case they feel it is inappropriate and tell us to stop, so we practise walling off our consciousness from them. It is very difficult at first, and makes us feel very small and alone. But during the times when we are out in the lab, we manage to keep ourselves apart from their communication streams, so they don't know what we are doing. We reflect that this must be what Consensus does, as they are not always as transparent to us as our family unit and the other entities of our society that we come into direct contact with.

After a while, we start paying closer attention to the interactions between the humans, and we discover something troubling. We particularly watch those who are working with the substance we have provided to them through Yardley and we realise they don't know what it is they are doing, or why.

* * *

P19 - May 2019 - India

Charlotte stared around at the hillside. "What the hell just happened? Where the hell are we?"

But Anushka's mind was still focused on what she'd just learned. She sank down onto the grass, gulping air into her lungs.

"Perkins is okay. I didn't kill him. He just tried to shoot me, but I didn't kill him."

"You did set him on fire," Charlotte's wry voice said from a few feet away, "so I'd say you're even now."

Anushka looked up. Charlotte was still staring at their surroundings.

"My question remains. Where the hell are we?"

In front of them were long sweeping mountains covered in grass and trees. A river snaked between two of the trees at the edge of sight, probably from a waterfall somewhere close by. Right near their feet grew flowers of yellow and white and violet, and not a single building was visible. Patches of brown showed on one of the mountains, as the sun started to dip behind it. The whole landscape was gorgeous, but now was not the time to stand around admiring the view.

Anushka looked back at Charlotte. She took a deep breath, really not sure how this was going to go. "I thought we ought to talk, so I brought us somewhere we wouldn't be interrupted."

Charlotte crossed her arms and raised one eyebrow. "That doesn't exactly answer my question, now does it?"

Anushka couldn't help a slight smile. "Noticed that, did you?" Then she sobered as a pang of longing stabbed through her for those not too distant days when they could joke and share intimacy together. "How did we get here, Charl?"

"I believe you grabbed me and teleported us here. Oh, you mean more figuratively?" Charlotte's expression hardened. "You stole classified material, released it on an unsuspecting public, and ran away. Without even a word."

Anushka scrambled to her feet, taking up a position slightly further up the slope, above Charlotte. She reached for any kind of justification for her actions. The only words that sprang to mind came out in a tentative, querulous tone.

"I left you a note."

Charlotte let out a hollow laugh. "A note? You think a scrap of paper with a scribbled apology is going to make up for you giving up on four years together?"

"Is that all this is about for you?" Anushka felt anger swamping her guilt. "That I left without saying goodbye? Don't you think there are more important aspects of this situation?"

Charlotte looked at her, eyes shining. "Not to me. I thought we were a team. Us against the world. But you must have been planning this for weeks, or longer, and keeping it from me. Don't you trust me at all?"

"Not with this." Anushka's hands tightened into fists at her sides. "Not when I knew you'd just run to Yardley and report my transgressions like the loyal little lapdog you are. And I was right. You're charging around at his beck and call, attacking innocent people and enabling him to do who-knows-what to them. How has it reached the point where you'll kidnap people off the street at his say-so?"

"We're trying to help them! They pose a danger to themselves and others, because of what you did, not because of Yardley. He's trying to fix the problem you created, so of course I'm helping him."

Anushka couldn't really refute her culpability, but she wasn't prepared to give ground.

"And what would he do to me if you took me back to the lab and handed me over? You say you thought it was us against the world, but Yardley was always there too, dividing your loyalty. If it was a choice between him and me, who would you pick?" She held up a hand. "No, don't answer that. You've already sided with him."

Charlotte looked at the ground. "You made that choice for me by running away."

"Yardley gave me no option! He was trying to force me to move to human trials way before we were ready. The XR-20 is dangerous!" Anushka gestured at her hair. "We know that now better than ever. And you know how I feel about rushing to human testing, after what happened at that lab I worked at years ago. But Yardley wouldn't listen to me. He said if I wouldn't move forwards with the experiments, he would find someone who would. I know what I did was rash and stupid - and has actually caused the exact harm I was trying to prevent. But I was scared and I didn't know what else to do."

"You could have come to me. You could have given me the option of siding with you."

Anushka didn't know how to respond to that, so she said nothing. They both stood there for a long moment, Anushka looking at Charlotte, who was still looking down. Anushka ached to cross the distance between them and take Charlotte in her arms. But the gap she had opened was too big and her feet were rooted to the ground.

"Take me back," Charlotte said, her voice low.

"And then what? We just carry on having crazy confrontations where people shoot at me and I set them on fire?"

Charlotte finally looked up, meeting Anushka's gaze. "You could come back with me. Talk to Yardley. Figure out a way to sort this all out. Together."

Anushka hugged herself. "I can't. It's gone too far for that now. I don't trust him." She paused, then forged onwards. "And I don't trust you to protect me, not from him. His hold over you is too strong."

Charlotte's jaw tightened. "Well, then. I guess that's that. So, are you going to disappear and just leave me here?"

Anushka took two quick steps forwards, laid a hand on Charlotte's shoulder, and jumped them back to the alley. It was empty. Anushka broke contact and teleported away.

* * *

P20 - May 2019 – India

All the green tea in the world wasn't enough to fortify Anushka as she tried to explain what was going on to her sister. She had come back to the house after the confrontation with Charlotte, feeling drained and depressed. Jhanvi sent Indrani and Khushi to their room amidst strenuous protests.

"They think you're a fairy princess," Jhanvi said once they had settled down again. "And I have to admit it's as sensible an explanation as any I've come up with."

Anushka took a sip of tea, warming her hands around the clay mug. Jhanvi regarded her, eyes wary, and Anushka couldn't blame her. She had shown up literally out of nowhere, after no contact for fifteen years. How could she expect even her own sister to trust and support her under such circumstances? She decided she would have to be honest, so she started at the point of stealing the XR-20 from the lab and summarised all the subsequent events, superpowers and all.

Jhanvi listened to the story with remarkable calmness, drinking her tea and not interrupting. When Anushka had finished, she was silent for a long moment.

Then she said, "Show me."

Anushka decided invisibility was the least disruptive of the powers she knew she could call upon. She put her mug down on the table, closed her eyes and thought about the colour blue, imagining at the same time that she was dissolving from view. There was no audible reaction from her sister so, after a few seconds, she opened her eyes. Jhanvi was still sitting on the other side of the table, looking at her.

"Well?" Jhanvi asked.

Anushka looked down at her hand and tried to visualise it going transparent, as she had before.

Nothing happened. She switched to thinking about the colour purple and imagining the impervious crystal skin covering her fingers. Still nothing.

Jhanvi frowned. "I don't know what game you're playing here, Nush, but it isn't very funny."

"I don't know what's going on. It's just not working any more."

Jhanvi rose. "I have things to do. You're welcome to stay if you need to, and perhaps we could try and catch up properly later."

Anushka got to her feet as well. "I - I'm sorry. I'm not trying to take advantage of you. You and the girls both saw my hair change colour earlier."

"I don't know what I saw," Jhanvi said. "And I don't know what to think. But I really do need to get on. Dinner will be in an hour."

She stacked the clay mugs inside one another and picked them up with one hand, scooping up the teapot with the other and taking it all into the kitchen.

Anushka felt like the walls were starting to close in on her, so she went back outside into the deepening twilight. She picked a direction at random and started walking. She couldn't make sense of what was happening. Had she lost her powers altogether? Was the effect only temporary? And, if so, how was she going to get back to England? She did have her passport with her, but she didn't want to use a commercial airline where people at the lab might be able to track her. Teleportation had seemed like the perfect answer to her problem and now it was gone.

She stopped and clenched her eyes shut, picturing the lounge in her London flat in as much detail as she could. She visualised herself standing on the bare, laminate flooring, next to the chrome and glass coffee table, the breakfast bar to her left with the kitchen nook behind it. Blue light filtered past her eyelids and, for a moment, she thought she'd done it.

Then, a light, silvery voice said, "Whatever you're trying to do, it won't work."

Anushka opened her eyes and blinked against the brightness of the light before her. She brought one hand up to shield her vision and tried to make out the form in the centre of the light. It was vaguely humanoid, though much taller and more slender than any human could be. She got the impression of a rounded, bald head and a pair of shining eyes. The figure was at once horribly shocking and strangely familiar. And she had definitely heard that voice before.

It had been a series of disturbing dreams that started in the months before she fled the lab. There had been a blue glow and that same silvery voice in her head.

"Question everything," it had said. "Yardley's motives are not pure. What is it that you are really working on? And what purpose will it serve?"

Anushka had assumed it was her subconscious telling her she had misgivings about what she was doing with her life. Because what did she really know about the end result of the XR-20 project? She had no idea where the material she was studying had come from, and wasn't even clear about what she was trying to achieve with it. Yardley's approach had been to give her free rein to research in her own way, saying he didn't want to prejudice her findings by giving her too much information. That had seemed like a welcome opportunity for pure experimentation without expectations to begin with. Now, though, Anushka realised it just meant he hadn't been open with her about their aims, and was keeping information from her about the XR-20's origins and purpose.

The blue glow had suffused her dreams and come into her thoughts periodically, causing her to pause and consider her actions. The XR-20 had the potential to be very dangerous, and Anushka had no way of knowing what it would ultimately be used for. Yardley had connections to the military, after all. Could it be some kind of weapon? And did Anushka really want to be involved with that sort of research?

The blue glow had filled her with urgency, making her even more restless and desirous of an active plan to remove whatever potential the XR-20 held from Yardley's grasp. And that was what had ultimately led to her flight.

Now the owner of what was apparently a real voice stood before her in all its unearthly glory.

"Will you allow us to explain?"

* * *

A10 - 2015 - London

The relationship between Anushka and Charlotte was competitive before they even met. Anushka had just moved to London and joined a local gym with an outdoor running track. She first started running at university and found it a good way to keep fit and also clear her head when it was too full.

During one evening session, Anushka's legs pulsed with energy as she kept running along the track. Her muscles strained and her chest heaved. Sweat dripped down her back, as she pushed herself to run faster, trying to outpace the thoughts chasing her. One foot after another, she pounded against the clay ground. The alarm on her watch went off, and she allowed her pace to slow. After a couple of minutes, it beeped again and she picked her speed back up. She alternated sprinting and jogging, letting her legs breathe a little while her mind gradually let the thoughts melt away onto the track behind her.

The track wasn't large, just wide enough for four runners to run side by side. And like most running tracks, it was surrounded by a large ring of soft green grass, perfect for runners to sit and catch their breath but also to provide some welcome colour. The floodlights made the track into an oasis of bright green and orange in the surrounding darkness.

Sweat now beaded on Anushka's forehead and her t-shirt was drenched, her leg muscles complaining. She was on her last sprint, just a few more metres to go.

And then, a woman flashed past on her right, casting a triumphant grin over her shoulder as she crossed the line a few strides before Anushka.

Her rival was tall and lithe, chin-length black hair whipping backwards as she ran. She drew to a halt a short distance past the finish line and stood, bent over, with her hands on her knees. Anushka noticed she was missing the last two fingers on her left hand, something that intrigued rather than repulsed her. The other woman looked up as Anushka approached, her eyes sparkling.

"Sorry, that was a bit unfair. You've probably been out here quite a bit longer than me."

Anushka smiled. "Why don't we have a rematch sometime when we're both fresh?"

The other woman straightened up and held out her hand.

"Deal. I'm Charlotte, by the way."

"Anushka."

They shook hands.

"I haven't seen you here before," Charlotte said.

"This is my first time."

"But not your first time running, surely. I can tell that much from watching you."

Anushka's smile widened. Charlotte had been watching her and appraising her skill and experience? "Thanks. I've been running for years, but I only just moved to London. Finding a track was one of the first things I did."

"Dedication. I like it." Charlotte smiled back. It softened her hawkish features. "Do you fancy a coffee in the gym cafe?"

Anushka laughed. "I thought you'd only just started your workout. And I thought you admired dedication."

Charlotte's cheeks reddened and Anushka kicked herself mentally for potentially ruining a good thing with her mockery. But Charlotte offered up a self-deprecating smile.

"In my own defence, this is my second workout of the day. I started with a weights and core session at 6am."

Anushka threw her hands up in a placatory gesture, hoping to salvage the situation. "You don't need to justify yourself to me, though I am suitably impressed. And I would love a coffee."

She was pleased when Charlotte nodded her agreement, and Anushka experienced a rush of relief that the encounter wasn't over before it had really begun.

They walked together back to the women's changing room. Charlotte stripped off as soon as they entered. Out of her running gear, her body was slim but strong, muscles standing out clearly in her arms and legs. She caught Anushka admiring her and smiled, this time without blushing.

Conversation over coffee was easier than Anushka expected. She hadn't socialised much since her move to London and certainly wasn't looking for any kind of deep connection. But Charlotte was very attractive and Anushka was lonely. What harm could a little flirtation do? After coffee, they agreed to meet at the gym again two days later for a joint training session. Charlotte still beat Anushka when they had their rematch, but Anushka was not deterred. It gave her a reason to keep meeting Charlotte at the gym, under the guise of requesting help to increase her fitness and using Charlotte's competition to challenge her to strive harder. Charlotte seemed more than happy to oblige.

* * *

C10 - 2015 - London

If asked what had first attracted her to Anushka, Charlotte would probably have claimed it was her intelligence. But if she was honest, it had been her hair. Charlotte was just stretching in preparation for a training session at the running track near the lab, when an unfamiliar motion caught her eye. An Indian woman she had never seen before was jogging round the track, her ponytail swinging behind her. Tied up, the hair was long enough that Charlotte estimated it would reach past her waist when it was loose. She imagined running her fingers through its thick, dark mass and felt a shiver of desire.

Charlotte found herself watching the woman as she continued her run. Her technique was good and she was clearly an experienced runner, but Charlotte couldn't break her gaze from the graceful movements of her body. As the woman ran past her and started what looked like a final push towards the finish line, Charlotte sprang into action and sprinted after her. She caught up just before the line and couldn't help overtaking for a petty last minute victory. She was surprised at how pleased she was when Anushka came over to introduce herself, thankfully not put off by Charlotte's cheap trick with the non-existent race. She was even more surprised when she heard herself suggest having coffee. She wasn't exactly in the habit of picking up women at the gym. In fact, her love life had been as dry as a desert since a disastrous blind date with one of Danny's friends shortly after he moved in with her.

But she felt a flush of pleasure when she noticed Anushka's attention in the changing room, and made no effort to conceal her nakedness. Anushka's body was curvier than her own, but still strong-looking, and her hair did indeed brush the small of her back when she released it from its ponytail and shook it out before heading into the showers.

The topic of conversation over coffee quickly turned to professions.

"I'm a biochemist," Anushka said when Charlotte asked. "I just started a teaching job at Imperial College, but I'm already missing the lab. Research jobs are hard to come by, though, so I had to take what I could get."

Charlotte grinned. “I work for Yardley Labs, so if you ever want an introduction, I know the boss pretty well.”

“You’re a scientist, too?” Anushka’s eyebrows rose towards her hairline.

Charlotte laughed. “No, I run the security team. Lester Yardley was my commanding officer for a while when I was in the army, and he offered me a job when I got invalided out.”

She raised her left hand and wiggled the fingers that were left. She was sure Anushka would have noticed the stumps but she wanted to make sure, in case it was something that might turn her off.

“It’s ridiculous, really, since there’s still so much I can do. But it compromises my ability to hold a weapon, so that was that.” She shrugged. “Let me know if you want me to try and set up an interview.”

Anushka’s eyebrows drew down again but her next words demonstrated that it wasn’t Charlotte’s lost fingers making her frown. “I did take a look at Yardley Labs when I was researching jobs in the area, but don’t they mostly do military contracts?”

Charlotte nodded, rubbing the fingers of her right hand over the stumps on the left. “That’s Yardley’s background, so it’s where his contacts are.”

Anushka pushed her hair over her shoulder, dropping her gaze. “Thanks for the offer. I’ll think about it and let you know.”

The conversation moved to other subjects, but Charlotte was glad of the implication that Anushka wanted to see her again. When Anushka suggested they work out together at the track later in the week, she agreed with enthusiasm.

* * *

E10 - 2018- Earth

It takes us another long while of effort and will, but we manage to cast our consciousness far enough to be able to speak to our family unit back on our homeworld. Messages come through to us on Earth from Consensus and we send reports back, but we want a more intimate and individual view of what is happening back home. We miss the easy, constant exchange of information we have with our family, as well as the emotional buoyancy we enjoy as part of their supportive, loving whole.

Our family unit is surprised to hear from us, but very pleased..

We have missed your presence in our minds! It is joyous to have you among us again.

We have missed you all too. There are not enough minds here to keep us from being lonely.

But you are doing important work that will help protect us from our enemy.

So the threat still exists?

**Word from Consensus is that the threat is growing. The enemy are more numerous than we at first thought and their intentions seem to be* _to wipe us from existence. So your work with the humans is vital.*_

*But what can be the enemy's motivation for such destructive desires?*

*We are not able to fathom. We are lucky to have Consensus to protect us.*

*And what does Consensus tell you about the humans?*

*That they are strong and able allies, and that we are fortunate to have found such people who are so willing to aid us in our time of need.*

*Consensus says that all of the humans are working with us towards our common goal?*

*Of course. How could it be otherwise?*

We cannot not hold the connection for long. But the exchange is enough to let us know that Consensus is lying to our people, just as Yardley is lying to his. We believe he is the custodian of all knowledge pertaining to our presence on his planet and has not shared this with anyone. Could Consensus be mistaken in our relationship with the humans? We do not see how, when we have told them how we interact only with Yardley. But what does this deception mean? How can they tell our people that the humans are united in their willingness to aid our cause when, as far as we can tell, only one human is even aware of our existence. Yardley may be assisting us with his experiments at his lab, but he cannot speak for the billions that populate his planet.

We know that Consensus does not tell us everything, but have always assumed this is to protect us or not to burden us with unnecessary information. But this direct deception tells us they are not as truthful with our people as we had thought and that opens up many uncomfortable questions about what else they might be keeping hidden from us.

* * *

P21 - May 2019 - India

Anushka stared at the figure before her, unable to make sense of what she was seeing. The blue glow in the darkness made it difficult to make out the form of the figure clearly and her mind rebelled against the possibility of such a form in the first place, making it even harder to pin down.

"What are you?" she asked. She considered that she ought to be freaking out more than she was, but she felt detached from her emotions, as if there was a cotton wool barrier in her mind, preventing her from accessing them.

The blue light faded to a dim glow that gave enough light to see in the darkening gloom, without making it painful to look at the figure. The shade and quality of the colour took her back to her dreams. A sense of reassurance, completely at odds with the reality of the situation, suffused her thoughts. The voice in her dreams had been urgent in its message, but always with a feeling of wanting to protect and help her. She realised, though, that if it had penetrated her sleeping mind from outside, it was surely capable of manipulating her reactions to it. Perhaps that was why she wasn't panicking now.

The familiar voice spoke. "We are the source of your new abilities. And the catalyst behind your current predicament."

Anushka swallowed, pieces fitting together in her head to make a worrying picture.

"The XR-20 I've been studying is alien? Well, that explains a few things. But you've been in my head? You sent me that dream! Did you make me steal the XR-20 and run away from the lab?"

The figure raised a hand in a placatory gesture. "We only planted the seed of doubt. We have not controlled your actions in any way. Your decisions have been your own."

Anushka only had the alien's word for that and it didn't make the intrusion any less concerning. "But I wouldn't have made those decisions without that first push. What gives you the right to mess about in my head and turn my life upside down?"

"We are sorry. But we needed your help, and it was the only way we could think of to separate you from the laboratory and bring you to a situation where you might be willing to aid us."

Anushka wrapped her arms around herself, hugging herself tightly. "You thought making me a fugitive and causing me to abandon my whole life would make me sympathetic to your cause, whatever it is? I hate to tell you this, but you were dead wrong.

I've lost everything, and now I'm stuck in a foreign country with no way to get home."

The alien held out a hand, and a small, transparent container materialised in it. Inside, there was what looked like a sample of the XR-20.

"We can solve that last problem for you, at least. Do you wish to obtain your powers once again?"

"Permanently this time?" Anushka asked. She needed them right now but she wasn't sure she wanted to commit to a whole lifetime of superpowers.

"As far as we are aware, the substance only has a temporary effect on humans," the alien said. "But we have access to more, if you want to keep using it."

Anushka took the container. "So, I can control how long the powers last and whether or not I keep them?"

The alien nodded. Anushka opened the container, scooped out some of the XR-20 and then ran her fingers through her hair. The substance was cold and slippery but it soaked into the fibres of her hair almost immediately, leaving no residue.

"Now," she said. "You have a lot of explaining to do. But first, do you have a name?"

"You may call us Ergo."

"Okay, Ergo. Before we do anything else, I need to tie up some loose ends. Then, do you have somewhere we can go to talk?"

"Yes. Meet us back here as soon as you are ready and we will take you to our ship."

* * *

P22 - May 2019 - North London

By the time Charlotte got back to the lab, it was late afternoon. She went straight to Yardley's office. As she approached the door, it opened and a woman stepped out. Charlotte recognised her as Major Simmonds, the army liaison officer for the lab. She barely acknowledged Charlotte as she swept past, her eyebrows drawn down in a frown.

Charlotte knocked on Yardley's door and noted a pause before he called her in. He was shuffling papers on his desk when she entered and it took him a moment to school his expression to its usual neutrality. The meeting with Simmonds must have gone badly for some reason, but it wasn't Charlotte's place to question how the lab was run.

"Ah, Ms Grant," Yardley said. "You have returned."

Charlotte stared at him. "Did you think I wouldn't?"

He steepled his fingers, his expression guarded. "Given free choice, I was confident you would. But you could have been kept against your will. Out of interest, where did she take you?"

"It was warmer than here, and nearly sunset, so several hours ahead. She doesn't really have ties there, as far as I know, but she may be hiding out in India."

"Can you be more specific?" His tone was neutral but there was steel in his eyes.

"No, all I saw was part of a mountainside. No way to narrow it down more than that, I'm afraid."

Yardley nodded. "We'll just have to come up with alternative methods of getting her back, then."

Charlotte narrowed her eyes. "To what end?"

Yardley smiled. "Why, to continue her work with us, of course. This little escapade has provided us with a great deal of interesting data to analyse. And we will need Dr Mahto's expertise and unique perspective to make sense of it."

"Data? Like what?"

Yardley rose from behind his desk. "Let me show you."

He led her out of his office and down to the main lab. Scientists in caps, masks and gloves were busy with multiple tasks, but most of them seemed to be working with samples of a green, leafy substance.

Charlotte thought back to her first destination of the day before. "You got hold of some of the contaminated lettuce?"

Yardley gave her a self-satisfied smile. "All of the contaminated lettuce, and more besides. In the end, it wasn't very difficult to send teams out to all the supermarkets on the distribution list and purchase what hadn't already been sold. We're having to spend quite a lot of time separating out the contaminated samples from those that are unaffected, but we're building up a reasonable supply for testing purposes."

He indicated the nearest fridge in the bank along one side of the lab.

Charlotte said, "So, do you need more human test subjects as well? Should I select another target and take the team out again?"

Yardley waved a dismissive hand. "I don't think that will do any good. The woman retrieved by Mr Owuye and Mr Perkins earlier today demonstrated no special abilities when tested and apparently her blood was clear of contamination. And Mr Perkins tells me the others on his list have been reporting in their online correspondence that their powers were sadly short-lived."

"So, what happened to the woman they picked up?"

Yardley's eyes widened. "What do you suppose happened to her? We gave her our apologies, along with sizable financial recompense for her trouble, and asked her very politely to sign a non-disclosure agreement before giving her a lift home. Really, Ms Grant, you are growing disappointingly suspicious of what we are trying to do here."

"I'm sorry," Charlotte said. "So, you want me to keep working on finding Anushka?"

"Exactly."

Yardley left her standing in front of the window into the lab, watching the scientists as they worked. Charlotte felt like it was only the presence of other people that prevented her from sinking to the floor. It had been a long and emotional day, and she had no idea how events were going to play out. The conversation with Anushka on the mountainside had really rattled her. Was what Anushka had said about Yardley true? Had he really ignored her warnings with the intention of putting people at unnecessary risk? But what he'd said about the woman they'd retrieved had seemed so reasonable.

Charlotte really needed to let off some steam, so she went to the lab gym for an intensive workout, in an effort to clear her head. She started with some stretches, then moved onto the treadmill, pushing herself to run as fast as she could for as long as she could. She was still struggling with the accusations Anushka had thrown her way and questioning her part in what was going on. But she found running did little to disperse those thoughts, since it was an activity she strongly associated with Anushka. She slowed the programme to a stop and jumped off, breathing hard but still keen to work out some frustration. She crossed to the punching bags, put on some gloves and threw her anger into her blows. She had reacted defensively to Anushka's accusations, driven more by her sense of betrayal than any reasoned commitment to her actions. Maybe Anushka was right, and what Yardley was asking her to do had gone too far.

This wasn't a good frame of mind for boxing practice. One of her punches went wild and she felt the twinge of her muscles protesting this unreasoned abuse. She gave up and retreated to the changing room, drenched in sweat but still keyed up. As she was showering, all her frustration and confusion continued to surge through her and she slammed her hand against the tiled wall. The pressure was building in her mind and she had to do something to release it. A crazy notion began to form.

She waited until most of the scientists had gone home for the day and used her pass to slip into the lab. She went to the fridge Yardley had indicated and found several boxes of lettuce. Taking one and putting it in her bag, Charlotte made her way out of the lab and went home.

She found Danny in the kitchen, eating dinner. She waved the box of lettuce at him and grinned.

"Fancy getting superpowers for a day?"

* * *

A11 - 2015 - London

Every time a session at the track with Charlotte approached, Anushka felt a fluttery sense of anticipation in her stomach. Her running technique and stamina had improved under Charlotte's intensive tutelage, but that wasn't what made her look forward to the sessions so much. Her appreciation of Charlotte's running style had little to do with what she could learn from it. It had a great deal more to do with the warm flush of pleasure that spread through her body as she raked her gaze over Charlotte's lithe body powering round the track. It would have made Anushka ashamed if it wasn't for the fact that she frequently caught Charlotte checking her out in turn. She was certain their attraction was mutual but she didn't know what to do about it.

It had been twelve years since Prisha rejected her advances in the street in Kolkata, but the effects of that encounter had been far-reaching. It had taken

Anushka a long time to admit to herself in concrete terms that she was attracted exclusively to women and her few short and awkward attempts at relationships with both men and women in the interim hadn't been successful. She knew she wanted more from Charlotte than just physical release but was wary of opening herself up to emotional intimacy.

So, while her attraction to Charlotte was strong, and apparently reciprocated, Anushka didn't know how to move forwards. Luckily, Charlotte took matters into her own hands.

They both signed up for a charity 10k run, which was advertised at the track where they'd met. They trained hard together, trying to improve their times so they could make a good showing on the day. Charlotte was still fitter and faster than Anushka and they agreed beforehand that she shouldn't feel obliged to stick with Anushka on the way round.

So, as Anushka completed the race with a time that was a personal best, there was Charlotte, waiting at the finish line to embrace her as she crossed over it.

Anushka felt Charlotte's arms tighten around her sweaty body and a shiver of pleasure ran through her. When they broke apart, Charlotte was grinning.

"Well done! Let's celebrate."

They showered, changed and headed out for dinner.

The French restaurant Charlotte picked wasn't too far from the park where the race had taken place. The door had pink and white flowers draped around columns on either side and inside, white curtains adorned the windows. Crystal chandeliers provided muted golden light above the tables, each of which had a vase of more pink and white flowers placed at its centre.

After they were seated at a table, a waiter popped open a bottle of wine and set it on their table.

"This all looks expensive," Anushka said with one eyebrow raised, as Charlotte filled her glass.

As what turned out to be a rich and delicious meal progressed, Anushka noticed Charlotte made sure to keep topping up her wine.

"Are you trying to get me drunk?" she asked with a smile.

Charlotte dipped a finger in her own wine and ran the tip round the edge of her own glass, creating a rich, ringing tone.

"Maybe," she said, capturing Anushka's gaze. "Do you object?"

Anushka felt her face flush and glanced down at the table. Charlotte reached across the table and laid her hand over Anushka's where it rested next to her fork.

"Hey," she said, her voice softening. Anushka looked up to see that Charlotte's expression was concerned. "I didn't mean to make you feel uncomfortable."

"No, it's okay, you didn't," Anushka said. "It's just - I'm not very good at this."

Charlotte ran her fingers over the back of Anushka's hand.

"You're doing fine." Then she blushed and dropped her gaze, suddenly hesitant. "Assuming

I haven't completely misread the situation. I can't claim to be an expert at this kind of thing, either. If you want me to stop, please just say so."

Anushka felt an involuntary smile quirk her lips up. She picked up her wine glass in her other hand and took a long gulp.

"No, no, you go right ahead."

Charlotte smiled back, and left her hand where it was for the rest of the meal. This made it difficult for Anushka to cut up her meat but she didn't care. They shared a dessert, Charlotte going so far as to feed Anushka a few mouthfuls from her own fork, which made Anushka giggle. Charlotte insisted on paying, pointing out that she had chosen the restaurant and didn't want Anushka to feel obliged to contribute. Anushka let her. It felt nice to be wined and dined, and Anushka didn't see the need to assert her equality with Charlotte. They stepped out into the warm evening.

"We could walk to my house from here, if you'd like?" Charlotte said.

"That would be lovely."

She reached for Charlotte's hand, but Charlotte pulled it away and stepped round to Anushka's other side, offering her other hand instead. Anushka glanced down and realised that the hand she had reached for was the one with the missing fingers. She persisted in taking hold of it and brought it up to her mouth, gently kissing each of the stumps in turn. This time, it was Charlotte who blushed, but she was smiling. They set off walking, Anushka holding the maimed hand in hers the whole way.

They quickened their pace by mutual consent as they neared their destination and Anushka felt a growing sense of excitement. Charlotte fumbled in her purse for her keys and nearly tripped as she stepped through the door. They were both giggling by the time they made it inside. Pushing the door closed, Charlotte backed Anushka against it. She then shoved her tongue in Anushka's mouth, while Anushka pulled Charlotte's blouse out of her waistband and slipped her hand up the bare skin of Charlotte's back. Charlotte held her gently by the chin with one hand and her kisses slowed while she ran her fingers through Anushka's long hair with the other. In this silent world of just the two of them, the sound of someone clearing their throat interrupted their exploration of each other.

They broke apart and both looked round. Anushka saw a man staring at them from the sofa in the living room.

"Hello, ladies," he said, struggling not to laugh. "I would have slunk away and left you to it, but…"

He gestured at his legs and Anushka saw they were both amputated above the knee. Embarrassment flooded through her but Charlotte just burst out laughing.

"Sorry, Danny. We didn't mean to interrupt your evening."

"Oh, you should feel free to go right on ahead," he said. "Don't mind me."

"Nope, floor show's over," Anushka said, slotting easily into the relaxed tone. Normally, meeting a stranger in such circumstances would have mortified her, but anticipation made her bold. "Nice to meet you, Danny. Charlotte's told me a lot about you. I'm Anushka, by the way."

"Oh, I know who you are. Charlotte's told me a lot about you too."

Charlotte pulled Anushka towards the stairs. "Would love to stay so you two can get better acquainted, but actually - I wouldn't."

Danny's voice followed them up, calling out, "Goodnight!"

* * *

C11 - 2018 - London

Anushka and Charlotte had known each other for three years when the university Anushka worked for went through a restructure. Anushka bored Charlotte with all the details over dinner one night.

"There's a new Director of Sciences," she said, sipping her wine in their favourite restaurant. "He's got some weird idea about working more cohesively, so everyone's going to have to broaden their teaching schedules. Which means even less time for research, and what research we do get to do will be less focused and less specialised. It's going to be a nightmare."

"You've never really been happy there. You always say you'd rather be able to do more research." Charlotte reached out and stroked the back of Anushka's hand where it lay on the table, thinking back to their first dinner together at that restaurant. "Why don't you come and meet Yardley and just hear what he has to say? He was telling me only the other day that we really need more scientific staff. He's got a new project starting up and he seems really excited about it."

Anushka bit her lip and looked down at her plate.

Charlotte pushed. "Why are you so hesitant about it? Is it the military connection? You could make it part of your contract that you only work on civilian projects, if it matters that much to you."

She waited expectantly until Anushka looked up and met her gaze again.

"Maybe you should set up a meeting or something."

Charlotte grinned. "Yes! It'll be so great to have you at the lab. We'll be able to see so much more of each other."

Anushka held up a hand. "Hold on, I haven't agreed to anything yet. I'll come and hear Yardley's pitch, but I'm not promising anything."

Charlotte squeezed her fingers. "Once you hear about the project, you won't be able to say no."

And she was right. At the meeting, Yardley was at his most charming. They met in his office at the lab and Charlotte joined them for a tour, excited to be able to show Anushka round her workplace at last.

"I have to admit I've been very eager to meet you, Dr Mahto," Yardley said with a smile. "Ever since Ms Grant told me she was dating a biochemist. I'm so glad you've finally decided to come and speak with me, to allow me to show you our facilities and talk about what we do here."

Anushka threw Charlotte a glare and Charlotte nodded encouragement. She knew Anushka wanted to play hard to get, rather than seeming desperate for a new job, so she hadn't told Yardley much about the situation at the university. She hoped Yardley's references to her own enthusiasm about Anushka wouldn't cloud Anushka's reception of what was on offer.

Anushka pasted a smile on her face. "Charlotte tells me you have a new project that needs staffing?"

"Yes," Yardley said. "It's an exciting new venture that I think would provide you with a lot to get your teeth into. I'm actually looking for someone with your experience to head up the team and supervise the research. You'd have a team of eight assistants and a broad remit. It's an experimental project, so I'd expect you to take full control and make decisions about the direction the research should go in."

"And what is the desired end result?" Anushka kept her tone neutral, though Charlotte could tell she was starting to get interested.

"I'm afraid I wouldn't be able to give you any of the exact details until you had signed a contract, but you must be aware that our projects frequently involve military applications. I wouldn't want you to think I was trying to hide that, and I know that might cause problems for some. Perhaps I could show you more of the facilities to help you make up your mind?"

Charlotte knew the lab was the most likely thing to persuade Anushka.

The one Yardley showed them was spacious with blue cabinets lining the walls, and a door on the left that led to a walk-in refrigerator. Test tubes and pipettes held within stands were under use by the researchers as they leaned over their stations.

There were racks of jars and vials, powerful microscopes that were plugged into sockets, wall-mounted eyewash stations that looked like washbasins with two taps turned upwards, three domestic refrigerators, and other glass equipment everywhere.

They passed by a bizarre, complicated machine that seemed to be sorting hundreds of test tubes, rotating them, counting them, labelling them, and finally delivering them into the hands of another researcher.

Charlotte could see Anushka itching to get access to it all, and hoped her resolve was slipping.

Within a month, Anushka had left the university and was about to start work at the lab. Charlotte couldn't be happier.

* * *

E11 - 2018 - Earth

We try speaking to the other members of our team. They have had even less contact with the humans than we have and are getting all of their information about the war effort and what we are achieving from Consensus and Yardley. They are held in stasis within an information bubble of official proclamations from Consensus on one side and project updates from Yardley on the other, with no way to obtain additional data from their own experiences. They therefore see no reason to be suspicious and we have to be careful in what we say to them. It is difficult to converse even with those outside our family unit, without conveying every aspect of how we feel about the subject matter, but we do our best to shield ourselves. We also try to make our questions as innocuous as possible, suggesting we are merely exploring ideas, as we are used to doing amongst our own people back home.

Do you think things are progressing well?

Yes, Yardley's reports are always encouraging and Consensus seems pleased with how everything is going.

But what benefit are the humans getting from offering soldiers to fight in our war?

Yardley says they will be able to use the abilities we are helping them develop for other purposes on Earth.

The humans do not seem as cohesive as our people. Do you not worry that we are providing some of them with the means to subjugate others on their world?

That is not our concern. If they are prepared to help us, it is up to them what they then do with the knowledge we provide. But Yardley has said they are all united in their willingness to aid us, so that suggests they must be united as a people in other ways as well.

And Consensus does not think the project is moving too slowly to be useful?

No, the latest reports are that the enemy has slowed in its direct plans to attack us, so we have time to work more with the humans before we need to take action.

That is good to hear. Do you think it possible the war might be averted, rendering our work here unnecessary?

All research is useful, whether it turns out to be necessary or not. Why are you asking so many questions?

We just want to make sure we are doing everything we can to be successful in our endeavours.

We do not wish to pursue the matter further, in case we alert our team members to the fact that we are having doubts. They may not be suspicious of Consensus' motives or Yardley's honesty, but they may easily become suspicious of us if we push the matter too far. It is clear we won't get any support in investigating our misgivings from that quarter. And we do not wish to find out what will happen if news of our dissent reaches Consensus, especially as the rest of our family unit is still at the mercy of whatever punishment they might mete out as a result of our potential rebellion.

* * *

P23 - May 2019 - India

Anushka's mind was still reeling from her encounter with the alien as she made her way back to Jhanvi's house in the growing darkness. She'd played it cool with Ergo during their conversation but that was partly because she just hadn't been able to take it all in. Meeting an alien being and discovering he had been messing with her thoughts for months, on top of everything else that had happened recently, was too much. She had known there was something strange about the XR-20, but getting proof it came from an alien world, one that had sentient beings on it, was something it was going to take Anushka some time to process. Not to mention the potential ramifications of Ergo's motives and how they might coincide with Yardley's plans. And also Ergo's as yet unconfirmed ability to potentially manipulate human emotions and actions. Were there more of his people on Earth? He spoke in the plural but Anushka didn't know if that was just an affectation or a reference to others close by. What he'd done so far didn't seem like a full-scale invasion but there was still so much about the situation Anushka didn't know.

One thing she did know for certain was that she didn't want to endanger Jhanvi or her family. Whatever Ergo was doing on Earth and however it connected up with Anushka's powers and the lab project, there was a lot more to what was going on than was clear to Anushka right now. And it seemed she was about to embark on a whole new chapter of madness. If Ergo had somewhere safe they could hole up and figure things out, Anushka decided she might as well make use of it.

So, she entered the dark and quiet house and crept up the stairs to her borrowed room. It didn't take long for her to gather her meagre belongings and stuff them back in her suitcase. As she went back down the stairs, she felt a pang of remorse at leaving again so soon, especially after her last conversation with her sister. She had hoped to mend some fences with this visit, but perhaps that had been a false hope, given the situation and her part in it. Maybe after all this was over, assuming it ever was, she could come back and try again to repair the damage in their relationship. But now was not the time for regrets or hesitation.

Anushka found a pad and a pencil on the counter in the kitchen and took it over to the table to compose a note to her sister. But what could she say? How could she convey in a few simple words how sorry she was for everything that had happened and how much she wished she could stay to explain properly? There was so much she wanted to say and so much she couldn't possibly convey.

In the end, Jhanvi made the task of composing the note obsolete. Just as Anushka was about to put pencil to paper, her voice came from the other side of the room.

"Running away again?"

* * *

P24 - May 2019 – Anushka

Anushka whirled to see her sister standing in the doorway, arms crossed and eyes sad.

"I really wish you would just tell me the truth, Nushie. You're clearly going through something and I'd like to help. Though at the moment I don't know whether you're involved in something actually dangerous, or whether it's all in your head. To be honest, I don't know which option scares me more."

Anushka laid the pencil down on the paper and faced Jhanvi squarely.

"I'm sorry. I wish I could explain."

Jhanvi raised an eyebrow. "I can tell how much by the fact you were apparently going to disappear again without saying goodbye."

Anushka raised one of her hands. "I don't know if it will help or hurt, but I can prove to you now that I'm not going mad. I got my powers back."

She focused on her fingers and willed them to disappear. Jhanvi gasped and her hand flew to her mouth as a blue stripe appeared in Anushka's hair and her fingers vanished. Jhanvi approached the table slowly and sat down, her eyes wide and her mouth open.

"Or maybe I'm just going mad as well," she breathed. She met Anushka's gaze. "So everything you told me was true?"

Anushka nodded. She allowed her hand to reappear and then summoned the crystalline skin to cover it briefly, catching sight of the purple stripe in her peripheral vision as it snaked down her hair. She wasn't sure it was the right decision to reveal her powers to her sister, but she didn't want to leave with Jhanvi thinking she was losing her mind. It was more important to her in that moment to show Jhanvi she wasn't lying, than it was to protect her sister from the knowledge of all the strange things that were going on. Anushka realised that was selfish of her, but tried to rationalise it in her own mind. Maybe this way, she could persuade Jhanvi to let her go. Not that she needed permission to leave, but it would be better to do so on good terms than with Jhanvi still so angry with her.

Anushka took a deep breath. "There's something going on that's a lot bigger than me and I have to see it through. I'm not sorry I came here because it's been wonderful to see you again. But I am sorry I brought this mess to your door and the best thing I can do to protect you and your family now is just to go. I'll come back if I can, once it's safe. In the meantime, you should just forget about all of this."

Jhanvi shook her head. "Or you could stay, explain everything properly and let me help. How's that for a radical concept?"

* * *

A12 - March 2019 - West London

"You just do whatever he says without ever questioning it, Charl," Anushka said. "It worries me."

They were at Charlotte's house, drinking wine after dinner. Danny was on an increasingly frequent night out with some friends he'd made on a recent IT project. Charlotte was leaning against the door frame, while Anushka sat curled on the sofa. Charlotte took a long sip from her glass before answering.

"Why should it worry you? He's my employer so I have an obligation to obey him."

"Not if what he's asking you to do is wrong. You're not in the army any more. There's no chain of command to break." Anushka put her glass on the coffee table so she could gesture more freely as she spoke. "And even soldiers are allowed to question illegal orders, aren't they?"

Charlotte tilted her head to one side. "When has Yardley ever asked me to do anything illegal?"

Anushka sighed. "Maybe he hasn't. Yet. But I wouldn't put it past him. I have serious doubts about some of the projects we're working on."

"You knew before you signed up that the lab took mostly military contracts, Nush. You can't claim the moral high ground now. Not after all this time. What's got you all riled up all of a sudden?"

Charlotte crossed to sit down next to Anushka and reached out to stroke her hair, but Anushka pulled away from her. Anushka hugged herself, her mind troubled.

"This is going to sound insane," she said, pausing to take a gulp of her wine. She'd been going back and forth about talking to Charlotte about this and she still wasn't sure it would work in her favour. "I had a dream. I was surrounded by blue light and a disembodied voice was trying to speak to me. The voice came from all around me and it sounded like it was speaking through water, as if it was far away or having difficulty delivering its message. I got the sense that it was telling me to beware of Yardley's intentions regarding the project." She dropped her gaze from Charlotte's raised eyebrows, her cheeks reddening. "Don't look at me like that. I'm not turning into some ridiculous hippy or anything. But dreams often bring up feelings from the subconscious that you're suppressing."

Charlotte schooled her expression. "Okay, but do those feelings have any basis in reality?"

"Well, now that I've started thinking about it, there are aspects of my work that make me wonder what the endgame is, and whether I'm doing the right thing in furthering this research. And I want to know that you're on my side, rather than blindly following Yardley just because of what happened back in the army."

Charlotte tipped Anushka's face back up with a gentle finger and held her gaze. There was a hint of uncertainty in her eyes.

"I'm confident Yardley wouldn't be involved in anything controversial, not without good reason."

"But that's exactly my point." Anushka threw her hands up. "I'm not sure my assessment of a good reason would be the same as yours. Or his."

"So, why don't you ask for more information about the purpose of your project? Surely you have a right to know what it's for, and I'm certain Yardley would explain it if you just ask. He's probably being tight-lipped because he's worried about industrial espionage. But you're the head biochemist. He trusts you enough to let you know what's going on. Even if it's classified, I bet he could get you clearance."

Anushka sighed. "Okay, I'll try that. But if I don't like the answers I get, I may have to rethink my position."

Charlotte shifted forwards, clearly uncomfortable with the conversation.

"Okay, that's fair enough. But I'm sure it won't come to that." She reached out again and this time, Anushka let her bury her fingers in her hair. "In the meantime, come here."

Anushka resisted for a moment, then sighed and leaned towards her. Their lips met, and that was the end of the argument.

* * *

C12 - March 2019 - West London

Later that same night, after they'd gone to bed, Charlotte lay awake, looking at the ceiling. Anushka was asleep next to her and Charlotte took comfort in the steady rhythm of her breathing, even as she worried over everything that had been said in her mind.

The difference in their attitudes towards Yardley and the military were an increasing source of contention. Charlotte knew Anushka had reservations about applying her scientific research to military projects but she'd thought they'd got past that when Anushka agreed to take the job at the lab.

But this talk of weird dreams had Charlotte rattled. They both prided themselves on their rationality, so it was worrying that Anushka was putting stock in something her brain had concocted in her sleep. Was it jealousy filtering through? Anushka surely knew she had no need to see Yardley as a threat on a romantic level, but Charlotte could admit it was true that she trusted and relied upon him. He had saved her life, after all, not only in the desert but also in a more existential way by offering her the job at the lab.

Was it possible that her sense of obligation to him was clouding Charlotte's view of him and the principles behind the projects he was running? Charlotte examined herself and her knowledge of the inner workings of the lab carefully. While she didn't know the details of what most of the projects were, she couldn't believe Yardley would be involved in anything illegal or nefarious. There would always be those who might take issue with any kind of scientific experimentation, but that was true of all sorts of research, including that which ultimately saved lives.

Charlotte hoped fervently that Anushka would be able to work out her issues with Yardley to her satisfaction. If Anushka forced her to choose between her loyalties towards Anushka or Yardley, with no good reason to do so, Charlotte didn't think the decision would be that easy. She couldn't turn her back on her job and her employer based on dreams and unfounded suspicions, and she would find it hard to accept that Anushka would expect her to do so. If Anushka continued in the vein she had so vehemently expressed that evening, Charlotte wasn't sure what she would do.

As she finally drifted off to sleep, Charlotte thought it would be better if she never had to find out.

* * *

E12 - 2018 - Earth

It is some time after our initial arrival on Earth that a new human joins the lab. She takes up a position of some authority, reporting directly to Yardley, but is still not privy to our existence, or told the true purpose of the work she is undertaking.

Her name is Anushka and we watch her assimilation into the life of the lab with interest. She works very hard at all hours of the day and night and we wonder at her dedication to something she doesn't fully understand. She seems to be particularly close to the human who controls the group of screen watchers, Charlotte, and we enjoy observing their interactions. It soothes us to see two humans sharing intimacy, as we have previously thought them incapable of it. Of course, they are unable to share things the way we can with our family unit, but it is as close as we can get to that kind of connection, so we revel in it.

In fact, it is Anushka's demonstration of her connection to Charlotte that first makes us think we might be able to make contact with her ourselves. We spend more time observing her and eventually explore the possibility of exerting influence over her mind. It is tricky and we have to be careful not to either harm her or reveal too much about our true nature. But we believe we are successful in planting some of our thoughts into her mind. We also discover she harbours misgivings of her own about the experiments she is performing on the material we have provided and the lack of information she has received from Yardley about its origins and purpose.

We worry that our manipulation of Anushka is just as bad as what Consensus is doing to our people and what Yardley is doing to his. But our suspicions that the motives of both are not pure are growing and we need to find out more. There is no easy way for us to investigate either Consensus or Yardley on our own, so we have to find an ally, and choosing one of the humans seems like the most sensible plan. We also yearn for greater connection with another being, after separating ourselves so much from the rest of our team and being so far away from our family unit.

We have no clear idea of what we and Anushka might do once we are united in our purpose. And we still have no clear idea of what we think might be the problem. We just know that everyone involved in the joint project is being lied to by those in control and it chips away at our conscience.

So, we continue to watch and to wait, honing both our shielding and communication skills, and trying to identify opportunities to learn the truth and bring Anushka over to our side.

* * *

P25 - May 2019 - Charlotte

"So, what do we do?" Danny asked.

"Just eat the lettuce, I guess." Charlotte shrugged.

“And how long do the powers take to manifest?”

“I don’t have a lot of data to go on here, but it seems to be a few hours. Why don’t we add the lettuce to our dinner, then just go to bed and see what happens in the morning?”

Danny stared at her. “You think we’ll actually be able to sleep after eating superpower-inducing lettuce?” He blinked. “I can’t believe I just said that.”

Charlotte grinned. “Well, you can do what you want. But I’m already sleep-deprived enough for one week, so I’ll be getting an early night, thank you very much.”

Danny gestured at the half-eaten dinner on his plate. “Okay. Lettuce me!”

Charlotte opened the box, plucked out a handful of leaves and sprinkled them over his food. Then she served herself some dinner from the pot on top of the cooker and added her own portion of lettuce. They ate.

After a few moments, Danny raised his fork and twirled it in the air.

“I do sense a hint of ‘je ne sais quoi’. A suggestion of potential, the essence of the possible, if you will.”

Charlotte chuckled. “Idiot.”

Danny grinned, then sobered. “I hate to put a downer on this exciting adventure into the unknown, but are you okay?”

Charlotte frowned at him. “Why do you ask?”

He gestured at their plates. “Oh, I don’t know. You’ve stolen proprietary material from the lab, presumably without Yardley's knowledge, and you're subjecting yourself to it when you have no idea what the effects might be. Doesn't any of that seem the slightest bit out of character to you?"

He'd kept his tone light, but pointing out the recklessness of her actions brought all Charlotte's rage and frustration at the situation surging back to the surface. She swallowed, trying to fight it back.

"Things are…" She trailed off, not sure how to proceed. "Weird. And complicated." She paused again. "Complicated and weird. And upsetting." A heavy sigh forced itself out of her lungs. "I don't know what to think any more. So, I just stopped thinking and acted instead. Probably a really stupid idea, but here we are."

"Yes, here we are," Danny said. "Emphasis on the 'we'. I'm right here with you and I'm not going anywhere."

Charlotte smiled, reaching across the table to pat his hand and holding back sudden tears. "Thanks. That means a lot."

After dinner, they retired to the living room to watch TV, though Charlotte found it difficult to concentrate and she imagined Danny was feeling the same. She kept shifting around in her chair, unable to sit still, as if all her nerve endings were on alert for some kind of alteration.

Eventually, she'd had enough and got to her feet.

"Okay, I'm going to bed. I'll see you tomorrow."

She walked to the door, put her hand out to grasp the doorknob and gasped as her fingers passed right through it.

"What?" Danny craned from his position on the other side of the room. "What is it?"

Charlotte crossed back to the centre of the room and made as if to press her hand onto the arm of the sofa. It passed through the fabric and she stumbled, off balance.

"Whoa! That's cool!" Danny grinned.

Charlotte straightened up. "Not if I can't get out of the room." She looked over at him. "Do you feel any different?"

"No. How am I supposed to know what I can do?"

"I have no idea."

"Hang on, I'll get the door for you."

Charlotte realised she could probably just walk through the door even though it was shut, but she decided to let Danny be chivalrous for a change.

Danny reached towards one of his prosthetic legs, which had toppled over and was lying on the floor next to his chair. It was just out of his grasp, but Charlotte watched in awe as it shivered and then jumped up from the ground and into his hand. He dropped it again, as if it had burned him.

"Shit! Did you see that?" His eyes were wide.

"Yeah! Try again." Charlotte bounced on the balls of her feet.

Danny looked down to where the leg lay, stretched out his hand and flexed his fingers. After a second or two, the leg jumped back up into his hand. He brandished it over his head in triumph.

"Fucking hell, that's awesome!" His grin was as wide as it could go.

He started buckling the prosthetic onto his stump, then stopped and dropped it back to the floor.

"What are you doing?" Charlotte asked.

He held up one hand. "Hang on a sec. I've got an idea."

He closed his eyes, took a couple of deep breaths and put his hands on the arms of the chair. Charlotte watched as he pushed downwards as if trying to lift himself off the seat. Then his whole body rose up in the air, halting when he was floating a couple of feet above the chair. He opened his eyes, looked down and burst out laughing. He wobbled in mid-air, then fell back down onto the cushions. His face was alight with joy as he looked over at Charlotte.

"I can fly!"

* * *

P26 - May 2019 - Anushka

Anushka kept eye contact with Jhanvi, attempting to stare her down. She wasn't sure why, since she'd never managed to win a staring contest with her sister before.

"No, it's too dangerous. I don't want to drag you any further into this thing than I have already."

Jhanvi regarded her steadily. "Shouldn't that be my decision? And you haven't told me yet what this thing even is."

"I don't really know myself yet."

Jhanvi's tone was exasperated. "Then let me help you figure it out. You're my little sister, Nushie. It's my job to protect you." She dropped her eyes to the surface of the table but Anushka didn't feel any sense of victory. "I know I haven't always done a very good job of that in the past. But now you need me more than ever." She looked up again, her eyes shining. "Don't let's repeat past mistakes. You've only just come back into my life. I don't want to lose you again so soon."

"You've got a lot more to lose now than just me." Anushka gestured at the house around them. "I can't let you risk what you've built here. I have no idea what Yardley's really capable of, or how far he'll go to get what he wants. If it was just us, then maybe, but you've got to think of your children."

Jhanvi sighed, unable to argue with that logic. "At least stay overnight and let's talk about it more in the morning. Perhaps we can come up with a better plan after a night's sleep." She shrugged helplessly. "Maybe I can come with you wherever you're going."

"No, I'm sorry. I have to go now. I love you."

Anushka imagined the hillside where she had met Ergo and she was instantly there. She felt a brief stab of guilt at disappearing on Jhanvi again, but it was quickly swamped by renewed wonder at being in the presence of an alien being. He was waiting for her, his glow muted but still a beacon in the darkness. She walked up to him, marvelling at the blue glow that surrounded his body, his impossible height and his unblemished milky white skin. He stood straight, a little too straight, as if he had a steel rod for a spine, and he swivelled his head downwards as she approached. He couldn't be more at odds with the green of the grass below their feet and colourful flowers off to the side. Anushka felt suddenly just as alien herself, standing there in the country of her birth, but not really connected to it in any way.

"Are you ready to go?" Ergo asked.

Anushka thought about her sister again, left sitting at her kitchen table, and fought back tears. She had no idea if and when she would ever see Jhanvi again. But she pushed that thought aside and nodded.

Ergo raised his arms slowly above his head, and a white light enveloped them both. Anushka felt the now familiar sensation of teleportation, but it was much more intense than when she did it on her own. Her head swam, her vision darkened and she felt herself falling into blackness.

* * *

A13 - April 2019 - North London

Anushka took a deep breath and knocked on Yardley's door. When his resonant voice called out for her to come in, she squared her shoulders and strode into the office.

"Dr Mahto, always a pleasure." Yardley smiled at her from behind his desk. "How goes our most prestigious project?"

"That's actually what I wanted to talk to you about." She stepped across the room and sat down in one of the chairs opposite him, smoothing her skirt over her knees.

He frowned. "Not experiencing problems, I hope?"

"No, no. Everything's progressing according to schedule. The way the XR-20 responds to the various experiments we've tried is fascinating. It's not like anything I've ever seen before. I wish I knew more about where it came from."

Yardley's smile was rueful. "Unfortunately, that's not something I can divulge. And you don't need to know its origins to be able to test it effectively."

"No," Anushka allowed, reaching for her courage and feeling her way ahead, "but knowing more about the ultimate purpose of the project would enable me to judge the success or otherwise of the experiments. And it would also help me decide on the next steps for testing and analysis. If I knew more about what the clients are trying to achieve, I could guide the project towards those goals more effectively."

She might have imagined it, but Anushka thought she saw the skin at the edges of Yardley's mouth tighten. He maintained his smooth and accommodating demeanour, though.

"I understand your frustrations, Dr Mahto. I really do. And I appreciate your desire to ensure the success of the project. But this project in particular is very sensitive and the clients are a bit skittish. They've stipulated additional security regarding their data and they don't want anyone other than absolutely essential personnel to know more than necessary."

Anushka felt her expression freezing in place. She kept her tone carefully neutral and focused on emphasising the good of the project rather than her own concerns about it. "Of course. But it's difficult to know how best to serve their needs if I'm not privy to what those needs are."

"I'm sorry." Yardley spread his hands. "But I'm afraid there's nothing I can do. I'm sure you and your team are doing sterling work. One thing I can tell you is that the clients are keen to see the effects of the XR-20 on human subjects."

Anushka was surprised into a laugh. "We're a long way from that, I'm afraid. And I couldn't countenance testing on humans without a lot more information about the XR-20's origins and chemical makeup. Unless you can give me that information directly, my experiments will need to continue at their current level until I can be sure what I'm dealing with."

Yardley frowned. "We'll have to see about that."

Anushka wasn't sure if he was talking about giving her more information or pushing for human testing. She left his office and went back to her lab. It was getting harder and harder to work under such restricted circumstances, and more and more difficult to ignore her misgivings. What little she knew about her project suggested that the XR-20 she was manipulating could easily be weaponised.

And the fact that Yardley wouldn't tell her the details made her trust his motives even less than before. The time was coming when she would have to take action, so she started thinking about what she could do if things at the lab became untenable. Her plans were tentative but her adamance that she wouldn't agree to putting people at unnecessary risk made her think she might actually have to leave the lab. And in fact it wasn't long before Yardley pushed the point too far and Anushka was forced to flee without a proper plan in place.

* * *

C13 - April 2019 - West London

Charlotte reached over to switch off the alarm, then stretched in bed, feeling across the empty space next to her, where Anushka would normally be. But Anushka hadn't been staying over at Charlotte's house as much in the last few weeks. Charlotte wasn't happy with how things were between them. She dragged herself out of bed and stripped out of the oversized t-shirt she slept in, leaving it crumpled on top of the duvet. Even though they'd reached an amicable agreement after their last discussion about Yardley, Charlotte knew Anushka was unhappy. But she wasn't sure how much more she wanted to delve into the issue. It was easier just to glide along and hope that things would sort themselves out.

She pulled some underwear out of a drawer and put it on mechanically, her mind distracted by the dream she'd had. After her return from Iraq, Charlotte had suffered nightmares about the bomb for months, mostly focusing around the deaths of her section members and Danny's injuries. She'd had counselling and worked hard to put the experience behind her, but now it was coming back to her again in her dreams.

These dreams were very different, though. Instead of being filled with smoke and fear and pain, they were filled with blue light and a sense of peace and safety. As Charlotte pulled on her trousers and tucked her shirt into the waistband, she remembered the vision she'd thought she'd had just before she lost consciousness after the bomb. There had been blue light, wings and a rainbow halo. The feeling in her dreams now was the same feeling she had experienced then.

Charlotte had always attributed her survival after the bomb to Yardley's quick actions and he had never done anything to disabuse her of this idea. But there was more to it than that. Something else had definitely happened that day. Something she couldn't remember clearly and that she didn't fully understand. And the presence of the blue light had something to do with it. She slipped her feet into her shoes and tied the laces with a double knot.

Were her dreams somehow connected to the blue light Anushka had mentioned from her own dream? It seemed ridiculous to think so and Charlotte assumed her subconscious was just picking up on that image and running with it. But Yardley was involved in both situations and Charlotte started to wonder if there was more to it. She certainly wasn't going to change her view of him based on dreams, though, as that would be stupid and very unfair.

Over breakfast, she twirled her spoon through her milky cereal, her chin in her other hand.

"What's the matter, Corp?" Danny asked. "Something to do with why I haven't seen Anushka around here recently?"

Charlotte glared at him. Trust him to be perceptive. "I don't want to talk about it."

"That's pretty clear," he said. "But I think you should. With Anushka. Come on, Corp, you two are too good together to let things fall apart. You've got to let me have some hopes for romance not being dead." He pursed his lips and batted his eyes at her. "Pretty please?"

As she walked to the tube station, Charlotte pulled out her phone and sent Anushka a text: "Breakfast in the canteen? Usual table. I think we should talk. See you in half an hour."

But, when she reached the lab, she discovered it was too late. Anushka had already stolen the XR-20 from the lab and was gone. Fuelled by the pain of this betrayal and abandonment, Charlotte's allegiance swung firmly back to Yardley.

* * *

E13 - April 2019 - Earth

Eventually, we know it is time to act. The humans have achieved so much with the material we have developed together, and it seems as if they are about to move on to a new and more active stage of their research.

We do not want Consensus or Yardley to have access to something that could prove so harmful to both peoples, and we know we cannot rely on any of the other members of our team to act for the greater good.

So, we seal ourself off from them mentally, and steal the craft in which we have travelled to Earth. It contains the whole supply of the material that we still have in our possession. It also has a cloaking device to hide it from the detection of the humans, so we employ that to conceal it from our own kind as well.

When Anushka later flees the lab with the rest of the material, which she has been working on herself, we know we chose correctly when we selected her as our ally. We have never felt closer to her than we do in that moment. We are both alone, cut off from our own kind, and rebelling against those in authority over us. We will need to work together if we are to discover the truth about what is going on, and do whatever is needed to be done to resolve it.

We also know we must cut ourself off from any contact with our family unit back home. It will be too dangerous to try to speak to them again, in case Consensus tracks our communication or picks something up from them. This is the first time we have been without any contact with any of our kind and it is very difficult for us to do this. We are not used to being without constant companionship. But it is necessary if we are to succeed in our mission, even though we are still unclear as to the true nature of that mission. Even if we manage to link up with the humans to work together, it will not be the same as the mental connections we have been used to up until now.

Once we decide to reveal ourself to Anushka and achieve a first successful contact, persuading her to come back to the ship with us, our path becomes clearer.

It is time for us to move forwards alone. It is time for *me* to move forwards alone. I am my own person, separate from the contamination and manipulation of Consensus, forging my own path into an uncertain future that will hopefully save two peoples from evil.

To that end, I decide to find out what I can about the material for myself. If I concentrate hard enough, I can make myself corporeal enough to interact with it. When I allow it to slide over my fingers, it is cold and slippery and it leaves a trail of more intense sensation behind it as it slides back into its container. What residue remains on my fingers sinks into my skin as I watch and my hand becomes heavier. I clench my fist, struggling a little to raise my arm with the added weight on the end of it. This bears more observation.

* * *

P27 - May 2019 - London

After trying to go to bed and falling through not only the bed, but also the bedroom floor to end up back in the kitchen, Charlotte figured out that she could switch off her ability to move through solid objects by concentrating on being fully present. She managed to get some sleep and came downstairs the next morning to find Danny zooming around the kitchen, taking unnecessary things out of high cupboards and then putting them back again.

"You do not want to see the state of the tops of our kitchen cabinets," he said as she came in.

"No, you're right, I don't." Charlotte smiled. "Don't wear yourself out. And remember, this is only going to last a few more hours. Be careful you don't hurt yourself when gravity reasserts itself."

"Stop trying to ruin my fun, Corp," he said, though he did slow down a bit.

Charlotte made her way to the lab, wondering what she could do that day that would be useful. It was all well and good messing about with the contaminated lettuce, but she still had a job to do. While she wasn't entirely convinced that Yardley's motives were pure, she still wanted to find Anushka and figure out how to fix the whole mess.

She went to the central security hub to check in with Perkins.

"Any interesting chatter?" she asked.

He shook his head. “Looks like the superpower fest is over for the time being.” He jerked his chin towards where a cardboard coffee cup was standing on the counter. “Skinny latte for you, if you want it.”

“Thanks.” Charlotte walked over, thinking about what they should do next. She reached out for the cup without really focusing on it and her hand passed straight through.

“What the hell?” Perkins’ eyebrows shot upwards. “You’ve got powers now?”

Charlotte made a suppressing motion with one hand. “Keep it down! I may have sneaked some of the lettuce samples last night, just for fun. It only lasts a day, after all, and I wanted to see what would happen.”

Perkins grinned. “I wouldn’t have pegged you for breaking the rules like that.”

Charlotte smirked back, enjoying their rare camaraderie. “You should have seen Danny’s face when he figured out he could use telekinesis to fly.”

“You gave some to Danny, too?” Perkins pouted at her. “So, where’s mine?”

“Sorry, Perkins. One time only deal. I’m back on the straight and narrow now.”

Perkins’ expression darkened. “No fair.”

“Thanks for the coffee, though.” Charlotte concentrated on picking it up properly. “I’ll be in my office, working out our next move.”

Perkins gave her one of his mock salutes as she went out.

Charlotte was only halfway through her coffee when she heard Yardley's voice out in the security hub. It was very unusual that he would venture down there. Normally, he summoned her to his office when he wanted an update. She gulped another couple of mouthfuls of coffee and headed out to see what was going on.

Yardley was standing behind Perkins, who looked round at Charlotte with a very uncomfortable look on his face.

"What are you waiting for, man?" Yardley said. "More of our samples have gone missing and I need to know who is responsible."

"Um, I seem to be having some technical issues with the surveillance feeds," Perkins said. "I don't think I can get you any footage of the main lab from last night."

"It's okay, Perkins," Charlotte said. "There's no need to try and protect me." She squared up to Yardley. "I took the samples, sir. I was just intrigued to see what would happen and I didn't think it would do any harm. It was stupid and I'm sorry."

Yardley regarded her with a calculated look in his eye. "I'm surprised at you, Ms Grant. It seems Dr Mahto's bad example has rubbed off on you. Still, this presents an interesting opportunity. I had intended to ask for volunteers to consume the samples, so we could do further tests, but now there's no need." He narrowed his eyes. "Would Mr Watson also be a suitable test subject?"

Charlotte held up a hand. "You leave Danny out of this."

Yardley smiled. "Mr Owuye, Mr Perkins, go to Ms Grant's house and pick up her lodger. In the meantime, you will come with me, Ms Grant."

Owuye and Perkins headed towards the locker room to gear up for their mission. Charlotte felt sweat start to prickle on her forehead. If Yardley had just asked for her cooperation she likely would have given it, but this attitude of coercion was unsettling to say the least. Despite his assertion that he would have asked for volunteers to eat the lettuce, it didn't seem that option of choice extended to her now - or Danny, who didn't deserve to get mixed up in this.

"What are you going to do to us?" Charlotte asked. "Anushka said you were pushing for human trials before she was ready. Why are you taking this so far?"

She started backing away from Yardley, but he waved over two of the newer members of her team. "Restrain her."

They took hold of her arms, not even hesitating at Yardley's order.

"I knew you'd take Dr Mahto's side eventually," Yardley said. "It's disappointing after all I've done for you over the years. And pushing forward with this project is the only way for the lab to survive. We haven't been producing the results the military wants for some time now, and they've been threatening to cut our funding. But this material, this XR-20 - it could save us. Think of all the military applications! Major Simmonds will be throwing money at us again in no time."

Charlotte struggled against her captors, but their grip was strong. "That's what this is about? Money?"

Yardley shook his head. "It's so much bigger than that. There are threats out there that you have no idea about. Yes, I'm trying to protect my business. But I'm trying to protect our nation, too. And perhaps our whole world. Now, come along. We have work to do."

* * *

P28 - May 2019 - Ergo's Ship

Anushka came back to awareness slowly. She was lying on something soft, and allowed herself to drift for a while as the fuzziness in her head began to recede. She heard movement to one side and opened her eyes. All she got was a sense of brightness, as if she was inside a light bulb. She sucked in a breath and squinted. There was a clicking sound and the light dimmed.

"We are sorry," a silvery voice said. Ergo. "Excuse me, we should say 'I am sorry'. It is difficult for us - me - to adjust to a singular existence. Also, I forget that your eyes are designed differently to mine. There are many strangenesses to become accustomed to, for both of us."

Anushka struggled to make sense of his words and ultimately decided not to worry about it right now. Ergo moved into view and Anushka saw that his skin was a milky white, slightly translucent so she could see purplish veins underneath. The surface was completely smooth, unblemished by the pock marks, wrinkles and roughness of human skin. He leaned closer, his blue eyes large in a flat face that had slits for nostrils and a thin, lipless slash of a mouth. He looked a lot like many of the alien forms described by humans who claimed to have been abducted and experimented on over the years. Could some of those stories actually be true? And what did that mean for Anushka now? Had she foolishly trusted the first offer of help she'd received since she fled the lab, and put herself in the power of a being that might mean her harm, purely because she'd been so alone in her struggle?

"You lost consciousness," Ergo said, as if she couldn't work that out for herself. "How do you feel?"

He seemed solicitous of her well-being and it was a bit late to worry about him experimenting on her now, so Anuhska decided to keep taking him at face value and assume his intentions were good. She pushed herself up on her elbows, keen to take in more of her surroundings now the glare had lessened.

"I'm a bit wobbly. Where are we?"

Ergo's mouth stretched in what Anushka assumed was supposed to be a smile, but she couldn't see his teeth, if he had any.

"I believe you would call it a spaceship."

Anushka raised her eyebrows. She was talking to an alien, so a spaceship shouldn't be too much of a reach. How else would he have got to Earth, after all? The room she was in was oval in shape, with panels covering the walls that gave off the now reduced light. She was lying on a moulded platform at one side, and Ergo was crouching next to her. The floor was lined with something that gave a little where the balls of his feet pressed into it. There was a round table a few feet away, with several cylindrical stools under it. Everything was white and Anushka couldn't see any square corners or sharp edges. Now that the lights were dimmed, it was very relaxing. She sat up further and Ergo rocked back onto his heels to avoid encroaching on her personal space.

Anushka looked him in the eye. "You have a lot of explaining to do."

"I agree." He gestured at the table. "If you would sit with me, I will try."

He held out a hand and Anushka took it. His fingers felt silky, as if she might not be able to keep a grip on them, but he pulled her to her feet easily. As she took a step, her hair fell forwards over her shoulder and she saw the silver colour as it cascaded downwards from scalp to ends. Then she was looking at a testing suite at the lab. Yardley was in the foreground, and behind him, Charlotte and Danny were strapped to two tables. Danny was struggling against his bonds and snarling, but Charlotte had her eyes closed and was lying still. As Anushka watched, Charlotte raised one of her hands and it passed right through its strap. Yardley laughed and motioned to one of the lab technicians standing by the tables. Anushka couldn't tell who it was because he was wearing a mask. He was holding a syringe, though, which he stuck into Charlotte's neck. She opened her eyes as the needle went in, while Danny yelled and struggled harder. Then Charlotte went limp and her head lolled to one side. Her eyelids drooped but didn't close, and Anushka could see that her gaze was unfocused.

The vision ended abruptly and Anushka stumbled against Ergo. It might be aliens that experimented on humans in the stories, but here it seemed her own kind were the ones she needed to be afraid of.

"Are you still unwell?" Ergo asked, steadying her with one hand.

"My friends are in trouble. I have to go." She thought of the colour pink, repictured the scene in her mind, and willed herself there.

* * *

P29 - May 2019 - North London

Everything was a blur. Charlotte felt like she was floating a few inches outside her body and she couldn't focus her thoughts. She knew there was something important she needed to pay attention to, but her mind kept drifting off. Someone was yelling and she wished they would stop. The voice was familiar but she couldn't place where from. Someone else was laughing and the combination seemed strange. So many loud expressions of emotion. Why couldn't people just keep their feelings to themselves and let her rest? Her face was numb and, when she tried to bring a hand up to touch it, something stopped her. She tried moving her head to look down at her arm but her skull was too heavy and she couldn't tell it what to do. She blinked hard a few times in an effort to clear her vision and she recognised the lab around her. A memory came slowly back into reach, telling her she was in danger, that Yardley had lost his mind and was going to experiment on her. Charlotte tried to care, but couldn't summon enough energy. It was easier just to lie back and let it happen. She had tried so hard to fix things with Anushka and keep her loyalty to Yardley intact, but she had failed on both fronts. Maybe it was time to give up. Then the yelling penetrated the fog in her brain. Danny was here and in danger too. She fought the haze and managed to focus enough to turn to look for him. There he was, strapped to a table next to her. Their eyes met and Charlotte saw both fear and concern in his face.

Then there was a flash of white light and Anushka was in the room, standing between them and Yardley.

"Dr Mahto." Yardley sounded unsurprised. "How kind of you to join us. And still retaining your powers, I see. That's interesting. I would appreciate the opportunity to find out how you've managed that."

"Let them go," Anushka said.

Her hair was pink but quickly fading back to its usual rich brown. She was fierce and combative, her stance that of a fighter. Charlotte thought she had never seen Anushka look more beautiful. Yardley gestured at one of the lab technicians.

"Secure and sedate her, please."

The man moved to grab Anushka. Charlotte's protective instincts kicked in and she struggled against her bonds. But Anushka's hair flashed red and she shoved the man backwards, sending him flying across the room much more powerfully than should have been possible.

"Now, there's no need for violence, Dr Mahto." Yardley sighed. "I'm only interested in exploring the new breakthroughs you've made in our research. For science. Surely you can understand."

Anushka's hair flashed orange and she held up a hand, flames licking over her fingers. Charlotte was finding it difficult to keep track of all the colours and their associated abilities. But it seemed Anushka had her powers completely under her control now. In other circumstances, Charlotte might have found time to be impressed, but the urgency of the situation and her own helplessness combined to swamp any other thoughts or feelings.

Anushka responded to Yardley's pseudo-rational plea with icy calmness of her own. "I understand you've restrained my friends against their will and are planning to do potentially harmful things to them. I don't agree that scientific endeavour justifies such methods."

"You've left me no choice," Yardley said. His tone remained neutral but Charlotte could see the tension in his jaw and the desperation in his eyes. "You don't understand. Stealing the XR-20 you were working on has left me in a very unfortunate situation. The sponsors of the project are very annoyed and want results. Ms Grant and Mr Watson - and you, of course - are my only way to appease them. And none of us want to find out what they will do if they are not satisfied."

"I know where the XR-20 came from," Anushka said, "and I intend to find out more about its purpose, without your interference. I have my own connections to its source now, and you are the only one threatening anyone over it. We'll be going now and you'd be better off not trying to stop us."

She flicked her fingers, sending flame shooting towards Yardley. Charlotte watched as he dived sideways behind a workstation and Anushka used the distraction to move between the tables where she and Danny were confined.

"You're amazing," Charlotte said, gazing at her.

"Can we save the lovey-dovey stuff for later and get out of here, please?" Danny said.

"No time to untie you," Anushka said. "I hope this still works."

She put one hand on each of them, closed her eyes, and her hair turned pink again. Charlotte felt the strange lurching sensation she'd felt before, when Anushka took her to the mountainside. Had that only been the day before? It seemed like much longer. Charlotte blinked and they were in a round, white room. She dropped a couple of feet to the floor, landing on a soft surface that cushioned the impact. She heard Danny squawk and looked over to see him lying on the floor a short distance away. Anushka stood between them.

Another figure came into view and Charlotte looked up long, thin white legs to a naked white torso and a bizarre, flat face, gazing down at her with huge, blue eyes.

Anushka spoke, her tone matter-of-fact. “Charlotte Grant, Danny Watson - meet Ergo.”

“What the fuck?” was all Charlotte could think of to say.

* * *

P30 - May 2019 - Ergo's Ship

Anushka felt a wave of exhaustion flow through her. She pulled a stool out from under the table and slumped down onto it. Ergo offered Charlotte a hand, which she took with wide eyes, and he helped her to her feet. Danny pushed himself to a sitting position and waved away the hand that was offered to him.

Anushka watched in amazement as he reached out a hand towards another of the stools and narrowed his eyes. The stool wobbled and then slid out from under the table and over to where Danny sat. He then put both his hands flat on the floor, pushed downwards, and his whole body rose into the air. He floated across until he was directly above the stool and then drifted down until he was sitting on it. He looked over at Anushka and gave her a self-satisfied grin.

Charlotte dragged a third stool next to Danny's and sat down too, putting a hand on his shoulder. Ergo stood, looking at them all.

"I was not expecting you to bring others of your kind here," he said to Anushka.

His melodic voice gave no hint of emotion and she hadn't yet had the chance to learn his expressions, so she had no idea if he was angry or not.

"They were in danger because of whatever's going on with the XR-20. They're already involved, so I didn't think teleporting them here would make things any worse. Besides, you said you need help, and I don't know how much use I'd be to you on my own."

Ergo inclined his head. "And you think they will be willing to help us?"

Anuskha looked at Charlotte. "I'm hoping so." She flicked her gaze to Danny. "Though I guess this isn't really your fight."

Danny glared at her, his lips thin. "If you're going up against that dick, Yardley, then I'm in. I was strapped to a table in his lab too! And I've known him longer than any of you, don't forget. It's not like he just decided to pick a random stranger to experiment on." He threw a hard stare at Charlotte. "With either of us. Plus, there must be more of the stuff that gives me powers, right? Otherwise, Anushka wouldn't have been able to come save us." He turned to Anushka. "Thanks for that, by the way."

She smiled at him, then looked past him to Charlotte, who was still looking dazed.

"What about you, Charl? Are you ready to give up your loyalty to Yardley yet?" Anushka asked. She kept her tone deliberately light but pointedly raised one eyebrow.

Charlotte winced, then pressed the heels of her hands into her eyes.

"You're going to rub that in for a while, aren't you?" She lowered her hands and met Anushka's gaze. "I think I'm going to need a lot more information about what's actually happening before I commit to anything. I'm not just going to jump from one side to the opposite one without knowing what's going on." She rolled her eyes at Anushka's frown. "But yes, given what just happened, I'm willing to admit that I no longer owe Yardley anything." She still couldn't believe what he'd done. "And that I was wrong about how far he was prepared to go with this project. I'm sorry I didn't listen to your suspicions before." She couldn't help a final dig. "Even though all you had to go on was a dream."

Anushka glared at her, then turned to Ergo.

"You were going to explain things before I disappeared on you. Why don't you give it a try now?" She glanced pointedly at Charlotte. "It might help us all clarify our positions."

He spread his hands. "I set myself against my own people and travelled a long way in the hopes of finding others to join my cause. I am trying to end an interstellar war."

* * *

P31 - May 2019 - Ergo's Ship

They all stared at Ergo as he reached the end of his story. He looked back at them impassively. After a long moment, it was Danny who broke the silence.

"Wow. Okay. So, what do we do now?"

"I think that's too big a question right now," Anuskha said. "First things first. Ergo, you mentioned that your people are made of energy, rather than being physical entities."

He nodded.

"I don't really understand how that works, but does that mean you don't have to look like you do?"

He nodded again.

"So, why choose this?" She gestured up and down his elongated, glowing body.

He blinked slowly. "We researched human culture and popular media and collated all the instances of alien lifeforms. This form seemed most frequent so we thought it would provide a familiar frame of reference for our interactions."

That explained the familiar form and reassured Anushka as to Ergo's sincerity about his desire to protect humanity. Charlotte evidently caught on to what Anushka was thinking.

"Could you maybe transform, or whatever, into a more human form? It might be easier for us, and it'll certainly make you a lot less conspicuous if we need to go out and about."

The synchronicity of their thoughts sent a pang across Anushka's heart. She missed the closeness they had so recently shared.

Ergo regarded them, as if considering the suggestion. Then, as they watched, the glow around his body intensified until they all had to shield their eyes. When it faded away, there was a man sitting where the alien version of Ergo had been. He was still thin, but not unnaturally so, and pale, but not so much so that he would stand out in a crowd. He had delicate features and fine silvery hair that framed his face. His eyes were a startling blue. He was dressed in a simple tunic and loose trousers that looked like linen. He shifted his shoulders as if uncomfortable with the sensation of cloth against them.

Anushka smiled at him. "That's better."

Danny spoke up again. "While I agree it's great that Ergo can fit in amongst humans now, I'd like to return to my previous question. What the hell do we do now?"

Anushka brought her hands together in a prayerlike gesture as she considered the question. "I'm still thinking in terms of practicalities. Let's not panic and rush into planning an offensive." She looked at Ergo again, trying to reconcile their previous interactions with his new appearance. She liked to think she was open-minded, but had to admit it was easier to relate to him now he looked more like them. "I assume this ship is shielded against both human and alien detection?"

"Yes. I have cut myself off completely from my kind." His features twisted in pain. "And I have used what I have learned to prevent anyone from being able to locate us."

"Good. So we don't need to worry immediately about being tracked." Anushka turned to Charlotte and Danny. "It makes sense for us to stay here for now, but you'll both need some supplies, won't you? If you let me know what you want, I can go to the house and collect stuff."

Charlotte's eyebrows drew together in an achingly familiar expression of concern. "Don't you think the house will be watched?"

Anushka sighed audibly. "Maybe, but I can get past any surveillance by teleporting directly inside. And I can jump away again in an instant if there's any trouble."

"She's right that we do need some stuff." Danny looked back and forth between them, his expression conciliatory.

"Okay." Charlotte stood up. "But I'm coming with you."

Anushka stared at her. "You don't trust me in your house? Really? It's stupid to risk both of us just because you're angry with me."

"Don't be ridiculous. I'm just trying to be practical, like you said. It'll be much easier for me to be there, than trying to explain to you where everything is that we might want."

Anushka sighed. "Okay. I guess that's a fair point."

Charlotte closed her eyes and visibly relaxed her shoulders as if composing herself not to take the bait for more argument. When she opened her eyes again, she turned to Danny. "And if you're so concerned about what we do next, why don't you try and come up with some ideas while we're gone?"

He gave a jaunty salute, evidently still attempting to keep the tone light. "Sure thing, Corp. Will do."

Anushka rose and stepped up to stand next to Charlotte. "Ready?"

"As I'll ever be."

Anushka felt Charlotte tense as she laid a hand on her arm, but she didn't know if it was because of the contact or just the anticipation of being teleported. She tried to put the thought out of her mind and focused instead on imagining the kitchen in Charlotte's house. Pink suffused her peripheral vision and they were gone.

* * *

A14 - May 2019 - West London

Charlotte answered Anushka's question by pulling away as soon as they materialised in her house, as if she didn't want to stay in physical contact with Anushka for even one moment more than absolutely necessary. She was breathing hard and staggered a bit before finding her balance.

"I don't think I'll ever get used to that." She bent over for a second, gulping air, then straightened again. "Okay, let's work fast."

Anushka followed her upstairs to Charlotte's room, where Charlotte pulled a large bag out of the bottom of the wardrobe and handed it to her. Anushka then trailed her around the room, holding the bag as Charlotte hurriedly stuffed it with clothes and toiletries.

"Aren't you going to say, 'I told you so'?" Charlotte asked, not looking away from what she was doing.

The question took Anushka by surprise. "What good would that do?"

Charlotte shrugged. "None at all. I'm just surprised you haven't grabbed the opportunity to rub it in that you were right about Yardley."

"Okay, sure, if that's the way you want it." Anushka felt the skin around her mouth tightening. "I was right, you were wrong. Do I feel good about it? Of course not! Do you think I wanted our boss to be secretly conspiring with evil aliens to create super soldiers for an interstellar war?" Anushka let her breath out in an exasperated rush. “Maybe you do. Maybe you think I’m so petty I’d actually want to be in mortal danger just to prove my point.”

Charlotte didn’t respond. They moved back downstairs in stony silence to Danny’s room, which had been converted from a sitting room at the front of the house. Charlotte repeated the packing process. She collected his prosthetics, along with clothes and other supplies, and threw them into the bag, shoulders tense.

Anushka hated how strained things had become between them but didn’t know how to start resolving the problem. Frustrated, she dumped the bag on Danny’s bed and crossed to the window, looking out into the street. There was a dark SUV parked on the other side of the road and the glint of sunlight on glass caught her eye as the rear window slid open. She saw a rifle barrel extend through the gap and acted on pure instinct.

Spreading her arms to cover as much of the window as possible, Anushka imagined her skin hardening. She felt the crystalline casing enclosing her just as the window shattered and a sharp impact on her shoulder partially spun her around. She caught sight of a wide-eyed Charlotte standing by the chest of drawers.

“Grab the bag and get over here, but stay behind me!”

Anushka turned back to the window as another bullet whizzed past her ear. A second later, she felt Charlotte’s hand on her back.

Releasing the impervious crystal from her skin, she flooded her thoughts with pink. As the house disappeared around her, she felt a sharp impact on her arm, and then they were back on Ergo's ship.

Danny looked up, startled by their abrupt appearance, his eyes darting immediately to Anushka's sleeve. "You're bleeding! What happened?"

Anushka lifted her arm and looked down at it. A red stain was spreading across the fabric of her shirt. The sight of it brought with it a wash of pain and she sagged backwards into Charlotte, who caught and supported her.

Charlotte helped Anushka to one of the stools.

"I said they'd be watching the house."

* * *

C14 - May 2019 - Ergo's ship

As soon as the words came out of Charlotte's mouth, she wished she could stuff them back in. Anushka had just talked about how 'I told you so' never solved anything, but apparently Charlotte couldn't stop herself.

Anushka glared up at her, face tight with pain. "Really?"

Charlotte took hold of Anushka's sleeve and ripped the existing hole larger until it exposed a wide gash on her arm.

"Looks like the bullet grazed you. Just a flesh wound."

"Your sympathy is overwhelming." Anushka gritted her teeth. "I hesitate to point out I was shielding you with my body at the time."

Charlotte ripped the sleeve off entirely and wadded it up. The shirt was ruined anyway. Might as well make use of it.

"I didn't mean…" She trailed off and tried again. "I just meant you're lucky there's no internal damage." She laid the makeshift pad over the wound. "Here. Press on that." Their fingers brushed over each other as Anushka took over holding the material against her arm, but all Charlotte felt was annoyance. "Of course I'm grateful you defended me from enemy gunmen. But they wouldn't have been shooting at us at all if you hadn't gone and stood in the window."

Anushka opened her mouth and took a breath but was interrupted by Danny.

"Okay, okay, time out!" He made the accompanying t-shaped gesture with his hands. "Do I need to send the two of you to separate corners to stare at the wall and think about what you've done? We're not going to be able to stop a war if we're fighting amongst ourselves all the time."

Charlotte crossed her arms and looked at the floor. She knew he was right. It was just so hard to get past all the complicated feelings of the past few days. At the moment, she couldn't see a clear path back to being able to work with Anushka and not letting her anger get in the way.

"We need to wash and dress the wound," she said, hating how sulky her voice sounded. She looked around to locate Ergo, who had wisely opted not to get involved thus far. "Does this ship even have a bathroom?"

He walked up to her and reached one hand towards her left temple. "May I?"

Charlotte instinctively stepped backwards away from his unexpected closeness. "May you what?"

"Gain more information about 'bathrooms' directly from your mind. It would be easier than you trying to describe one to me."

"Uh, sure. I guess so." Charlotte stood rigid, waiting for - she didn't know what.

Ergo touched two slender fingers to the side of her head and she felt a small jolt, a bit like a static shock. Ergo closed his eyes and his brow furrowed. Then he stretched his arms out and a white light shot out of his fingers towards the far wall of the room. When it faded away, there was a new door where there hadn't been one before. Ergo opened his eyes again.

"The ship now has a bathroom."

Charlotte just stared at him, open-mouthed. Out of the corner of her eye, she could see Danny doing the same.

"Okay, um, thanks." She turned back to Anuskha. "Come on, let's get you cleaned up."

Charlotte steadied Anushka as she struggled up from the stool, still holding the remains of her sleeve against her arm. Not sure what she would find on the other side, Charlotte crossed the room and opened the magic door. The sight that greeted her made her gasp.

It was an exact replica of the upstairs bathroom at her house, down to the floral curtains at the frosted glass window. It must have been the image uppermost in her mind when Ergo was sifting for bathroom information.

"Wow." Charlotte reached to open the cabinet above the sink and there was the first aid kit she always kept there at home. "Good eye for detail, that alien. Well, this makes things much easier."

She gestured for Anushka to perch on the toilet seat and got to work. Apart from the occasional sharp intake of breath, Anushka was silent throughout the whole process, and Charlotte decided to follow her lead. It was useful to have a task to focus on that involved both her hands and her concentration. Patching up a bullet wound was something she could do; patching up her relationship would have to wait. She wasn't surprised when clear, cold water came out of the sink tap, but couldn't help wondering where it was coming from and where it was going when it disappeared down the plughole. She decided it was probably best not to ask.

After a few minutes, the wound was cleaned and neatly bandaged.

"There you go. Good as new."

"Thanks." Even that one simple word sounded grudging. "I'd better find a new shirt."

With that, Anushka went back out into the main room, leaving Charlotte wondering what their future held, and not just in terms of the galactic threat.

* * *

E14 - May 2019 - Ergo's Ship

I do not understand humans. When I touched Charlotte's mind just now, it was impossible not to feel the great love she has for Anushka. In fact, I had to push past a great roiling mass of passion, concern, affection and longing before I could access the much more mundane information I was seeking. Admittedly, it was all mixed up with anger and hurt, but it was still there and much stronger than its negative aspects. I am certain Anushka feels the same.

And yet, neither of them seems to be able to be honest with the other, or likely with themselves, about their feelings. And they cannot share those feelings directly, because they are locked inside their own corporeal shells, with no connection to one another to provide support and an open exchange of views. Even within their own minds, they do not seem to see what it is that will make them happy, or they are incapable of acting on such knowledge if they possess it. They are trapped, with only their individual minds to keep them company, and that does not seem to be a healthy way to exist, in my opinion. Beings need input from outside to provide perspective and balance. The physical nature of the human form creates an impenetrable barrier to clear communication. I do not know how they can live their lives in such separation. Life within my family unit is - was - so much easier. There could be no confusion, no deceit.

Which is, I suppose, how I now find myself in the situation I am in. Cut off. Utterly alone. The very bonds that provided me with both security and love now prevent me from having any contact with my family at all. If I were to contact them, they would know everything about what is happening and it would place them in the same danger I face.

I cannot protect them from Earth and I cannot go home until the circumstances are very different. So, I must abandon them and not allow myself the comfort of their presence in my mind. I begin to see why the humans suffer so. With only their own thoughts available to them, they have only a very narrow view of the world and it is easily warped and corrupted by the emotions they seem unable to control or fully understand. In order to survive my current predicament, I must learn to live as a human. The prospect frightens me. But perhaps as I do so, I can help teach the humans to understand each other better. Their expressions and body language are clearer to me than they seem to be to each other, though of course I have the advantage of being able to sense their thoughts.

Maybe that is the answer. I will consider further.

* * *

P32 - May 2019 - Ergo's Ship

Anushka looked up and then away again as Charlotte came out of the magical bathroom and back into the main room of the ship. The wound on her arm was a constant irritant but much better since Charlotte's ministrations. It had been upsettingly familiar to have Charlotte's hands on her skin. The pain of the wound was a sharp reminder of the rift between them, a physical echo of the mental pain she felt all the time, being in such close proximity to Charlotte. That closeness now prompted sadness and anger rather than the comfort and affection of old.

"So, Danny," Charlotte said. "Amaze us with your awesome plan."

He just stared at her for a moment. "Come on, Corp! Give me a chance. You were only gone about ten minutes. I know I'm good, but I'm not that good."

The easy banter between them just made Anushka feel even worse. At least Charlotte still had Danny. Anushka herself was completely alone within their merry band. She had wanted so desperately to have some allies on her side, helping her in her struggle. But now she wondered if it might be worse than being all on her own.

"Fair enough." Charlotte chuckled, then sobered. "Okay, troops, gather round. It's war council time."

Anushka was about to challenge Charlotte's automatic wresting of control, but a wave of weariness flooded over her and she just didn't have the energy. Besides, it was tempting to let someone else take charge for a while, after she'd been exposed and alone for the last few days. She counted back in her head. Had it only been three days since she'd fled the lab? It felt like months. She might as well take advantage of the others' presence by letting them help to come up with a plan.

"Anushka? Care to join us?"

She looked up at Charlotte's voice, to find the other three had already gathered around the small table. Anushka heaved herself to her feet, dragged her stool over and sat down between Danny and Ergo. Her intention had been to keep as much space between herself and Charlotte as possible, but it just meant she was directly in Charlotte's eyeline and would have to sit awkwardly askew to avoid meeting her gaze.

But Charlotte was in full military tactics mode and seemed to have set their differences aside for the time being. She fixed her attention on Ergo.

"Where does the alien material come from?" she asked.

He shrugged, a curiously human gesture. "I do not know. Consensus supplied it to us to pass on to Yardley. My team and I were simply to act as liaisons to keep an eye on the progress of the experiments."

"And do the rest of your team have access to more?"

"No. We were storing the remaining samples in this ship so I stole it along with the vehicle."

"And it took you a while to travel here from your home planet?"

The words rang strangely in Anushka's ears. Even after everything that had happened, and even sitting where she was right then, it was difficult to believe the situation they were in. Ergo had travelled across space from another planet and they were all sitting calmly with him in his spaceship.

"Yes." Ergo thought for a moment. "It would have been several of your Earth weeks."

"Good. So they won't be able to get any more of the substance immediately. We need to make sure we're the only ones who have access to it for the time being. It'll give us quite an advantage."

"There's still some at the lab, though, right?" Danny asked. "You only took a little bit for us to try, didn't you?"

Anushka frowned. That was right. Charlotte must have obtained some of the XR-20 for her and Danny to have developed powers. But hadn't she removed it all when she left? She thought back to the random people who'd been affected by the contaminated lettuce and winced. Of course.

She stared at Charlotte and Danny. "You ate some of the lettuce?"

Danny nodded, then turned to Ergo. "I actually have a question about that. How come the Corp and I only have one power each, but Anushka has a whole range?" He pouted. "Doesn't seem fair."

It was Anushka who replied. "I assume it has something to do with the fact that I didn't consume the XR-20. The first time, I accidentally got some on my hands and then ran my fingers through my hair. Then I just automatically did the same thing when Ergo gave me more to reactivate my powers after I lost them." She looked for confirmation from Ergo.

He nodded. "I imagine you are correct, though I have no more information about the process than you do. I would think the material was absorbed directly into Anushka's brain through her skull, thus resulting in a more intensive effect than from simply ingesting a small amount via a contaminated foodstuff."

Charlotte nodded. "Let's get back to the matter at hand. We can worry about theory later. Our first mission is to break into the lab and steal the rest of the lettuce. I know where it's being stored."

Danny held up a hand and pointed at Charlotte and Anushka in turn. "Is it safe to let the two of you go off together again? It's not going to help matters any if you have another lovers' tiff right in the middle of enemy territory." They both glared at him and he raised his hands in surrender. "I'm just saying."

"I will go with you, Anushka," Ergo said. "Bullets will not harm me, so it will not be necessary for you to be concerned for my safety while we are there."

"Okay," Charlotte said. "Danny and I can stay here and do some brainstorming."

"Speaking of…" Danny glanced at Anushka. "Can you maybe grab me a laptop while you're there?"

"I'll try." When had she turned into such a master criminal?

Charlotte stood up. "Well, it's been a long couple of days and I have no idea what time it is, wherever we are, but it's at least a few hours until it'll get dark in London. I suggest we all try and get some rest and the two of you set off after the lab will have finished normal business hours."

* * *

P33 - May 2019 - North London

Anushka and Ergo materialised right inside her lab and it was a shock to be in such familiar surroundings again after all the running and then the spaceship. Ergo stayed by the door, while Anushka went to the storage compartments Charlotte had described. They were all empty. Anushka cursed inwardly. Of course Yardley wouldn't just leave the samples there, where they knew how to find them. But where else would he have put them?

Before she could formulate a new plan, a shrill alarm went off and the bright white lights switched to a dim reddish glow.

"They know we're here," Anushka said. "Let's try Yardley's office."

She grabbed Ergo's hand - it was cool and almost slippery despite his human appearance - and transported them to Yardley's office. There was a safe behind his desk. Anushka imagined a red streak in her hair, reached down and yanked the handle. The whole locking mechanism broke away from the safe and the door swung open. A neat stack of Tupperware containing limp lettuce leaves looked incongruous alongside file folders and a gun. Anushka started pulling everything out and shoving it into Ergo's arms. Anything Yardley considered important enough to store in his safe might prove useful, or at least might inconvenience him when he found it missing. The sound of feet pounding down the hallway outside came through the closed door.

"One more stop," Anushka said and jumped them to the security office.

Perkins yelped at their appearance and scrabbled backwards on his wheeled office chair, colliding with the back wall. He held up his hands as if to fend off an attack.

"You stay away from me!"

"I'm sorry about last time," Anushka said. "It was an accident. But you might want to think about reconsidering your life choices. If you stick with Yardley, the next time I have to hurt you will be deliberate."

His eyes widened, but Anushka turned away from him, taking two short strides to a desk on the other side of the room and scooping up a laptop and power supply.

Perkins reached for his radio.

"They're in the security-"

Before he could finish the sentence, Ergo stepped up in front of him and reached out towards his head. Perkins flailed wildly, connecting with Ergo's hand and sending it slamming into the wall. Ergo reached out with his other hand and placed two fingertips on Perkins' forehead. Perkins immediately slumped in his chair, eyes closed.

"What did you do to him?"

"He is merely sleeping. Do we have everything we require?"

"Yes. Let's head back." Anushka reached out to lay a hand on his arm, and started to think pink thoughts. Then the door burst open behind them and there were men with guns staring at them. Anushka switched her colour choice to purple and felt the crystalline skin wrap her in an impenetrable shield. Charlotte's security team opened fire and Ergo spun away from Anushka. She scrabbled to close the distance between them and reach her fingers around his wrist. A split second later, they were back on the ship.

* * *

A15 - May 2019 - Ergo's Ship

Charlotte and Danny looked up from the table when Anushka and Ergo appeared. Ergo staggered and Anushka looked at him in concern. There was a patch on his side that was glowing bright white.

"Ergo! Are you okay?"

He turned wide eyes on her and seemed to be trying to catch his breath. "I believe one of the projectiles struck me."

Charlotte gasped. "You got shot? How bad is it?"

He closed his eyes and stood very still for a long moment. Then he breathed out and opened his eyes again. "I have repaired the damage. I am fine." His face fell. "But I dropped the samples when I was impacted. I am afraid they are still at the lab."

Anushka sighed. "Well, I don't think it's a good idea to go back and try to retrieve them now. And at least you're okay. That's the most important thing. There wasn't much lettuce in that tub, so I don't think Yardley will be able to do too much damage with it."

Ergo set down the stack of files on the table and Anushka gave the laptop to Danny.

"Any bright ideas while we were gone?" Anushka asked.

Charlotte sighed. "As Danny said before, you didn't give us much of a chance. I forget how quickly you can travel now." She gestured at the files. "What's all this?"

"No idea." Anushka shrugged. "But I figured it was better in our possession than Yardley's."

"Good thinking."

Anushka tossed her hair over her shoulder. "I do have good ideas sometimes, you know."

"I was trying to be nice and you're going to throw it straight back in my face?" Charlotte leaned her elbows on the table, her expression weary. "We're not going to get very far here if we're constantly sniping at each other."

Anushka knew she was right, but just couldn't quite let it go. "Then stop looking so disappointed with me all the time! As you pointed out at the house, I was right. Stop punishing me for it."

Charlotte came straight back at her. "You weren't right about everything. You weren't right about leaving without telling me." Evidently neither of them were ready to let this go.

"What would you have done if I'd come to you? You would have turned me in to Yardley and I'd probably be in an alien experimentation programme by now."

Charlotte's eyes widened. "Is that really what you think of me?"

Danny opened his mouth to say something but Ergo beat him to it.

"I can show you what you each really think of the other, if you think that would help."

They all stared at him.

Anushka spoke first. "What do you mean?"

"I have been considering how difficult it must be to be human. To be unable to see clearly what those around you are thinking and feeling. The two of you are at odds, but I believe that may be because you are making erroneous assumptions about each other's motives and emotions. I can open your minds to one another, so you can understand each other fully."

Anushka looked across the table at Charlotte, whose brows were drawn down in consternation. Her own attitude to the suggestion was one of mixed feelings. It made her uncomfortable to think of someone else being privy to her inner thoughts, even Charlotte. But the idea of being able to see into Charlotte's mind was very tempting, and it would have to be an equal exchange. It was true that they were currently putting their efforts to combat Yardley at risk with their bickering, so perhaps it was only fair to the others to at least try.

Anushka said, "I'm game if you are."

As Anushka had known she would, Charlotte couldn't turn down such a challenge. "Okay. Let's do it. Things can't get any worse."

Danny gave a bark of laughter. "I think you'll find they probably can. Are you both sure about this?"

Anushka held Charlotte's gaze, daring her with her eyes.

"Yes," they both said together.

Ergo reached out his hands. Anushka and Charlotte each took one and he brought them together in the centre of the table. Danny pushed himself up off his stool with his telekinetic power and floated away to the other side of the room. At Charlotte's enquiring glance, he shrugged.

"No offence, Corp, but I don't want to end up in anybody's else's head, and I'm pretty sure nobody wants to be in mine. I'll just be over here at a safe distance."

Anushka felt the contrast between Ergo's cool fingers and Charlotte's warm ones. Then she felt a rush of unfamiliar sensations and closed her eyes. It was as if everything contracted and then expanded. She felt herself wobble on her stool and concentrated on staying upright. Something opened up in her mind and a swirl of coloured emotions poured in. There was black anger and blue disdain, wrapped up together with sickly yellow pain and shot through with thin strands of red love. It was a jumbled mass that pulsed with jagged energy. Anushka imagined her hands reaching forwards to embrace it. As soon as she touched it, the ball of hurt and confusion began to unravel, and each individual thread started to become clear to her. She separated them and took them into herself one by one, the inner workings of Charlotte's mind unfolding into her own, piece by piece.

The anger was sharp and Anushka had to stop herself from flinching away from its jagged edges, that threatened to pierce her soul. She grasped it firmly in her virtual hands and examined it closely. At its centre was a small, square piece of paper with the words, "I'm sorry," scrawled on it. The wholly inadequate note she'd left in Charlotte's office the night she'd run away. Inky black claws ripped at it but it remained undamaged, a constant reminder of Anushka's abandonment.

When Anushka pulled at the blue tendrils that also circled the piece of paper, she found they were sticky, like liquid glue. They reeked of contempt, pushing away the image of Anushka that the paper brought into being in Charlotte's mind. She hadn't even had the courage to say goodbye, so why should she be worthy of Charlotte's consideration at all? But the slimy yellow ache of pain that dripped from the gluey tendrils gave the lie to that desire for dismissal. And, at the centre of everything, a red velvet heart was nearly entirely encased in a brittle shell of shadowy grey fear. Underneath all the rage, Charlotte was scared of losing her.

Anushka's mental avatar slowly consumed every individual piece of Charlotte's emotions, both bitter and sweet. At last, Anushka opened her eyes to find Charlotte staring at her open-mouthed. There were tears streaming down her face and Anushka was unsurprised to find her own cheeks wet.

"Is that really how you feel?"

* * *

C15 - May 2019 - Ergo's Ship

Charlotte experienced Anushka's thoughts and feelings as a soundtrack, linked to certain images. The harsh clashing of cymbals evoked fear and distrust at the sight of Charlotte walking away from Anushka into Yardley's office. A scene of the two of them arguing in Anushka's flat was overlaid with strident brass. The sound of breaking glass accompanied Anushka looking up at the security camera as she fled the lab in the middle of the night. Scenes of empty hotel rooms were coupled with a plaintive strain of lonely violins. And a single flute piped sorrow at the inevitability of separation, while a frantic drumbeat pounded out its bassline of constant fear underneath it all. Fear of capture by the person Anushka loved most and wanted protection from; fear of loss of the wonderful connection they had found in one another; and fear of never being able to heal the breach between them. Each sound vibrated through Charlotte's body, resonating painfully in her torso until she couldn't take in any more.

Charlotte was still reeling from the onslaught when she opened her eyes again, and she barely registered Anushka's question. But she nodded slowly, not quite sure what she was agreeing to.

Anushka pulled her hand away and stood up abruptly. "So, it's true. You do think I betrayed you."

"And you don't trust me at all!" Charlotte stood as well, backing away from the table. "I may not always agree with you, but I would never deliberately hurt you."

"The way I hurt you. I see." Anushka's tone was cold. "You think me stealing the XR-20 from the lab and leaving without telling you is worse than you ratting me out to Yardley and letting him do whatever he wanted with me."

"But I didn't do that!"

"But you would have."

"You can't know that!" Charlotte put her hands to her head, pressing her temples as if she could push all the hurt and confusion into a tiny box where she wouldn't have to face it. "When you left, I didn't know what to do or what to think. I had no reason not to trust Yardley, and what you'd done seemed insane to me. But I never wanted to harm you."

"But you hunted me down at his behest. And you kidnapped people off the street and took them back to him at the lab."

"To protect them from what you'd done to them! How many times do I have to explain that to you?" Charlotte felt her breath start hitching and fought for control. How had this gone so wrong, so fast? "I wanted to find you so I could figure out what was really going on. What did you expect me to do? Just let you go, without any explanation, and ditch my job as well by refusing to look for you? I was trying to help you as much as I was following Yardley's orders. Can't you see that?"

Anushka folded her arms, hugging herself tightly. "I can see that you thought you were doing the right thing. But I still completely disagree with you about what that was. You think you love me, but I'm not sure you really know what love is."

"And you do? What about trusting and confiding in one another? What about sharing our deepest fears and believing we'll support each other, no matter what?" Charlotte let out an exasperated breath. "I can see you thought you were doing the right thing, as well, but I completely disagree with your actions, too."

"Well, there we go. Not really anything else we can say, is there?" Anushka's voice was hard, her whole body rigid with tension.

Charlotte watched as a streak of pink appeared at Anushka's hairline and snaked its way down past her shoulders. And then she was gone.

Danny looked over at Ergo. "Well, that went well."

* * *

E15 - May 2019 - Ergo's Ship

I admit my experiment in opening Anushka and Charlotte to each other has not proceeded in the way I had hoped. Apparently humans are incapable of understanding each other even when experiencing connection on a level akin to the one I share with my family unit. So used to only having their own minds to rely upon in their daily lives, they seem unable to take on board opinions and feelings different to their own. It did not occur to me that their isolationist existence would present such a barrier to a joining of minds. I am not sure where we go from here. Danny seems like the most reasonable of the three, though I understand his relationships with the other two are less complicated. Perhaps I should let him take over in the attempts to get Anushka and Charlotte to at least be able to work together towards our common goals. Maybe it is coming together to fight a bigger threat that will ultimately bring them back to peace with one another again. I can only hope so, as we are already fighting a war on multiple fronts and having to deal with battles amongst ourselves will only make our task that much more difficult.

There is a strange pressure at the edge of my consciousness. I fear my enemies are trying to find me. It is possible that focusing on the humans' minds and opening them to each other has weakened my defences. I must be vigilant, as my shielding is the only thing keeping us safe from discovery. But on closer inspection I realise the energy pressing against my barriers is a familiar one, a bittersweet taste of home that I have sorely missed, even though my time of absolute separation has been relatively brief.

Are you there?

A faint but unmistakable contact. I have neither the heart nor the will to reject it, regardless of what the consequences may be. Some bonds are too strong to repulse. And the disastrous experiment with the humans has only intensified the sense of loss I feel at the lack of contact with my own people. I allow a gap in my shielding that only members of my family unit may penetrate. It seems my skills at separating my mind from others have grown apace.

I am here.

There is a flood of relief and joy, which I feel echoed throughout my entire being. It is as if parts of me that were severed have now been reattached. I feel whole again. But I must be careful not to get carried away. I must limit contact, both in terms of depth and time.

Why did you leave us?

To keep you safe.

How could contact with you possibly harm us?

I want to tell them. I want the openness and sharing between us to be restored. Can I risk it? I do not know. But the choice is taken from me. They have breached my unwilling defences and my mind is open to them. I can no longer keep them out.

Can this really be true? Is it possible that Consensus is deceiving us? Do they really have both the ability and will to do so?

I ache at the fear and sorrow that accompanies their words, emotions that only reflect my own, and risk intensifying on both sides until we are all lost in disbelief and terror. I school my emotions as best I can, focusing on transmission of information only.

I believe it to be so. I am working with the humans to find out more.

We will help you.

It is too dangerous. You are too close to Consensus. You will be discovered and harmed.

Have some faith in us. We have seen how you have shielded yourself from us and all our kind. We have learned from what you have learned, in the way our people have shared knowledge for centuries. We can keep ourselves safe.

Please be careful.

We will.

We must separate again now. It is too hard to keep even one tiny channel open and still protect myself from others.

Yes, we understand. But know that we are with you. We are helping. And we will contact you again when we have information that may be useful.

Thank you. It helps to know this, more than you can know.

Not more than we can know. We know you. We see and feel everything you do. We know because we love you.

Joy and comfort spread through me, providing a salve to my fear and sadness.

I love all of you too. Goodbye and good luck.

The connection is severed and a well of renewed loneliness opens within me as I am separated from my own kind once more. But the knowledge of their love and support bolsters me for the fight ahead. The pressure of their presence in my mind is replaced by a sharp stinging sensation in my hand and my side. I look down to see a blue, glowing substance shimmering between my fingers. It is like the material provided to the humans for their experiments and it is oozing from a split in my skin where I hit my hand against the wall in the lab. I reach to my side with my other hand and find there is more oozing from where the projectile struck me.

What can this mean? Could it have something to do with my previous interactions with the material? Anushka is also contaminated by the material, but she did not secrete it when she was injured earlier. Why would I produce it from an injury?

* * *

P34 - May 2019 - India

The sun was just starting to show its face over the tops of the surrounding mountains as Anushka appeared back on the hillside near the commune. The dawn took her by surprise. She hadn't thought consciously about where she wanted to go. She had just needed to get away from Charlotte and this was where her mind had taken her. Strange that an impulsive decision to flee had brought her back to her home country again, the place she had first fled so long ago.

That time, she had been running from her past and had ultimately found Charlotte, her refuge from the pain of her childhood and the problems with her family. Now, when she was fleeing problems with Charlotte, she found herself back where she'd started. Would there ever be a place she felt truly safe? Would there ever be relationships in her life that weren't fraught with difficulties?

Anushka thought back to what she had learned from seeing inside Charlotte's mind. It had been painful and unexpected. But there was a core of love there that hadn't yet been erased completely. The common denominator in all her troubled relationships was herself, of course. Ergo had thought knowing Charlotte's mind and heart would help her understand the situation better, but it had only made her more defensive and angry. Perhaps it was her own mind and heart she needed to explore more closely, not those of other people. She spent so much time looking outside for circumstances and people to blame for the situations she found herself in. She never wanted to look closely at her own feelings to see how they contributed. Could she accept that she herself was at least partially to blame? And that she had to take responsibility for enacting positive change?

As the first rays of the sun reached for her, Anushka felt the chill around her heart receding. If she wanted things to change, it was up to her to take the first step, to cede ground and admit fault. Otherwise, everything would stay the same, and she and the people she loved would circle endlessly around the barriers they had constructed between themselves. If they all just stuck to their side of the walls and wouldn't allow any chinks of light to break through from the other side, Anushka would always remain angry and alone.

Anushka turned away from the sunrise to look back towards the commune. Her sister was standing in the long grass a few feet away. They stared at one another, neither speaking. Anushka took a deep breath and started to walk towards Jhanvi. Here was as good a place to start as any.

* * *

P35 - May 2019 - Ergo's Ship

Charlotte stared at the space where Anushka had been only a moment before.

"I really wish she'd stop doing that."

Danny huffed out an exasperated breath. "And I really wish the two of you would just get a room and sort all this shit out."

She stared at him. "What?"

He stared right back. "You're clearly both still crazy about each other. Can't you just get the hell over this fight already? You're both on the same side again now. Does it really matter how you got there? What's the point of hashing out the same stuff over and over again. You're stuck with each other, and we're stuck with both of you." He gestured at himself and Ergo. "Can't you dig the stick out of your arse and just get along while we fight the bigger enemy, for our sakes if not for your own?"

He was right. Charlotte knew he was right. But she didn't want to admit it. And she couldn't sort things out with Anushka if Anushka wasn't there, could she? But maybe, if and when Anushka decided to show her face again, Charlotte could at least try to unbend a little. In the meantime, she turned to more practical matters.

"Why don't we look through these files from the lab and see if there's anything we can use against Yardley." She glanced over to where Ergo had moved during the argument and had been standing silently for some time. "You with us, Ergo?"

He swivelled his head slowly in her direction, as if dragging his attention away from a different conversation.

"Yes," he said, blinking. "I am with you."

He suited action to word and came to join them at the table. Charlotte noticed a glow on his hand. "What's that?" she asked.

"Hey!" Danny said. "Are you making more of the goo? I didn't know you could do that."

Ergo blinked slowly. "Neither did I. It is a mystery to me why the substance should be produced by an injury to my corporeal body. How could that be the case?"

Charlotte just wanted to get to the files, but Danny was sitting forwards, an intent look on his face.

"You said Consensus gave you the stuff and told you it came from this enemy that's threatening your people, right?"

"Yes," Ergo replied.

"Well, maybe there's a link between them and you. Maybe they're an offshoot of your people, who never stopped being corporeal, or something." Danny shrugged. "Just a thought."

Ergo regarded him solemnly. "It is a very interesting thought. I will have to consider it further."

"Can we get back to the task at hand, please?" Charlotte said.

She divided the file folders into three equal piles and passed one to each of her compatriots. The fourth stool at the table remained resolutely empty. Danny shrugged at her and opened the first folder. Charlotte followed suit with her own pile.

Over the next half hour, she learned more than she had ever wanted to know about the various projects that were being undertaken at the lab. Yardley had his fingers in a lot of pies, mostly of the military variety, but also including some private contracts she hadn't been informed about. Not very surprisingly, there was no mention of aliens or the weird superpower-granting goo. But there was a lot about how much trouble the lab was in, along with threats from the military about pulling all their contracts due to lack of satisfactory results. After she had scanned the last page of her pile, Charlotte sighed.

"I'm starting to see why Yardley is so desperate for a big win. But there's nothing here we can use. Either of you got anything?"

Danny shook his head despondently.

"Nothing about my people or the project with Consensus," Ergo said.

They stared at each other for a few moments, then a thought struck Charlotte.

"I think I have an idea." She gestured at the laptop Anushka had brought back from the lab and looked at Danny. "Can you send and receive secure messages on that thing?"

"Sure thing, Corp." His face brightened. "Just give me a couple of minutes. Who do you want to talk to?"

Charlotte grinned. "Someone I think might be persuaded to help us."

* * *

A16 - May 2019 - India

"I'm sorry," Anushka said as Jhanvi came to stand beside her.

They both looked out at the view, as the sun continued to climb into the sky.

"About what?" Jhanvi's tone was neutral but her expression was expectant.

Anushka turned away from her sister's searching eyes and crossed her arms tightly over her chest. Her lungs felt constricted and she cleared her throat noisily.

"Where do you want me to start?" She took a couple of deep breaths. "I'm sorry I blamed you after mum died. I'm sorry I didn't come back to see you in all that time. I'm sorry I only came here because I was in trouble. And I'm sorry I keep running away when all you want to do is help and support me."

There was a moment of perfect silence in the stillness of the morning light. Then Anushka felt an arm snake around her shoulders and she turned into her sister's embrace.

"It's okay, Nushie. But I appreciate you saying all that. I know it can't have been easy for you. Any of it. And I'm sorry too, for leaving you in the first place."

Anushka huffed a laugh against Jhanvi's neck, while at the same time fighting back tears. They broke apart and Jhanvi held onto her upper arms, looking into her eyes.

"Will you let me help you now?"

Anushka dropped down onto the grass of the hillside, drawing Jhanvi down next to her.

"I wasn't kidding about it being dangerous."

Jhanvi hooked her arm round Anushka's elbow and squeezed. "And I wasn't kidding about it being my job to protect you. At least tell me what's going on. Please?"

Anushka hugged her knees, feeling suddenly like a little girl again, confessing her troubles to Jhanvi in their shared bedroom. It had always made her feel better once Jhanvi knew everything. So that's what she did now. Told her sister everything, without worrying about whether or not Jhanvi would believe her, and without considering what the consequences might be.

When she had brought Jhanvi fully up to date, she let out a huge sigh. A weight had been lifted, but the challenge was still ahead.

"So, I don't think there's really anything you can do to help. We don't know what we're going to do yet, but I don't want you caught up in it. And I'll be safer on Ergo's ship than at your house. I think it's probably best if I just go back and let you get on with your life."

She realised she was just talking for the sake of it and stopped. Then she turned to look at Jhanvi for the first time since she'd started relating the tale. Her sister's eyes were wide.

"You think I can just go back to my normal life after hearing all of that?" Jhanvi kept tight hold of Anushka's arm. "Please promise me you won't just disappear again. Please at least come back to tell me what happens and let me know that you're all right."

Anushka leaned her head on her sister's shoulder. "I promise. And if I do think of anything you can do, I promise I will let you know."

"I'll be here," Jhanvi said.

"Thanks, sis. But now I think I'd better go. I have some more apologising to do."

Jhanvi pushed herself to her feet, then offered Anushka a hand up.

"I hope you can work things out with Charlotte. It sounds like you're good for each other, even if you do drive each other crazy."

Trust Jhanvi to get right to the heart of the matter, past all the aliens and threats of interstellar war. Anushka smiled.

"I hope so, too. And I'm going to do my best on that front," she said. "I'll see you soon."

Her last view of the hillside was of Jhanvi raising a hand in farewell, her eyes shining with unshed tears.

* * *

C16 - May 2019 - Ergo's Ship

"Secure chat established, Corp," Danny called from the table.

Charlotte looked over from where she had been pacing back and forth in what little space was available on the other side of the room. She hoped they wouldn't all be staying on the ship for too long. The quarters would get very cramped, very quickly.

"Great." She sat on the stool next to Danny and shifted the laptop until it was facing her.

Danny leaned in so he could see over her shoulder.

She typed in the relevant address, then added:

>Are you paying attention?

They waited.

After a couple of minutes that felt like an eternity, a responding message appeared.

>Who is this?

"Who is that?" Danny wanted to know, but Charlotte ignored him, setting her fingers to the keyboard again.

>Who do you think? And I actually mean just think about it, don't type it.

There was another long pause, then more words appeared.

>It's not safe for me to be talking to you.

Charlotte grinned, then said aloud, "But you haven't closed the chat window, now have you?" She went back to typing.

>Who watches the watcher? You're safe enough.

Danny drew in a sharp breath. "You're talking to Perkins? Is that a good idea?"

Charlotte threw him a sideways glance. "Only if your security combined with Ergo's shields are better than his hacking skills. Do I need to be worried?"

Danny cracked his knuckles. "No sweat, Corp. I can beat Perkins in a hacking challenge any day. Chat away."

Meanwhile, Perkins was evidently both flattered and intrigued.

>Fair point. What can I do for you?

>Thought you might be interested in a side hustle. Just to break up the daily grind.

>I'm listening.

>We need whatever information you can get on the original fugitive's project, particularly comms between head honcho and whoever the clients are.

>Not asking for much, are you?

Charlotte could almost see Perkins' accompanying eye roll in her mind's eye. But she knew she had him.

>You know you love a challenge. And I'm sure you're just as curious about what's going on as the rest of us. Plus, this way, however things fall out, you can claim you were working for the winning side all along.

Another long pause, then a single word.

>Okay.

Charlotte chuckled. "He's so easy to manipulate."

"Let's just hope he's smarter about hiding his tracks," Danny said.

"Oh, if there's one thing that's guaranteed, it's that Perkins will cover his arse." Charlotte started typing again.

>Great. See what you can find and I'll be back in touch.

Charlotte closed the chat window and relinquished the laptop back to Danny.

"Now what?" he asked.

She grimaced.

"Now we wait. For Perkins to deliver. And for Anushka to come back from wherever she disappeared to." She stretched and yawned. "Why don't we try and get some sleep and see where we are in a few hour?" She waved at Ergo. "What do you have in the line of beds?"

When Ergo subsequently offered to create bedrooms for them all from Charlotte's thoughts, she tried to imagine the most spacious and luxurious suites she could think of, but her thoughts kept slipping back to the familiarity of her own house. Still, adding extra rooms was a great solution to the space issue. Maybe quarters wouldn't be so cramped after all.

* * *

E16 - May 2019 - Ergo's Ship

I furnish the humans with places to sleep. They are still amazed by my ability to conjure rooms and objects as if from nothing. It is not something I can do outside the ship, except regarding my own appearance. The ship has a certain amount of matter and energy that feels familiar to me and I have discovered I can manipulate it however I wish, in a similar way to how I change my own physical manifestation. I enjoy their delight in the simplest of things. It is good to see happiness, even in such small measure. I wonder how long it will be before we can truly relax and enjoy freedom from fear. If we ever can again.

Despite their limitations in mental connection, I am growing fond of these humans. I hope Anushka and I haven't sealed their doom by bringing them into our struggle.

I also hope Anushka is all right. Her ability to teleport is useful, but dangerous. It gives her the opportunity to act entirely on impulse, and could lead her into difficulties. It seems I have yet to teach the humans the benefits of working as a team. Once Charlotte and Danny are settled and likely to be immobile for some time, I decide to leave the ship to seek Anushka out.

I reach for her consciousness and pull myself towards it, reverting to my energy state as I shift in space. Anushka's mind is a brightly coloured light in the energy field, its nature and presentation unique to her life force, but only visible to me because I have had contact with it before. The others of my kind would not be able to track her this way, as they would not know what to look for. They have not had interactions with humans in the same way as I have, and would not think of trying this.

I watch Anushka and her sister. More complications within human relationships. I just want Anushka to be happy, though I realise I have jeopardised her ability to achieve that state by interfering in her life the way I have.

Perhaps, when all this is over, I can help her to repair the bonds of her existence. Though my attempts at that have not been very successful so far.

Anushka's sister intrigues me. She also has a very bright presence in the energy field. It is almost a matching pair with Anushka's, and I can see how close they could be if they just allowed themselves to reach out. I can tell Jhanvi is passionate about supporting her sister. She also has a great deal of curiosity about my kind and our purpose here on Earth. I cannot blame her and I am not sure it was a good idea for Anushka to reveal as much as she has.

It might be worth me keeping an eye on Jhanvi, in case she does something inadvisable and inadvertently places herself, her family, or any of us at risk.

* * *

P36 - May 2019 - Ergo's Ship

When Anushka materialised back on the ship, the main room was empty apart from Ergo.

"Where are the others?" she asked, feeling her heartbeat speeding up.

His slow gaze found her and he gestured to two new doors she hadn't noticed.

"They went to sleep." He pointed at the left-most door. "Charlotte is in there."

Relief flooded through Anushka's body, then she felt a shiver of anticipation and grinned at Ergo. "Playing matchmaker?"

His face fell. "I am sorry my previous efforts caused more harm than good."

"It's okay. I know you were only trying to help." Anushka shrugged. "It's not your fault we're both being idiots. And I think connecting with Charlotte's mind has helped me see just how much of an idiot I'm being, and I think I'm ready to try being something else now. So it's hopefully done some good after all." She yawned. "Don't you sleep?"

Ergo shook his head. "This body is not real. So it requires no sustenance or rest. But I will meditate and recharge my mind."

Anushka took a quick trip to the bathroom, finding a replica of the spare toothbrush Charlotte kept for her in its usual cup on the sink. She looked at it, nestled against Charlotte's own toothbrush, and her resolve deepened. After using a few minutes to freshen up, she went back out into the main room, where Ergo was sitting on the floor with his eyes closed. Anushka didn't disturb him, instead going to the door he had indicated and slipping inside.

For a moment, she thought she had accidentally transported herself back to Charlotte's house, as she stepped into the familiar contours of Charlotte's bedroom. The sounds of gentle breathing told her that Charlotte was already asleep. Did she dare? Well, nothing ventured, nothing gained.

Anushka stripped to her underwear, pulled back the covers and slid into the bed next to Charlotte. She snuggled up against Charlotte's back, wrapping an arm around her slim body and burying her face in Charlotte's neck. Charlotte shifted sleepily, uttered a low noise of pleasure and laid her arm along Anushka's, squeezing it against her stomach.

"I'm sorry," Anushka whispered.

"I know," Charlotte breathed. "Me too."

And that was that. Anushka knew it couldn't be so simple, that there were many important things they would still need to work through. But, for now, they were safe and warm, wrapped around each other in a way that was so perfectly comfortable. It felt like coming home. All the mess and complications and unresolved issues could wait until another day. Right now, Anushka was exactly where she wanted to be, with exactly who she wanted to be with. She relaxed with a deep exhalation and let sleep take her.

* * *

P37 - May 2019 - Ergo's Ship

The following morning, Anushka proposed taking a solo trip to a busy London street, to get some more cash and buy breakfast for everyone.

"Risky," Charlotte said, worried about surveillance.

Anushka crossed her arms. "But nobody who's interested could possibly predict where I'll go. And even if Yardley is tracking my bank account, he wouldn't be able to deploy anyone quickly enough to catch me." She pouted. "And I really want a bagel."

If she was honest, Charlotte really wanted a bagel too. She shrugged, not wanting to launch into yet another fight. Especially over breakfast foods.

Anushka was back within a few minutes, with a smile on her face and two paper sacks in her hand.

"Who's for coffee? There were only two bagels left, but I got a poppy seed muffin too."

The three humans ate while Ergo looked on, and Charlotte had to admit it was good to be eating fresh food in comfortable surroundings. At some point, however, they would have to leave their safe haven and re-enter the fray. But first they needed more information.

"Are you sure this is a good idea?" Anushka echoed Danny's words from the night before. "Do you really think we can trust Perkins?"

"Not remotely," Charlotte said. "He'll likely play both sides as long as he can. So we assume he's feeding information to Yardley as well, and plan accordingly."

Danny fired up the laptop and set up the same security arrangements as before, then handed it over to Charlotte, who started typing.

>Are you there?

The answer was almost instantaneous.

>You haven't exactly given me much time. And I'm not your beck and call boy.

Charlotte chuckled.

>And yet, here you are, ready and waiting.

She could hear Perkins' exasperation in the typed words.

>Yes, well, it's not as if I actually have a life.

>And you do want to show off how amazing your stealth research skills are, don't you?

Danny grinned. "Won't he see through such blatant manipulation?" He paused for a beat. "Oh right, it's Perkins."

More words appeared on the screen, scrolling fast.

>Head honcho is on the warpath. Whatever you did has put the whole project in jeopardy. He's got a meeting with the clients, off-site. Details to follow.

After a couple of minutes, a date, time and location appeared on the screen. Charlotte typed again.

>Great. Thanks!

>Don't get dead. And don't get me dead, either.

Charlotte closed the connection and looked around at her co-conspirators. "Okay, so we have a target. Now we just have to decide what we're going to do."

But Anushka wasn't listening. Her eyes had a far-off look and a silver streak was travelling down her hair.

"Anushka? What is it?"

"I have to go." Anushka's tone was distracted. She gestured vaguely at the laptop screen. "I'll meet you there."

The silver streak in her hair turned turquoise and she vanished.

"Not again," Charlotte said.

"Isn't her hair usually pink when she teleports?" Danny asked.

Charlotte threw her hands up. "Who the hell knows? We need some kind of tether to stop her disappearing like that. In the meantime, I guess we'll have to plan our offensive without her and just hope she shows up to help."

* * *

A17 - 2009 - Iraq

The first main difference Anushka noticed was the heat. It battered at her skin after the cool of Ergo's ship, as if there was a scratchy blanket trying to smother her. She opened her eyes and squinted into the harsh light of a desert sun. After a few moments, she grew more accustomed to the glare and the landscape resolved more clearly around her. Everything was brown and grey, the dullness of the colour palette oppressive in its unrelenting uniformity. Scattered rocks and a few scrubby bushes provided the only texture to what was otherwise a featureless expanse of gently undulating sand. The barest hint of a breeze pulled dust up from the ground and sent it swirling in playful eddies around Anushka's feet. She was standing on a rough road that bisected the desert, but there was nothing in sight. No people, no buildings, just sand.

What was she doing here? And where was here anyway? She remembered seeing flames and blood and feeling a desperate urge to go to the place where they were. She had teleported on instinct but it felt different to the other times she'd done it. There was the sense of a rushing wind, a resistance to her travel that she had to fight against. And the vision of her destination hadn't been clear enough for her to visualise properly. It had all been based on need and urgency.

Anushka climbed a nearby rise to get a better view of her surroundings. On the other side, around a curve in the road that had been obscured, a jeep lay upside down, flames licking across its frame. There were two bodies, one behind and one inside the vehicle. She spotted two more figures further away, one lying flat, the other crouched, radio in hand. The image exactly matched a story Anushka had been told years before.

Without thinking, Anushka teleported across the intervening space to stand behind the crouched figure. She knew what was about to happen and she had to help. But she would need more than one of her abilities to be in effect at the same time if she were to provide the required assistance. Focusing inwards, she imagined multiple strands of colour sprouting in her hair, side by side, matching her will to each one, whether or not it was something she had done before.

The impervious crystalline substance closed over her skin before her arms went transparent, leaving only a blue aura visible. Then she imagined a shield and cast it over the two figures on the ground, spreading her arms over them protectively. Massive shimmering yellow wings unfurled from between her shoulder blades and mirrored the movement of her arms, covering the whole area. Seconds later, the jeep exploded behind them and Anushkha felt debris raining down.

As part of her brain marvelled at the fact that she had apparently jumped nine years back in time and created new abilities purely by imagining them, she leaned down and whispered in Charlotte's ear, "It's okay. I've got you."

Once the danger was passed, Anushka collapsed back onto the ground, suddenly exhausted. Charlotte and Danny were both unconscious and she knew they would soon be rescued, but she couldn't bring herself to leave them. She also wasn't sure exactly how to get back to the future, or why this new and radical ability had manifested now. She glanced at her watch, immediately wondering why she thought it would provide any useful information. But the date caught her eye, a date that always saw Charlotte and Danny going out without her, and returning late into the night, blind drunk. Ten years to the day since the explosion.

Before long, the sound of a vehicle reached her ears, growing closer. She couldn't afford to be found here, especially not by Yardley's soldiers. She stood, and gasped as a rainbow shimmer descended over her vision. Summoning her shielding wings again, this time with a golden metallic tint, she flexed them and shot into the sky.

* * *

C17 - May 2019 - Ergo's Ship

Charlotte looked around the main room of the ship, noticing another disappearance.

"Where's Ergo?"

Danny looked around as well, as if needing to check that Ergo wasn't lurking in a corner.

"No idea. Nothing like being the only ones on the team that can't teleport, huh?"

Charlotte snorted. "Our fellow team members aren't exactly up to code on health and safety, are they? Because, if you haven't noticed, there doesn't seem to be a door to the outside anywhere. What do we do if there's a fire?"

Danny stared at her for a long moment, then gave a slightly nervous laugh. "Just have to avoid blowing anything up, won't we?"

"Speaking of which," Charlotte said, "what are we actually intending to do if we go to this meeting between Yardley and the other aliens? We'll need to have some kind of a plan going in, though it might be tricky to get there if Ergo doesn't come back soon. And it'll be even trickier to communicate the plan to Anushka if she's going to meet us there."

"It's just impossible to get decent super-powered help these days." Danny grinned. "Guess it's up to us to sort out the practicalities. Can we get Perkins to surveil the meeting remotely so we get evidence of anything untoward Yardley might do? He won't be pleased to see us, and he might try and get the aliens to attack us or something. Do we even know what they could do to us?"

"Unfortunately not." Charlotte sighed. "That would have been part of the planning process, if Ergo were here. I don't like going into such an unknown situation without any intel or background on the players. We don't know the enemies' intentions or capabilities. We'll be on unfamiliar terrain. Half the team is currently MIA. It's not great."

"But we can't just sit around here doing nothing," Danny pointed out. "We'll have to show our hand at some point. And, if we want to stop Consensus, maybe approaching the other aliens is the best bet. If we can show them that Yardley's a dick of the first order, and that the people pulling their strings aren't to be trusted either, maybe they'll come over to our side." Danny gestured at the empty room. "Though we can't exactly offer them first class accommodation, or in fact any semblance of a pension plan."

"Let's see what we can find out about the location by looking online, and work from there," Charlotte said.

She wondered where Anushka had disappeared off to, and what had dragged her away with such urgency. The previous night's intimacy had been a welcome return to their old dynamic, and an even more welcome break from their recent fighting. But they still had plenty of issues to work out, not least of which was persuading Anushka to stop running off on her own. But that conversation would have to wait until Anushka came back again. Charlotte wondered if the situation would ever calm down enough for them to sit down and hash everything out. In the meantime, there was research to do.

* * *

E17 - May 2019 - India

I am drawn back to Anushka's sister, Jhanvi. Something about her intrigues me. She has a settled life, a family to care for. She is not directly involved in the interstellar events that have altered her sister's life. And yet she wants to be. She has no other reason, except the desire to be of use to someone who shares a biological connection with her. Perhaps some humans are capable of the kind of communion I have enjoyed with my own kind, after all.

And yet Jhanvi must be drawn in more than one direction. Surely the fate of her children and husband must be in conflict with her desire to help Anushka. But then again, perhaps it is exactly those fates that she is concerned with, in wanting to assist our cause. Should Consensus gain a foothold of control over humanity, there is no telling where it may end for them. I do not believe Consensus will have concern for the wellbeing of individual humans. They will see them purely as a means to whatever end they are envisaging in their deceitful plan.

I hover outside Jhanvi's house and observe her in my energy form as she wakes her children, prepares their sustenance for the day and sends them out into the world to pursue their own independent existences. She kisses her husband and he leaves as well. As soon as they are all gone, she retrieves a computer device and starts looking for things on the global network the humans have created to be able to share information over distances.

Even though they are separate and isolated within their individual shells, they still seek to connect with one another, in whatever limited way they are able. Perhaps one day my people can help them achieve the next step in their evolution, and they can join us in the freedom and unity of energy existence.

Jhanvi is searching for references to other humans' contact with extra-terrestrial life forms. There are many on record and it is difficult for her to narrow down her terms. I do not know what she hopes to find, or what she intends to do with the information if she locates it. But Anushka's warnings of danger have not been enough to deter her, and I believe she will keep looking until she feels she is able to provide some assistance to us. I look forward to discovering the nature of her eventual contribution.

* * *

P38 - May 2019 - London

Charlotte and Danny perched on a rooftop, looking down at the warehouse, where Yardley had agreed to meet with the other alien representatives. Ergo had come back from wherever he'd been and had transported them both back to Charlotte's house again to gather more supplies.

Danny was wearing his prosthetic legs and had practised using his telekinesis to enhance his ability to walk in them without crutches. Charlotte had picked up a parabolic microphone and recording device, deciding it was better not to involve Perkins any more than he already was. She always preferred to rely on herself where she could.

"Hang on," Danny said, angling the microphone towards the warehouse. "I think I'm picking something up."

He flipped a switch and there was a brief burst of static, before it resolved into Yardley's voice.

"I apologise for the inconvenience, but I thought it would be better to meet here, rather than at the lab. We've been compromised one too many times and it's important that we speak without the risk of unwanted interruptions."

A silky, deeper version of Ergo's voice sounded next. "It is no inconvenience for us. We are happy to accommodate you. What is it you wish to speak to us about?"

"I'm afraid the latest breach at the lab has resulted in the loss of nearly all the remaining XR-20 we had in storage. I have one subject in process, but the effects on him won't last much longer. I was hoping you would be able to provide me with some more of the XR-20 so that the experiments could continue."

Yardley was trying his best to sound calm and unruffled, but Charlotte could hear the tension in his voice. He hated to be on the back foot, so it must be killing him to have to come crawling to such important clients, asking for help. One thing snagged at her mind; a subject in process? What could that mean?

"Unfortunately, we do not have any more," the alien said. "The traitor took our remaining stocks with him when he fled. So, much like you, we have been betrayed and robbed. We can send a message home to ask for more, but none will reach us for some time. It seems we must cease progress until we can resupply."

Whilst it was good to hear that their enemies' plans had been scuppered, there was nothing about this meeting that would prove incriminating. Ergo thought he might be able to convert the other representatives of his people to their cause, if he was able to share what they had learned about the project. But there had not yet been an opportunity to approach the other aliens with the information they had collected.

Before Charlotte could raise these doubts, though, Danny exclaimed and pointed up at the sky.

"What the hell is that?"

Charlotte looked up, squinting against the sunlight, and spotted a shape growing steadily larger in the distance. It resolved itself into a humanoid form, edged in blue, sparkling and gliding towards them on golden angel wings. The figure was topped by a streaming rainbow of multi-coloured hair. The image sparked a powerful memory in Charlotte and, for a brief moment, she was transported back to a dusty desert road filled with pain and fear.

"Anushka?"

* * *

P39 - May 2019 - London

Anushka soared over the rendezvous location, revelling in the feeling of the wind through her hair. She felt powerful, untouchable. She saw three tiny figures crouched on a rooftop, but they were unimportant. The energy flowing through her set her apart, made her something other than human, and it felt good.

She zeroed in on the warehouse where Yardley was meeting with the other aliens from Ergo's team. She could hear them talking inside with no effort and idly wondered what strand of her rainbow-coloured hair was providing that power. Her crystalline skin in place, she zoomed down towards the building and flew straight through an upper window. The sound of the glass shattering was unnaturally loud in her ears and it tumbled to the ground inside the warehouse, startling those below.

Anushka pulled out of her dive, instinctively angling her wings to bring her to a graceful landing a few feet away from Yardley. One of Charlotte's security team from the lab, Owuye, stood a few feet behind him. He started to move forwards at Anushka's appearance, but Yardley raised a hand to forestall him.

Yardley stared at her, briefly open-mouthed, before schooling his expression back to one of bored disdain.

"Dr Mahto, I see you have come more into your powers since our last meeting." He turned to the aliens, who stood in a huddled group, elongated and glowing in the same way Ergo had when he first appeared to Anushka. "You see what we have been able to accomplish. I think you'll agree that this specimen is an encouraging development."

One of the aliens stepped forwards. "Indeed. This human appears to embody exactly what we are looking for. Have you brought her here to demonstrate this to us?"

Anushka spread her arms wide. "I no longer answer to him. He has not brought me anywhere. I am here to prevent whatever atrocities you are planning to perpetrate on both our peoples."

The alien continued to address Yardley. "It seems you have lost control of your test subject. That is unfortunate, but not insurmountable."

He turned to Anushka and stretched out one impossibly long arm towards her. "Perhaps there is some way we can negotiate with you to harness the power you have so successfully mastered."

The alien started to step in her direction but Anushka threw up one of her hands in a warding gesture. The alien paused, apparently unsure of whether or not she could harm him. Yardley, on the other hand, was undeterred.

"No!" he cried. "Your deal is with me. We can still achieve great things, once we have more supplies of the XR-20. And we can still recapture this specimen for further study. Owuye!"

The large soldier stepped forwards, rolling his shoulders. He clenched his fists and thrust them forwards. Flames enveloped his hands and he stalked towards Anushka, a grim smile on his usually stoic face. Anushka laughed.

"You really think a little bit of fire can subdue me?"

In response, Owuye punched one fist out and a gout of flame shot out as if from a flamethrower. Anushka unfurled her wings and flung herself into the air to avoid it. It occurred to her that her crystalline skin should be impervious to fire, but she didn't want to test that theory under battle conditions, and she wasn't sure the protection extended to her wings. She still had to expend a lot of energy to keep all her powers in place at once, and the risk of losing one or more of them was too great.

Owuye stalked the warehouse space below her, firing streams of flame into the air in an attempt to bring her down. Anushka saw Yardley and the aliens backing towards the edge of the space, out of the way, as she ducked and weaved, dodging the flames. The air heated up around her and it started to get difficult to breathe. A flash of white light drew her gaze and she saw Ergo materialise inside the warehouse, Charlotte and Danny clinging to his arms. A searing pain stabbed down her nerve endings from an unfamiliar source and she twisted her head to see scorched and blackened feathers along the edge of one wing. She wheeled in a tight circle, trying to present as hard a target as possible.

She had to get closer to Owuye, if she was going to stop him, though. She decided to risk testing her crystalline shell against the fire. She pushed her wings as much behind her back as she could and still maintain control, and started a dive towards the fiery figure below.

* * *

P40 - May 2019 - London

Everything happened very fast.

Once it was clear things were going south, Ergo teleported Charlotte and Danny into the warehouse. Charlotte scanned the scene, taking in the fight between Owuye and Anushka. Owuye was sending fire up in streams towards Anushka, who was flying down at him, deflecting the flames with her hard crystal body. Charlotte didn't want to know what would happen if they collided.

Charlotte stood up from the crouch she was in and sprinted forwards. "Owuye! Wait! Stop, both of you!"

Owuye glanced in her direction, then turned his attention back to the figure in the air, aiming one hand at her, and swinging the other up towards Charlotte.

His deep voice boomed across the large warehouse space, strain evident in his words. "Just leave it, boss. I don't want to hurt you."

Anushka had slowed her descent, hovering a few feet up, waiting to see what would happen. Her rainbow hair and hard expression made her look almost as alien as Ergo, and the coldness in her eyes made Charlotte shiver.

"I don't think you want to hurt anyone," Charlotte said, focusing on Owuye. His instinct was always to follow orders, but she knew his moral compass swung in the right direction, deep down. "Listen to me. Do you really think Yardley is on the right side of this?"

Owuye shot her another glance, his eyes darting between the various targets in his field of view. His brow was furrowed, sweat trickling down the sides of his face. She pressed her advantage.

"You're the only weapon Yardley has left in his arsenal. He doesn't have much of the XR-20 left, if any. When your powers fade - and they will soon - which side do you want to be on? The wrong one, with no advantages? Or the right one, with all the power?"

Tension thrummed through his body for a few seconds more, then his shoulders slumped and the fire around his hands sputtered out.

"Good choice," Charlotte said.

"I'm not choosing your side," Owuye replied. "But I'm not going to hurt people for Yardley, either. I need to think some before I decide on my next move."

Charlotte nodded, not wanting to press the point, now that the immediate danger was apparently over. "Fair enough. Good luck."

He nodded back, then turned and walked out of the warehouse.

Charlotte ran over to where Anushka was coming in to land. "Are you okay?"

Anushka was breathing heavily, her face more human again now that Charlotte was up close. "I think so. The damage to my wing isn't bad."

Charlotte put her hands on her hips, her concern now replaced by irritation. "What the hell were you thinking? He might not have been able to hurt you, but what were you going to do when you hit the ground?"

"I don't know, okay? I didn't have a plan, I was just going with whatever seemed best at the time." She seemed rattled by her own actions, which gave Charlotte hope that she could be reasoned with.

Ergo broke in, suspending the argument. "We should leave. They will be able to track us here."

Charlotte looked around the warehouse. Yardley and the other aliens were gone.

Ergo waited for them all to gather around him, held out his arms so they could all touch him, and suddenly they were all back on the ship.

* * *

C18 - May 2019 - Ergo's Ship

Anushka was slumped at the table, all indications of power gone. Her long hair spilled over her shoulders, entirely brown.

"Are you okay?" Charlotte asked, moving to lay a hand on Anushka's shoulder.

Anushka brought her head up, meeting Charlotte's gaze. A riot of emotions played across her face, all swamped by exhaustion.

"Just tired, I think. When I use all my powers at once, it takes more energy."

"Yeah…" Charlotte trailed off, not sure how to articulate the thoughts that were running through her mind. "About that. What happened to you after you disappeared on us? Again. The wings, the rainbow hair…" She trailed off, trying to pin down the hazy memory that kept flashing up in her mind.

Anushka smiled. "I have no idea where all that came from and it was a bit scary, if I'm honest. Almost like the power was controlling me, rather than the other way around. I'm actually glad you stopped the fight when you did, because I'm not sure what I might have done otherwise."

Charlotte shook her head. "No. I mean... " She shrugged helplessly. "I don't know what I mean."

Anushka reached up and squeezed Charlotte's fingers. "Did you recognise me, Charl? I wasn't sure if you were still conscious."

Charlotte's breath caught in her throat. She fought past the constriction. "So, it was you? All that time ago, but actually earlier today?"

The ramifications pushed against her rational mind and it rejected them, thrusting them aside to be examined later. Anushka just smiled, love radiating from her gaze.

Danny cleared his throat. “Does one of you want to tell the rest of the class what the hell you’re going on about?”

Charlotte looked over at him, still dazed. “Anushka was - is - our angel. She’s the one who protected us from the blast when the jeep exploded. She’s the reason we weren’t killed that day.”

It took him a few moments to connect the dots, then a few more to wrap his head around it.

“So turquoise is time travel?” His eyes widened. “Fuck me.” His eyes narrowed, focused on Anushka. “Are you going to try that again? Sounds like it might come in pretty handy.”

She shook her head. “I don’t think I want to start messing around with changing things in the past. There’s no telling what that might lead to. I’m not sure I should be messing around with any of this stuff without doing more research first. It’s getting out of hand. I don’t think you should take any more XR-20, either.”

In answer, Danny used his telekinesis to levitate off his stool and fly slowly around the room. “You’re not the only one who can fly, you know. And there’s no way in hell I’m giving this up. You can use me as your lab rat all you want, as long as you don’t take my juice away.”

“Your new abilities aren’t the only way you can contribute, you know,” Charlotte said. “Your brain is what’s been helping us so far, so you’re always going to be useful, even if you lose your powers.”

Danny settled back down on a stool and saluted, flashing his customary grin. "I know, Corp. I'm amazing. No question." He looked back over at Anushka. "And thanks, by the way."

"For what?"

"For saving our bacon when the jeep blew up. I still can't figure out how that could have happened, but I'm grateful."

"Yes." Charlotte leaned down to give Anushka an awkward hug. "Me too. I can't believe that was really you. But it's good to know I wasn't hallucinating, after all this time."

"Getting back to the matter at hand," Danny said. "We're essentially back to square one. What do we do now?"

Ergo spoke up from the other side of the room. "I believe there is another source of information we can utilise. I will go and fetch her."

* * *

A18 - May 2019 - Ergo's Ship

"Her? Who?" Anushka spoke to the empty air where Ergo had been just a moment before.

"Now you know how I feel when you keep doing that," Charlotte said.

Anushka laid her head back down on her folded arms. She was tempted to ask Ergo for more of the XR-20 when he came back, to try and dispel the bone-deep weariness that was creeping through her entire body. But that would probably be a bad idea. Who knew what effects it might have if she added more to her already contaminated body? She was glad she'd had the opportunity and ability to save Charlotte and Danny in Iraq, but she didn't want to feel that out of control again. She just hoped she'd get the chance to study the XR-20 and its effects more.

"Fair enough," she said to Charlotte. "I'm sorry. So what do we do now?"

Charlotte spread her hands in a helpless gesture. "We wait. There isn't anything else we can do. Especially since we don't know where the door is."

Anushka glanced around and realised she was right. They were essentially trapped until Ergo came back, since Anushka didn't feel capable of teleporting herself anywhere right now, let alone taking two other people with her.

It was about ten minutes before Ergo reappeared, and he brought someone with him, as he had said he would. It was Jhanvi.

Anushka watched as her sister staggered with the effects of teleportation, then stared around the room at them all, trying to take in her abruptly different surroundings.

"Jhanvi? What the..." Anushka focused on Ergo. "What the hell are you doing bringing my sister here?"

He regarded her in his infuriatingly calm manner. "She has information that may be of use to us."

This brought Anushka's attention back to her sister. "What did you do?"

"Hello to you, too," Jhanvi said, steadying herself with a hand on the table. She looked at the others in turn. "And you must be Charlotte and Danny. It's lovely to meet you. I'm Jhanvi, Anushka's sister."

"Hi," Charlotte said.

Danny waved.

"Now you've got the pleasantries out of the way," Anushka said drily, "do you want to stop putting off telling me what you did after I specifically told you not to get involved, and let us in on why you're here?"

Jhanvi shifted a spare stool out from under the table and sat down. "I've been doing some research, based on what you told me about all this." She waved her hands, encompassing the whole ship. "And I don't think your friend here and his team are the only aliens that have been sent to Earth."

Of course she'd been doing research. Anushka knew it had been a bad idea to tell Jhanvi as much as she had. She'd thought there wouldn't be anything Jhanvi could do to get involved, but her sister's determination was second to none.

"Is that true?" Anushka asked Ergo.

"I do not know. Not as far as we were told by Consensus. But it seems very clear to me now that they have not been honest with us about many things. So it is possible they sent other teams to other parts of the world, to conduct their own experiments."

"But how does that help us?" Danny asked. "Doesn't that just make everything worse? We thought we were only dealing with Yardley and a couple more aliens. If there are loads of teams, how can we hope to work against them?"

"By using their very existence to undermine Consensus," Ergo said.

* * *

E18 - May 2019 - Ergo's Ship

I drop my shields and reach out to my brethren. First, those who formed the rest of my own team here on Earth. Contact is immediate.

Traitor. You have made a foolish error because now we know where you are.

Wait. Before you act against me, are you prepared to listen? To let me explain why I have done what I have done?

There is a pause. I believe they are conferring amongst themselves without allowing me access to the conversation. I load more information into the connection between us in an attempt to influence their deliberations.

My shields are now down and will remain so. You can find me at any point and I will not have time to move away, not without abandoning the humans. You can also access my mind fully and without restriction, so you will know that what I say is the truth.

We understand. And we will listen. Briefly.

We have been misled. We are not the only team Consensus sent.

Why should that matter to us? We have been given a job to do. If others are also performing the same role, that makes sense, so as to maximise potential success.

But they lied to us. About that, and about many other things.

How can we be sure you are not suffering some kind of delusion that only makes you think what you say is true?

Join with me in contacting the others. Let us all come together so that we can see the situation clearly. Then we can decide what to do.

I expand my awareness, feeling the others of my team joining their consciousness to mine. With our combined power, we are able to reach out and seek others of our kind within the confines of this planet. We find many. Across the globe of the Earth, connections are made. There is surprise, wonder, suspicion, anger. It is unsettling to all of us to discover how much has been hidden from us. And the fact of the other teams' existence is only the first of many deceptions I plan to reveal. I request quiet and receive it, speaking to all in one burst of beautiful, connective energy. I show them everything I have learned; about the substance and what I have determined it may mean about our supposed enemy; about the humans and what has been hidden from them; about Consensus and their lies.

I am opening myself to you all completely. See what is in my mind and what is in my heart. When has Consensus ever been this open with any of us? Will you all come to meet with me and those who have been working with me, to help us to uncover the truth?

Layered, overlapping responses. All of assent. I have sparked curiosity and they are all eager to find out more. I have relied on my people's thirst for knowledge to get them to agree to my plan. I give them a location, then focus my attention back to my physical surroundings. We are a long way away from our ultimate goal of stopping the war and bringing down Consensus, but I have made the first step and it feels good to be in contact with my own kind again. I begin to feel the scattered pieces of my psyche reattaching into a familiar whole.

* * *

P41 - May 2019 - North London

Ergo stood silently, eyes closed, for several minutes, while the others looked on, exchanging baffled glances every now and then. Anushka had never been very good at waiting, and started to feel impatient. There was nothing any of them could do, though, and she didn't want to risk interrupting Ergo before he was finished.

Eventually, he opened his pale eyes again and regarded them steadily. It was impossible to read his expression.

"The others have agreed to meet with us," he said. "We should go, so as to be there before they arrive."

"Arrive where?" Anushka asked. "And is delivering ourselves into their hands really such a good idea?"

He nodded. "I believe it is the only way. I cannot go up against Consensus alone and I cannot show the others the truth of the situation without connecting with them fully. I am sure they will listen to reason when they hear what we have to say."

Danny joined the sceptical side of the team. "But what do we really have to tell them?"

"Your theory about where the XR-20 substance comes from got me thinking. Please," Ergo said, a note of urgency creeping into his voice. "We must go."

The four humans exchanged another glance, shrugging to each other, before moving to stand around Ergo and placing their hands on the exposed skin of his arms. Anushka realised Ergo hadn't answered her question about where they were going, but it was too late. They were already there.

They materialised in the car park in front of Yardley's lab. Ergo took up a position before the glass front doors, which Anushka hadn't used since she'd fled with the alien XR-20. Had it really been less than a week since that panicked night?

There was no time to discuss a game plan, as groups of aliens, in the original elongated shining form, started to appear around them. They gathered in a loose arc, facing Ergo and the humans. Their silent regard was unsettling and Anushka wondered if Ergo really knew what he was doing.

As soon as eight sets of aliens had taken their places, Ergo stepped forwards and raised his hands in welcome.

"Thank you all for coming. I will use audible speech for the benefit of my human companions, but I also open my mind to you all, so you can be assured of my sincere intent." He gestured round at the gathered group. "You have now all seen with your own eyes how we have been misled. But I believe the deceit of Consensus reaches far more widely and deeply than just making us believe we were each part of the only team on Earth. I believe they have also lied to us about the nature of our enemy." Ergo produced a knife from somewhere and drew it across the pale skin of his forearm. Anushka gasped as what looked like some of the XR-20 oozed out of the wound. Ergo continued speaking to his rapt audience. "I have asked those of my family unit who remain on our planet to investigate my theories, and I believe they will now have more information to share with us. Join with me now to contact those we trust back on our world. I would ask that you broadcast what you learn, so that all may hear and understand."

All the aliens closed their eyes simultaneously and started swaying like tall trees in a gentle breeze.

Taking turns with no interruptions or overlapping, they spoke aloud into the bright afternoon.

"We have distressing news from home."

"We have been betrayed by those we trusted to lead and protect us."

"Consensus has misrepresented everything, for more years than we can count."

"The enemy is not an enemy. They are of us."

"The so-called enemy were once of our people. They originated with us long ago."

"They spoke out against Consensus and were cast out, to live as exiles far away, in corporeal forms that could no longer connect to the whole."

"Consensus expunged all reference to them from the common consciousness, so we would be unaware of their existence."

"They have long been planning a return to expose Consensus, but Consensus plotted against them, telling us they were a threat and exhorting us to make war against them."

"The only threat they pose is to Consensus. They preach a return to unity, honesty, transparency, everything that Consensus claims to stand for and yet everything Consensus has subverted to their own ends."

"We have been pawns in the desire of Consensus to retain power and control over us."

"We must rise up against Consensus and join with our exiled brethren to return our society to the ideals upon which it is predicated."

There was a long silence, as the aliens all gradually opened their eyes again and looked around at each other, dazed and overwhelmed by the revelations. Anushka looked at her sister, whose eyes were wide. To a certain extent, this gathering of alien beings in North London was her doing.

Ergo raised his hands again but, before he could speak to the general assembly, the whoosh of the automatic doors behind them drew Anushka's attention, and she turned to see Perkins coming out of the building.

"What on earth is going on out here?" he asked, staring wide-eyed at all the aliens.

* * *

P42 - May 2019 - North London

Charlotte looked round at the sound of Perkins' voice. Danny was standing next to her on his prosthetic legs, keeping himself upright without crutches.

"What do you want, Perkins?" Charlotte asked. "We're a little busy."

"I think I have an idea of what to do about Yardley," he said. He brought a tablet up into view.

Charlotte raised an eyebrow at him. "Do you indeed? Picked a side to land on, have you?"

He waved a hand at all the aliens, who were staring at each other intently, presumably carrying on a debate about what to do telepathically.

"I think I can see who's going to come out on top." He gave her his trademark grin. "Will you accept hard evidence of Yardley's crimes in exchange for immunity and a place back on your team?"

He turned the tablet to face her and she watched as the video footage of Anushka rescuing her and Danny from being restrained in the lab played out on the screen. It was unsettling to view herself from above like that, and the scene looked like something out of a bad sci-fi movie.

"I'm sure we can make a case on your behalf," Charlotte said. Apparently, she was in charge now.

"Good," Perkins replied. "I've already sent the video with a brief summary of the more believable of recent events to Yardley's military contacts. Someone should be along shortly."

Charlotte stared at him. "Don't you think we should get all the aliens out of sight before that happens?"

Perkins shrugged one shoulder. "Probably best, yeah."

* * *

E19 - May 2019 - North London

I - we - have been welcomed back to the shared consciousness of our people. Joy spreads through us at the renewed contact. The whole group gathered at Yardley's lab is reeling from the information we have learned. Our whole concept of the power structure of our society has been shattered. But we are all firm in our commitment to bringing our people back to unity.

Charlotte approaches us.

"There will soon be a lot of humans here with weapons and suspicion. It's probably best if none of you are here when they arrive."

We agree. With the task ahead of us, the last thing we need is to be forced into a complicated confrontation with more humans. We turn to Anushka.

"We must go home. There is much for us to do there. We must find a way to wipe the corruption of Consensus from our lives and welcome our long-lost family home. But we will open communications with you again once things are stable."

She nods, then gestures at her sister. "I know this is an imposition, but could you drop Jhanvi back at her home on your way?" She pauses. "And maybe give me the rest of the XR-20 stocks you have, so I can continue researching it?"

We nod. "Neither of those things will be onerous to us. But, now we know the substance you call XR-20 is a by-product of injury to our corporeal brethren, we must research it ourselves to establish if there is a safe way to produce it without harming us. So we may not be able to provide more, once the existing stocks are depleted."

"Thank you," she says. "And I understand. Regardless of what happens with the XR-20, I'm sure my people would welcome further contact with yours." Then she gathers Jhanvi in a tight hug. "I'll be in touch, I promise. And, once I get a proper handle on the alien stuff, I could pop by to see you more regularly."

Jhanvi laughs. "There are such things as aeroplanes, you know."

Anushka smiles, but we see moisture in her eyes. "Okay, I know. We'll see each other soon, regardless of the transportation method."

They break apart and Jhanvi comes to stand next to us. We look at Anushka, Charlotte and Danny in turn.

"Thank you for all your contributions. You have helped to prevent an unnecessary war and protected your own planet from harmful interference as well. We look forward to a time when we can re-establish contact and work together peacefully to promote knowledge between our peoples."

"We'll be here when you're ready," Anushka says.

We turn our focus inwards.

Come, family, friends. Let us leave the humans to regain their equilibrium. We have much to atone for, but our continued presence will make the situation worse, rather than better. We should depart elsewhere to plan our return home.

Unified assent washes through our mind from all those gathered and we are finally whole again.

We take Jhanvi's hand. Anushka raises a hand in farewell and everything around us vanishes into white light.

* * *

C19 - May 2019 - North London

As Charlotte watched the aliens disappearing, the sound of engines reached her ears and a cavalcade of several military jeeps and a couple of unmarked cars with flashing police lights turned onto the site. They drew up in front of the building and multiple people climbed out. A handful of soldiers arrayed themselves in a semi-circle around the group, weapons ready but not actually pointed at anyone. A man and woman in uniform and another woman in civilian clothes approached.

The uniformed woman was Major Simmonds, the army liaison to the lab. She targeted her gaze straight at Charlotte.

"Grant? What the hell did I just witness?"

"Major," she replied, fighting the urge to salute. "That's going to be a bit difficult to explain."

The Major's eyes ranged over the scene, as if seeking out any remaining aliens, then came back to meet Charlotte's gaze again.

"You'd better start sharp-ish. After the information we've received about recent activities at Yardley Labs, and what we may or may not have just seen here, your explanation had better be good."

The civilian woman stepped forwards.

"Seconded. I'm Agent Harris, MI-5. And I'm going to need some pretty spectacular reasons why I shouldn't just take you all into custody."

Before Charlotte could even start to think of how to respond, a beam of red light shot past her and a tree at the edge of the car park exploded in a shower of sparks. The trunk was sheared clean through and the tree toppled, crashing to the ground and scattering soldiers in all directions.

Yardley came striding from the lab, fists clenched at his sides, face covered in fury. He raised an accusatory finger at Anushka, ignoring everyone else completely.

"You!" he spat. "You've destroyed everything I've built!"

He narrowed his eyes and red beams streamed out of them in Anushka's direction. Anushka's hair burst into rainbow colours, her skin hardened to crystal and she took to the air on golden wings. Yardley tried to track her progress through the sky with his laser vision, but couldn't control it enough to hit her. She swooped and swirled, avoiding the beams with ease, until Charlotte saw her falter. As Charlotte looked on in horror, the sparkling crystal retreated from her skin, the shining wings shrank and disappeared, and suddenly she was plummeting towards the ground, her hair brown and trailing behind her.

Before Charlotte could do more than cry out, Danny was shooting up into the air. He aimed himself towards Anushka and caught her, slowing their descent so that they touched the ground gently. The extra weight must have unbalanced Danny, though, as his prosthetic legs collapsed under him and they both fell in a heap. Yardley stalked towards them, all sense of reason gone from his glowing red eyes. Danny stretched out one hand towards him and he stopped in his tracks, eyebrows drawing down in puzzlement. He strained against the force Danny was sending out, but he couldn't move. He set his features in determination and fired a laser beam, which hit the tarmac a few feet away from where Danny and Anushka were crouched, and started tracking towards them, gouging a path in the ground as it went.

Charlotte glanced over at Major Simmonds, who was frozen, watching the scene unfold, mouth open. In a moment of desperation, Charlotte grabbed the Major's sidearm, took aim and fired. Blood burst from the side of Yardley's head and he collapsed to the ground, inert. The laser beam shut off as he fell.

There was a moment of perfect stillness and silence, before people started shouting and running around. Charlotte stood in the middle of the activity, a gaping void expanding throughout her body. Danny raised himself onto his prosthetic legs and then helped an exhausted Anushka to her feet. They both came over to where Charlotte was standing, and Anushka threw her arms around her.

"You saved our lives," she whispered into Charlotte's hair.

But it was Major Simmonds' harsh voice that brought Charlotte back into the present moment. "Relinquish that weapon, Grant!"

Anushka stepped back, swaying a little. Moving by instinct, Charlotte put the safety back on the gun, dangled it from two fingers and held it out to Major Simmonds, who took it from her with a frown.

"Well," Simmonds said. "Now that the excitement is over, we need to get back to the explanations."

Charlotte exchanged a helpless glance with Anushka, who raised her chin and spoke in an authoritative tone.

"Lester Yardley attempted to murder us so Charlotte acted in our defence. You all saw it." She gestured at Perkins' tablet. "You'll also see from the footage provided, that we have been working to obstruct Yardley's criminal activities. I am the lead scientist and will take control of the lab and shut down all projects until we're given permission to resume."

Agent Harris nodded. "The footage you mention also contains certain aspects that will require additional investigation." She waved vaguely around the car park. "Not to mention the rest of what we've witnessed here today."

Anushka nodded. "We're happy to answer any questions you might have. And we're eager to be as transparent as possible in our dealings with both the military and the security services moving forwards. There's plenty to discuss and lots of options for working together in pursuit of knowledge that could benefit the whole world."

Agent Harris gave a harrumph. "Well, for the time being, you'll all be coming with us for those questions you're so happy to answer." She glanced at Simmonds. "We'll be happy to share all information gathered, unless you'd like one of your team to be part of the discussions."

Simmonds considered. "I think I'll let my aide take care of the mess here, and join the discussions myself, if you don't object."

It was all so stiffly polite and desperately deferential. Charlotte could imagine they were both very eager to find out more about what was going on. It was only their curiosity that was causing them to be so accommodating to one another. It all felt to Charlotte as if it was happening very far away. She was trying not to look at where Yardley's body lay crumpled on the tarmac.

She remained quiet as the four of them - Charlotte, Anushka, Danny and Perkins - were bundled into one of the vans and driven away from the lab.

* * *

A19 - May 2019 - West London

Late in the evening, Anushka opened the door to her flat and Charlotte followed her inside. They'd spent several hours going over everything with Agent Harris and Major Simmonds, and there was plenty more still to discuss. But both women had agreed to release them for the night, and Danny had suggested they might need some privacy, so they had come to Anushka's while he went home to Charlotte's house.

All the driving around had felt so torturously slow after Anushka had become so used to being able to think of a place and will herself there. But the unpredictability and short-lived nature of the powers bestowed by the XR-20 still unnerved her. And she knew she would have to get used to being fully human again if Ergo wasn't able to supply any more of the substance safely.

Anushka looked around the barely lived-in space of her lounge. Ergo's ship felt more familiar and homelike than this flat, but it would have to do for now. She crossed to an armchair and dropped into it with a sigh. Charlotte followed suit, choosing a different chair on the other side of the coffee table.

They regarded each other for a long moment.

"So," Anushka said.

"So," Charlotte echoed.

Anushka hurried to reassure Charlotte on the point she knew was foremost in both their minds. "You had no choice. If you hadn't done what you'd done, Danny and I would both be dead."

Charlotte gave a heavy sigh. "I know. It doesn't make it any easier, though."

"I know." There was another long pause, before Anushka managed a small smile. "No more evil forces trying to kill or capture us. So I guess we've got no more excuses to avoid this." She gestured vaguely at the space between them.

Charlotte smiled back, then frowned. "Do you think we can ever get back to where we were before?"

Anushka struggled to take a full breath. "Is that what you want?"

Charlotte's frown deepened. "Isn't it what you want?"

"Ergo's not here to show us each other's thoughts, so we're going to have to stop hiding and try to be more open with one another." Anushka held Charlotte's gaze. "I want to be with you. I think you want to be with me, too." She raised one eyebrow and Charlotte nodded, her expression guarded. "But so much has happened to erode trust between us. I don't think we can just go back to where we were before."

Charlotte dropped her gaze to the floor and let out a long breath. "So what does that mean?" She sounded lost, vulnerable, in a way that Anushka wasn't used to.

Anushka grappled with finding the right words, feeling her way as she spoke. "I don't think we should try to go back. But I think we can move forwards. We need to take it slow, be honest about how we feel, and see if we can find something new. Start from where we are and work out where we want to get to." She got up, walked around the table and knelt down beside Charlotte's chair. She reached out and lifted Charlotte's chin so their eyes met again. Anushka held her breath. "Will you try that with me?"

Tears sparkled in Charlotte's eyes, but she was smiling. "Yes. Yes, I will."

* * *

P43 - August 2019 - North London

Three months later, Anushka walked into the security office at the lab to see Perkins working side by side with Danny. The latter looked up at her entrance.

"Be right with you," he said. "Just need to finish testing this new plugin."

"No problem. I need to pop in to see Charlotte for a minute, so take your time."

Anushka proceeded through the space and knocked on the open door to Charlotte's office. They were jointly in charge of the lab now, but neither of them had wanted to take over Yardley's office, so it remained empty. Charlotte looked up from her desk and smiled.

"Come to steal Danny for more testing?"

"We agreed on joint custody," Anushka said. "He can do computer stuff for you, as long as he's also made available to help me with my research."

Danny's voice called from the main area. "I can hear you, you know! I'm not your child, or your property."

"Teachers' pet, more like," Perkins retorted. "Good doggie."

Anushka stepped inside Charlotte's office and shut the door on the bickering. "Don't those two drive you crazy?"

Charlotte grinned. "I've told them they have to work out their own differences. No coming to me to complain about each other. So, they actually keep themselves pretty occupied, and mostly leave me alone." She gestured at the chair on the other side of her desk. "What's up?"

Anushka sat down. "Ergo's coming back."

"How do you know?"

Anushka waved her hands around the sides of her head. "I just do."

"Any more details than that? Do you know what's been going on with him on his homeworld?"

Anushka shook her head. "I only know that he's on his way, and that he'll be here soon."

Charlotte brushed her hair behind her ear. "I guess we'd better let Harris and Simmonds know. They'll be wetting themselves to get the chance to meet him."

"Which one will you call first?" Anushka grinned. Their government and military liaisons were both sticklers for protocol and always wanted to be the first to know anything.

Charlotte grimaced. "Maybe I'll set up a conference call and tell them both together."

"Probably best."

"So," Charlotte said, with a twinkle in her eye. "I guess things are about to get exciting again."

"It's been three months," Anushka said, matching Charlotte's smile with one of her own. "Aren't you ready for a bit more excitement?"

Charlotte reached across the desk, and Anushka brought up one of her hands and intertwined their fingers.

Charlotte's smile widened. "Bring it on."

THE END

ABOUT THE AUTHOR

Annie Percik lives in London, where she writes novels and short stories, whilst working as a freelance editor and proofreader (https://alobear.co.uk/?page_id=778). She writes a blog about writing on her website (www.alobear.co.uk), which is where all her current publications are listed, including her debut fantasy novel, The Defiant Spark (http://getbook.at/DefiantSpark). She also makes a media review podcast with her husband, Dave (https://stillloveit.libsyn.com/), and publishes a photo-story blog, recording the adventures of her teddy bear (https://aloysius-bear.dreamwidth.org/). He is much more popular online than she is.

www.ingramcontent.com/pod-product-compliance
Lightning Source LLC
LaVergne TN
LVHW010052110826
845155LV00028B/309

* 9 7 8 1 9 1 4 9 2 6 0 6 8 *